HANNAH'S JOURNEY

HANNAH'S JOURNEY

Anna Schmidt

CHIVERS

British Library Cataloguing in Publication Data available

This Large Print edition published by AudioGO Ltd, Bath, 2013.
Published by arrangement with Harlequin Enterprises II B.V./S à r.l.

U.K. Hardcover   ISBN   978 1 4713 2568 7
U.K. Softcover   ISBN   978 1 4713 2569 4

Printed and bound in Great Britain by
MPG Books Group Limited

For Yahweh has heard
the sound of my weeping,
Yahweh has heard my pleading.
Yahweh will accept my prayer . . .

— *Psalm* 6:8–9
(New Jerusalem version)

To those who have
dared follow the beat
of the different drummer.

CHAPTER ONE

Sarasota, Florida, May 1928

Levi Harmon pushed aside the piles of bills littering his desk and swiveled his high-backed, leather chair toward the series of leaded glass-paned doors that led outside to the front lawn. The room had been designed as a solarium, but Levi had seen little use for such a space and instead had located his Florida office in the room with its tiled terrazzo floor, its arched doors opening to the out-of-doors that he loved so much. After all, what was the use of being rich if not to live as you pleased?

He walked out onto the terrace and leaned against the stone railing. Before him the lawn stretched green and verdant past the swimming pool and rose garden, past the mammoth banyan trees that he'd insisted the builder spare when constructing the mansion and on to the gatehouse that was a miniature version of the mansion itself.

He'd worked hard for all of this and had thought that by now he might be sharing it with a wife and children, but work had consumed him and he had never found a woman that he thought suited to the kind of vagabond life he'd chosen.

He'd come outside to think. Perhaps he should take a walk along the azure bay that most of the mansion's rooms looked out on. That always calmed him whenever business worries piled up. And indeed, they had begun to pile up — not just for him but for many men who had taken the cash flows of their businesses for granted these past several boom years. He had started down the curved stairs to the lawn when he noticed a woman he did not recognize walking up the driveway.

She moved with purpose and determination, her strides even, her tall slender frame erect, her head bent almost as if in prayer. As she came closer, he saw that she wore a dark gray dress with a black apron and the telltale starched white cap that was the uniform of the Amish women. How was it possible that she had not been stopped at the gate, detained there while the gatekeeper made a call to the house?

At that same moment he heard the phone in the foyer jangle. He moved back to the open office doorway and continued watching the woman even as he half listened to his butler, Hans, hold a quiet conversation with the gatekeeper. The woman was even with the pool when Hans came onto the terrace to deliver his report.

"She is Mrs. Hannah Goodloe," Hans said.

"She's Amish — probably lives out near the celery fields," Levi said impatiently. "What business could she possibly have here?"

"She would not say, but insisted on speaking with you personally. Shall I . . ."

Levi waved him away and went inside, rolling down the sleeves of his white shirt as he retrieved his jacket from the hall tree in his office. "Show her to the Great Hall," he said as he ran his fingers through his copper brown straight hair.

"Very good, sir," Hans murmured, but his words came with little approval. "May I remind you, sir, that your train . . ."

"I know my schedule. This won't take long."

"Very good, sir."

Levi listened to the tap of his butler's leather heels crossing the marble foyer to take up his post at the massive double front door. By now she should have reached them

11

and yet neither the bell nor the door knocker sounded. Had she changed her mind?

He crossed his office and peered outside. No sign of her retreating. Assuming she was standing on the front steps, perhaps gathering her courage, he could simply walk around to the front of the house and encounter her there. But for reasons he did not take the time to fathom, it seemed important that this woman — this stranger — enter his house, see the proof of all that he had accomplished, marvel at the beauty of his self-made world in spite of her religion's stand against anything deemed ostentatious.

And even as the chime of the front doorbell resonated throughout the house, Levi thought not so much of the present, but of a time when he was not so different from this plain-living woman who now stood at his door.

Just by coming to the winter home of the circus impresario, Hannah had probably violated several of the unwritten laws of the Ordnung followed by people of her faith. In the first place, the minute the gatekeeper had turned his back to make the call to the mansion, she had slipped past him and started her walk up the long drive. Surely that was wrong. But she had to see the only man capable of finding her son.

All the way up the drive, she kept her eyes on the ground half expecting to hear the gatekeeper running to catch up with her as she followed the pristine, white-shell path until it curved in front of the massive house itself. Only then did she glance up and her breath caught. The house soared three stories into the cloudless blue sky, its roof lined with curved terra-cotta tiles sparkling in the late-morning sun. Curved iron balconies hung from large arched windows on the second and third stories, and everywhere the facade of the house had been festooned with ornate carvings, colorful tiles and stone figures that were as frightening as they were fascinating.

Hannah dropped her gaze and started up the front stairs, avoiding the detailed iron railing that lined either side of the wide stairway and refusing to be tempted to admire the tiered fountain where water splashed like music. Even the stairs were a rainbow of colorful marble in pink and purple and pale green. She supposed that for a man like Levi Harmon — a showman known for his extravaganzas and exotic menagerie of animals from around the world — a little purple marble was to be

13

expected. She sucked in her breath, straightened her spine and prepared to knock.

But the massive wood door was covered by a gate, a barricade in filigreed iron that boasted twin medallions or perhaps coats of arms where she might have expected the obvious door handle to be located. Perturbed more than amused at this need for such material grandeur, Hannah took a step back and studied the house. Determined not to be daunted in her mission, she made a detailed study of the entrance. After all, the man entertained guests, did he not? Surely those people had to at some point enter and exit the house.

The doorbell was housed in the uplifted hand of a bronze sculpture of a circus clown located to the right of the door. Hannah took a deep breath, uttered a short prayer begging God's forgiveness for any misdemeanor she might be committing and pressed the button. When she heard a series of muffled bells gong inside the grand house, she locked her knees rigidly to keep them from shaking and waited for the doors to open.

"Good morning, Mrs. Goodloe," a man dressed in a black suit intoned as he swung open the inside door, and then opened the wrought-iron screen for her. "Please come in. Mr. Harmon is just completing some business. He asks that you wait for him in here."

The small man of indeterminate age led the way across a space that by itself was larger than any house she'd ever seen. Hannah avoided glancing at her surroundings, but could not miss the large curved stairway that wound its way up to the top of the house, or the gilt-framed paintings that lined the walls.

"Please make yourself comfortable," the man was saying as he led her down three shallow steps into a room easily twice the size of the space they had just left. He indicated one of four dark blue, tufted-velvet sofas. "Mr. Harmon will be with you shortly."

"Is that . . ." Hannah stared across the room at a wall of polished brass pipes in a range of sizes and the large wooden piece in front of them.

"The Butterfield pipe organ? Indeed," the man reported with obvious pride. "Mr. Harmon purchased that when they demolished the old Butterfield Theatre in London. He had it taken apart, labeled, then shipped here to be reassembled. It makes the most wondrous sound."

"I see." She had no idea what he was talking about. She had simply been taken aback to see an enormous pipe organ in a private home.

"Actually, the organ was Mr. Harmon's gift to me, ma'am." And then as if reminding himself that he was not to offer such information, he cleared his throat. "May I offer you a cool glass of water, ma'am?"

She had walked the five miles from her father-in-law's house near the celery fields down Fruitville Street, and then along the bay to the Harmon estate. But she had not come on a social call. "No, thank you," she replied as she perched on the edge of one of the sofas and folded her hands primly in her lap.

Seconds later, the silence surrounding her told her that she was alone. If she liked she could walk around the grand room, touch the furnishings, peer at the many framed pictures that lined the tops of tables and even satisfy her curiosity to know what the bay might look like seen through one of the multi-colored panes of glass in the sets of double doors that lined one wall. But an Amish person was never truly alone. One was always in the presence of God and as such, one was always expected to consider actions carefully.

Hannah focused on her folded hands and

considered the rashness of her action in coming here. But what other choice did she have? Caleb was missing and she had every reason to believe that he had run away. Oh, she had been foolish to think that taking him to the circus grounds the day before would somehow dampen his romantic ideal of what circus life was like. She had thought that once the boy saw the reality of the dirt and stench and hard work that lay behind the brightly colored posters, he would appreciate the security and comfort of the life he had. She had even thought of promising him a visit to his cousins in Ohio over the summer as a way of stemming his wanderlust. But when she had gone to his room to rouse him for school this morning, he hadn't been there and his bed had not been slept in.

She laced her fingers more tightly together and forced herself to steady her breathing. She would find Caleb even if she put herself in danger of being shunned to do it.

"Mrs. Goodloe?"

She'd heard no step on the hard, stone floor and yet when she looked up, Levi Harmon was standing at the entrance to the oversized room. He was a tall man, easily topping six feet. He looked down at her with eyes the color of the rich hot chocolate her mother used to make. "I understand there is a business matter we need to discuss," he added as he came down the shallow stairs, and took a seat at the opposite end of the sofa she already occupied. "I must say I am curious," he admitted, and his eyes twinkled just enough to put her at ease.

"My son, Caleb," she began and found her throat and mouth suddenly dry. She licked her lips and began again. "My son, Caleb, is missing, Mr. Harmon. I believe that he may have run away."

"Forgive me, ma'am, but I hardly see . . ."

". . . With your circus," she added, and was relieved to see his eyes widen with surprise even as his brow furrowed with concern.

"It would not be the first time," he said more to himself than to her as he stood and walked to the glass doors, keeping his back to her. "What does your husband think happened to the boy?"

"My husband died when Caleb was four. He's eleven now. This past year he has . . ." She searched for words. "There have been some occasions when he has tested the limits that our culture sets for young people."

"He's been in trouble," Levi Harmon said.

"Nothing serious," Hannah hastened to

18

assure him. "Then last month I found one of your circus posters folded up and hidden under his mattress. When I asked for an explanation, he told me that he wanted to join your circus. He had actually spoken to one of the men you employ to care for the animals."

"And what did you say in response to this announcement?"

"I tried to make him see that the poster was nothing more than paint on paper, that it made the life seem inviting but it was not real. That nothing about the circus is real."

She saw him stiffen defensively. "Oh, I know that it's your livelihood, Mr. Harmon, and I mean no disrespect. But for people like us — for a boy like Caleb — it's a life that goes against everything we believe."

"What happened next?"

Hannah was surprised that he did not question her further, but rather seemed determined to get at the root of her story. This was the part that was hardest for her because in the seven years since her husband had died, she and Caleb had never had a harsh word between them. "He became quite unlike himself," she said almost in a whisper. "He was sullen and stayed to himself. I went to our bishop but he said that time was the great healer."

"And you believed that?"

"For a while," she admitted. "But when nothing changed I decided to go against the bishop's advice and take action."

He turned to look at her. "What did you do?"

"I took Caleb to your circus, Mr. Harmon."

Levi tried and failed to disguise his shock that she would do such a thing. "You saw the show?"

"No. I took him to the grounds after the matinee yesterday. I wanted him to get a glimpse of what living the life of a circus worker would really be."

"My performers and crew are well cared for, Mrs. Goodloe. They have chosen this life for any number of reasons and . . ."

"I did not mean to imply otherwise, sir. However, a young boy's eyes are often clouded by the color and excitement associated with that life — the parades and the applause and such." She stood up and moved a step closer as if she needed to make her point and yet the tone of her voice remained soft and even solicitous. "I wanted Caleb to see that a life of traveling from place to place could be a difficult one."

He could find no argument for that.

Instead, he turned the topic back to her reasons for coming to him. "That matinee was our last show of the season down here," he said. "At this moment the company is on its way to our headquarters in Baraboo, Wisconsin, with stops along the way, of course."

"And I have reason to believe that my son is on that train," she said. "I have come here to ask that you stop that train until Caleb can be found."

"Mrs. Goodloe, I am sympathetic to your situation, but surely you can understand that I cannot disrupt an entire schedule because you think your son . . ."

"He is on that train, sir," she repeated.

"How can you be so certain?"

"Because besides the fact that Caleb was not in his bed when I went to wake him this morning, there were two other things missing from his room."

Levi waited but she had his full attention. He had never met a woman whose outward demeanor was so gentle, even submissive and at the same time, her eyes reflected an inner strength and certainty that she would not back down.

"About the time he began to have problems within the community he began wearing an old hat he found once. A fedora, I

21

believe it's called. That hat was not on its usual peg this morning."

"So, the boy went out and wore his hat," Levi said, resisting the patronizing smile he felt about to reveal.

"That's true," she said, "but he had also taken a jar of coins that he's been saving for months now, adding to it almost weekly after taking on odd jobs for others in the community."

Levi flashed back to his own packing the day he decided to run away. He, too, had taken money carefully squirreled away for months as he planned his escape. "Still, neither of those items ties my circus to his plan. He could have just . . . left."

She smiled and it was unsettling how that simple act changed everything about her. Suddenly, she looked younger and more vulnerable and at the same time, so very sure of herself. "Caleb would never leave without a plan," she said. "From the time he was four or five, Caleb has planned his days. Then it was that he would spend the morning at play and then have the noon meal with his grandfather before spending the afternoon helping out at his uncle's carpentry shop. Once he entered school he would write out a daily schedule, leaving it for me so that I would not worry."

"Am I to assume there was no schedule this morning?"

"No. Just this." She produced a lined piece of paper from the pocket of her apron and handed it to him. In a large childish script the note read,

Ma,
Don't worry. I'm fine and I know this is all a part of God's plan the way you always said. I'll write once I get settled and I'll send you half my wages by way of General Delivery. Please don't cry, okay? It's all going to be all right.

Love, Caleb

"There's not one word here that indicates . . ."

"He plans to send me part of his wages, Mr. Harmon. That means he plans to get a job. When we were on the circus grounds yesterday, I took note of a posted advertisement for a stable worker. My son has been around horses his entire life."

Once again, Levi found it difficult to suppress a smile. "I believe that posting was for someone to muck out the elephant quarters," he said and saw that this was news she had not considered.

"Oh. Well, Caleb also saw that posting

although he tried hard to steer me in the opposite direction and frankly, it did not occur to me that there might be a connection until I arrived at the grounds before coming here and saw the sign lying in the sawdust where the tent had been."

"And on that slimmest of evidence you have assumed that your son is on the circus train that left town last night?"

She nodded. She waited.

Levi ran one hand through his hair and heaved a sigh of frustration. "Mrs. Goodloe, please be reasonable. I have a business to run, several hundred employees who depend upon me, not to mention the hundreds of customers waiting along the way because they have purchased tickets for a performance tonight or tomorrow or the following day."

She said nothing but kept her eyes — a startling and unexpected shade of forget-me-not blue, he realized — focused squarely on him.

"Tell you what I'll do," he said without the slightest idea of how he might extricate himself from the situation. He stalled for time by pulling out his pocket watch, glancing at the time and then snapping the embossed silver cover shut and slipping it back into the pocket of his vest. "I am leav-

24

ing at seven this evening for my home and summer headquarters in Wisconsin. Tomorrow, I will meet up with the circus train and make the remainder of the journey with them. If your boy is on that train I will find him."

"Thank you," she said, her head slightly bowed so that for one moment he was unclear whether or not her gratitude was directed at him or to God. She lifted her gaze to his and touched the sleeve of his suit jacket. "You are a good man, Mr. Harmon."

"There's one thing more, Mrs. Goodloe."

Anything, her eyes exclaimed.

"I expect you to come with me."

CHAPTER TWO

"You can't . . . that is . . . why . . . I could not possibly. . . ."

"Those are my terms, Mrs. Goodloe. Assuming you are correct and your son is traveling with my circus, then it is my duty to find the boy and return him to you. However, as I mentioned, I have a business to run and other people who must be considered. Once the boy is found it would only be right for you to take charge of him from that point forward."

Without her being aware of moving, Hannah suddenly realized that Levi Harmon had escorted her back into the foyer where his servant stood by the door. "Hans, please make sure that Mrs. Goodloe has all of the information she needs to meet us at the railway station tonight." He turned back to Hannah then and took her hand between both of his. "I wouldn't worry, Mrs. Goodloe. The likelihood is that by the time you are reunited with your son he will be more than happy to come home, and any concerns you might have about his wanderlust will have been cured."

"Shall I call for your car to take Mrs. Goodloe home?" Hans asked.

"I . . ." Hannah searched for her voice which seemed to have been permanently silenced by her shock at the recent turn of events.

"Mrs. Goodloe and her people do not travel by motorized vehicle," Levi explained. "Unless, of course, the situation is an unusual one." His eyes met hers just before he entered the room off the foyer and closed the door.

The man called Hans seemed every bit as nonplussed as Hannah was. "I believe we have a bicycle," he said. "Would that be all right?"

"Thank you, Mr. Hans, but I walked here and I can walk back." Squaring her shoulders and forcing herself not to so much as glance at the closed door where Levi Harmon was, she marched to the open front door.

Hans scurried to open the iron gate for her. "It's simply Hans, ma'am," he said.

Hannah paused and looked at him. "You have no last name?"

"Winters," he managed, "but . . ."

"Thank you for your kindness, Mr. Winters."

"Mr. Harmon's private car will be attached to the train leaving for Atlanta at 7:02 this evening, ma'am. You really only need to pack a single valise. Everything you may need will be provided. Mr. Harmon is extraordinarily good to his guests." His voice was almost pleading for her to not think too badly of his employer.

"Thank you, Mr. Winters." She shook his hand. "It was my pleasure to make your acquaintance." She started down the drive and, although she refused to look back, she was suddenly certain that Hans Winters was not the only one watching her go.

By the time she reached the edge of the celery fields with their cottages in the background, it was midafternoon. The five-mile walk had given her ample time to consider the possibilities before her — and to pray for guidance in choosing correctly.

Instead of stopping at her small bungalow, she went straight to her father-in-law's bakery. As she had suspected, he was still there — as was his eldest daughter Pleasant, who had helped him run the business since the death of her mother. Hannah frowned. She had hoped to find Gunther

28

Goodloe alone. Pleasant was the antithesis of her name. A spinster, she seemed always to look on the dark side of any situation. Hannah could only imagine how she might react to the idea that Hannah needed to travel — by train — to find Caleb.

Hannah took a deep, steadying breath, closed her eyes for a moment to gather her wits, then opened the door to the bakery.

"We're closed," Pleasant barked without looking up from her sweeping.

"Hello, Pleasant. Is Gunther in the back?"

"Where else would he be?"

Hannah saw this for the rhetorical question it was and inched past her sister-in-law. Her father-in-law was a short and stocky man with a full gray beard that only highlighted his lack of hair. "Good day to you," Hannah called out over the clang of pans that Gunther was scrubbing. She took a towel from a peg near the back door of the shop, and began drying one of the pans he'd left to drain on the sideboard.

"The boy took off, did he?"

Hannah nodded.

"Any idea where he went?"

"Yes." She inhaled deeply and then told her father-in-law her suspicions.

"The circus? Well, he wouldn't be the first." He shook the water from his large

29

hands and then wiped them on a towel that had once been a flour sack. "Do you want me to go down there and fetch him home?"

"You can't. The circus company left before dawn."

Gunther raised his bushy eyebrows but said nothing.

"I went to see Mr. Levi Harmon," she admitted.

"Why would you do such a thing on your own, Hannah? Why wouldn't you have come to me — or the bishop — right away and let us handle this?"

"Because Caleb is my son."

"Nevertheless . . ."

"It's done," she interrupted, "and now we must decide what to do next."

"What did Harmon have to say? He can't have been any too pleased to have you accusing him of harboring a runaway."

"I didn't accuse him of anything. I simply asked for his help in bringing Caleb home. He leaves this evening and plans to meet up with the company tomorrow and travel the rest of the way back to Wisconsin with them."

"So if Caleb is with the company, he'll send him back?"

Hannah swallowed. "He's agreed to look for Caleb."

"And if he finds him?" Gunther looked at her with suspicion.

There was no use beating about the bush. She met his gaze. "He expects me to come with him and bring Caleb home myself."

"You cannot travel alone, child." The older man ran his hand over the length of his gray beard.

Hannah held her breath. He was not saying she shouldn't go.

"I think this is a matter for the bishop to decide," he said finally. He took down his hat from the peg by the side door. "Pleasant? Hannah and I will be back shortly."

Pleasant cast one curious glance at Hannah and then returned to her sweeping. "I'll be here," she said.

They found Bishop Troyer at home and Hannah stood quietly by the front door while Gunther explained the situation. The two men discussed the matter in low tones that made it difficult for Hannah to hear. Twice the bishop glanced directly at her, shook his head and returned to the discussion. *I should have simply agreed to go with him,* she thought and then immediately prayed for forgiveness in even thinking such a thing. *But this is my son — my only child and I . . .*

"Hannah? The bishop would like a word

31

with you."

Her legs felt like wood as she crossed the room and took a seat on the hard straight-backed chair opposite Bishop Troyer. She folded her hands in her lap more to steady them than to appear pious and kept her eyes lowered, lest he see her fear.

"This is indeed an unusual circumstance, Mrs. Goodloe, but at the core of it all is the undeniable fact that a boy — one of our own — is missing. And although you may be right in surmising that he has run away with the circus, we must be sure."

Hope tugged at her heart and she risked a glance at the kindly face of the bishop. His brow was furrowed but he was not frowning, just concentrating, she realized. He was trying to work out a solution that would serve the purpose of finding Caleb and bringing him home without going too far afield from the traditions that governed their community.

"It seems to me that Mr. Harmon's offer is a kind and generous one."

"Oh, he is a good man, Bishop, I'm certain of that," Hannah blurted.

This time there was no mistaking the frown that crossed both the bishop's face and her father-in-law's. Gunther cleared his throat and when she glanced at him, he shook his head as if warning her to remain silent.

"I have given my permission for you to take this journey as long as your father-in-law and your sister-in-law, Pleasant, travel with you."

Hannah's heart fell. "But the bakery," she whispered, knowing there was no one else Gunther would trust with his business.

"I have some time," the bishop replied, "as well as some experience in managing a business. I have offered to watch over the store while you are away."

She could hardly believe her ears. The bishop's offer was beyond anything she might have imagined possible. She glanced at Gunther who had offered the bishop a handshake — a contract in their society as binding as any piece of paper.

"Well, child, we must go. You said the train will leave at seven?"

Hannah nodded, unable to find words to express her joy and relief.

"Then come along. You and Pleasant can see to the packing while the bishop and I go over some of the particulars of managing the business for a few days."

Levi had spent the rest of the day in his office tending to the mountain of paperwork in preparation for vacating the Florida house for his more modest home in Wisconsin. For the next few weeks he would conduct his business from his private railway car. The Florida staff would see to the closing of his Sarasota residence and the opening of his home in Baraboo. With the exception of Hans who would travel with him, others of his household staff would travel directly to Wisconsin while he and Hans caught up with his company and made the scheduled stops with the circus for performances along the way.

He'd tried not to think about the Goodloe woman. He was fairly certain that she would not — could not — meet his demand that she travel with him to find her son. It had been ridiculous to even suggest such a thing and yet there had been something about the way she had looked at him as he dismissed her and returned to his office that made him uncertain.

The boy had run away and perhaps had inherited his wanderlust from his mother. It was intriguing to think that she was the parent with the adventurous streak. Over the years he had spent living the circus life, never once could he recall a female running away to join the troupe. Of course, Mrs. Goodloe was not exactly planning to join the traveling show. She simply wanted to find her son. But would she defy the counsel of her community's elders to accomplish that? He doubted it.

And he had no more time to give to the woman's problem. No doubt the boy had stowed away on the train. No doubt he would be discovered. No doubt that by week's end he would be back in his own bed. Levi knew that his managers would see to that. Besides, he had other far more serious matters to consider. How was it that when his circus had just completed its most successful season yet in terms of sold-out performances, the numbers did not reflect that? Expenses had risen to be sure but it seemed impossible that the cost of feeding and housing a menagerie of exotic animals and a hundred-plus performers and crew could explain such a disparity in revenue.

"Your car is waiting, sir," Hans announced with a meaningful glance at the nineteenth-century, gilded French clock that dominated the narrow marble mantel of the fireplace. The manservant was dressed in traveling clothes and holding Levi's hat as well as his own.

Levi gathered the papers he would need and stuffed them into the valise that Hans had brought to him earlier. "I should change," he muttered irritably and then wondered why. It was unlikely that there would be anyone at the station to see him off. Levi was a generous supporter of many charitable groups throughout this part of Florida, but he was known to be a reclusive man and most people had learned to respect that — even though they openly commented on the paradox that a man known for his extravagant entertainments and lavish lifestyle should be so protective of his personal privacy.

"Let's go," he told Hans as he headed for the door.

The weather had deteriorated. The air was steamy with humidity and the sky had gone from blue to a steel gray that held the promise of rain. He thought of Hannah Goodloe, imagining her walking back to the small Amish community east and north of the train station. For reasons he could not fathom, he felt the desire to make certain she arrived home before the rain began. He should have insisted on having his driver take her back. Surely she was there by now. Surely she had taken precautions for the weather.

At the station his private railway car was attached to the train that regularly made the run from Sarasota to Tampa and then from there to points north. Once the train reached Jonesville on the Florida/Georgia border, his car would be disconnected from the regular train and attached to his circus train. By the time they reached Baraboo, they would have performed in a dozen towns across half a dozen states and it would be June in Wisconsin.

"All aboard!" the conductor bellowed as Levi strode the length of the hissing and belching train to where his car waited. He passed clusters of passengers that had gathered on the platform to say their good-byes and board the public cars. Not one of them paid the slightest attention to him but he could not help scanning their faces to see if she had come after all.

"Ridiculous," he muttered, but while Hans handed the rail attendant Levi's valise, Levi looked back, down the length of the now almost deserted platform.

"Board!" The conductor's call seemed to echo and exaggerate the fact that she was nowhere in sight.

"Sir?" Hans stood at his elbow waiting for him to mount the filigreed metal steps to enter his car.

Levi nodded and climbed aboard but took one last look back. And there, out of the steam and fog, he saw three figures — two women and a bearded man — consulting with the conductor who pointed them in Levi's direction.

He felt a strange sense of relief that bordered on victory. She had come after all and apparently with her family's blessing, assuming her two companions had accompanied her to see her off. "Make sure the guest stateroom is prepared," he said to Hans as he stepped back onto the platform and walked toward the trio. "Mrs. Goodloe," he said, removing his hat and smiling broadly.

"Mr. Harmon, may I introduce my father-in-law, Gunther Goodloe, and my late husband's sister, Pleasant."

It was only when the older man shifted a worn cardboard suitcase from one hand to the other in order to accept his handshake that Levi realized they were all three carrying luggage. "I see you came prepared to stay for some time, Mrs. Goodloe. However, if your son is . . ."

"My father and sister-in-law will be accompanying me on the journey, Mr. Harmon. The conductor tells us that the regular seating is filled and I apologize for not notifying you sooner of the extra passengers, but . . ."

Levi turned his attention to the man. "I

38

assure you, sir, your daughter-in-law will travel in comfort and there is no reason at all for you to . . ."

"Our bishop has given his permission for this unusual trip," Gunther Goodloe said in a gentle but firm tone, "and he has done so only on the understanding that our Hannah will not make this journey alone." He smiled and shrugged as if he'd just made some observation about the inclement weather.

"I see." He could feel Hans watching him nervously, waiting for instruction. He could see the conductor checking his pocket watch and casting impatient looks in his direction. "Well, come aboard then and let's get you all settled in." He waited while the three-some climbed the stairs and then turned to Hans. "Prepare my quarters for the gentle-man. The two women can stay in the larger guestroom."

"Very good, sir." Hans knew better than to question his boss, although the question of where Levi would sleep was implicit in the look he gave his employer. He walked to the far end of the car and boarded from there. Levi was well aware that while he was giving his guests the grand tour of the view-ing room, the dining room and the parlor, Hans would be organizing the staff to prepare the rooms.

Once Levi had left the ladies and Gunther Goodloe to rest before dinner in their staterooms, he let out a long sigh of relief. The older man made him nervous. Not intentionally, of course. Gunther was the epitome of polite reserve, but it was that very reserve that brought back memories Levi had thought he'd long ago laid to rest. Memories of his late father — a man who, like Gunther, said little in words but spoke volumes with his half smile and expressive pale blue eyes. And his grandfather, whose strict household where Levi had lived after his parents died had been the deciding factor in his decision to run away.

"Mr. Harmon?"

Levi had been so lost in the past that he had not heard the young widow come in. Of course, even within the quiet of his luxurious car, there was always the steady rumble of the train moving over the tracks. He fixed a smile on his face and turned to greet her. "I trust everything is to your liking, Mrs. Goodloe?"

"It's very . . ." She hesitated, studying the pattern of the Oriental rug that carpeted the combination dining and sitting room. She drew in a deep breath, closed her eyes for an instant, then met his gaze directly. "I'm afraid that the accommodations simply

won't do," she said. "Not at all. My family
and I simply cannot stay here."

CHAPTER THREE

"We are on a moving train, Mrs. Goodloe." His head was throbbing. Would these people never be satisfied?

"I appreciate that," she replied without a hint of the sarcasm he'd infused into his comment. "I only thought that my father-in-law could perhaps share whatever accommodations Mr. Winters uses."

"Mr. Winters? Hans?"

"Yes. I am thinking that his accommodations are . . . plainer and would be more comfortable for my father-in-law."

"And where would you and Miss Goodloe stay?"

Her brow furrowed slightly. "I hadn't thought that far ahead," she admitted. "It's just that Gunther — Mr. Goodloe — seemed troubled by his surroundings. He's of the old school and . . ."

"You and your sister-in-law are not?" Levi felt the twitch of a smile jerk at one corner of his mouth. He could see that she had not considered this in her zeal to assure her father-in-law's comfort, but after a moment she offered him a tentative smile.

"We can perhaps make do if you would agree to certain minor changes that would allow Pleasant to feel more at ease."

"What kinds of changes?"

"If we might have some plain muslin cloth — perhaps some linens that are plain, we could cover some of the more . . ." Her voice trailed off.

Levi closed his eyes in a vain attempt to get control of his irritation and found himself thinking about the room he had given the women for the night. The cabin had ample room for two. A sofa upholstered in Parisian brocade that folded out into a bed and an upper berth. Above the cabin door hung a painting from his collection in a thick gilded frame. The dressing table was stocked with a variety of toiletries in elegant crystal bottles, each set into a specially designed compartment to keep it secure when the train was in motion. The lighting in the room came from wall sconces that sported laughing cherubs and the floor was outfitted with a thick sheepskin rug. For people like the Goodloe family, he could see that the place might come across as anything but "plain."

"Could we not do the same for Mr. Goodloe in my room?"

"I suppose. It's just that he's beginning to
think that we made a mistake in accepting
your kind and generous offer." To his shock
her eyes filled suddenly with tears. "Oh, Mr.
Harmon, I want so much to find my son
and bring him home but if my father-in-law
decides we've made a mistake and the train
stops to take on more passengers and . . ."

A woman's genuine distress had always
been Levi's undoing. "Hans!"

The manservant appeared immediately.
"Sir?"

"Mr. Goodloe will be bunking in with you
for the duration of our trip. I apologize for
any inconvenience but it's necessary."

"Very good, sir. I'll see to it at once. Will
there be anything else?"

"Yes, while we are at dinner, please see
that Mrs. Goodloe's stateroom is refur-
bished. Remove anything that shines or glit-
ters or smacks of flamboyance. Use plain
linens to make up the beds and see if you
can locate a couple of those rag rugs you
use at the mansion for wiping our feet inside
the garden entrance to put by each bed."

"Yes, sir."

"And cover the paintings and mirrors,"

44

Levi added as Hans hurried off to do his bidding. "They are bolted to the walls," he explained when he saw Hannah's puzzled look.

"I'll go and let the others know. May God bless you, Mr. Harmon." She was halfway down the narrow corridor when he called her back.

"Mrs. Goodloe?"

This time her face was wreathed in a genuine and full-blown smile that took his breath away. He had intended to reassure her that her son would be found and before she knew it, she and her family would be safely back home. But the attraction that shot through him like a bolt of adrenaline before a tightrope walker steps out onto the wire for the first time made him react with the same philosophy by which he had lived his entire life. *Never let the other person believe he — or she — has won.*

"I am a businessman," he began, and saw her smile falter slightly. "I rarely if ever do anything without expecting something in return." The way her spine straightened almost imperceptibly and her chin jutted forward with just a hint of defiance fascinated him.

"I thought you had invited us here as your guests, sir."

45

"That's true."

"Then what is your price?"

"I would like to know your given name and be allowed to call you by it when we are alone."

Her lips worked as if trying to find words. Her eyes widened. And then to his delight she burst out laughing. "Oh, that's a good one, Mr. Harmon. You had me going there for a moment."

"I'm serious."

She sobered. "My name is Hannah."

"Hannah," he repeated. "Well, dinner will be served in fifteen minutes, Hannah. And I assure you that the food will be plain enough even for your father-in-law." He turned away, busying himself by flipping through a stack of messages Hans had left for him on the sideboard. He was aware that she remained standing in the doorway to the corridor but he refused to turn around.

"I'll tell my family," she said, and then added in the lowest possible tone to still be heard clearly. "Thank you, Levi."

All the way back to her room, Hannah sent up pleas for forgiveness. From childhood on she had been known for her impish personality. But she was a grown woman now — a mother, a widow. Surely such

46

mischievous behavior was beneath her. Levi Harmon could have turned her away at the door of his lavish Sarasota estate. He could have thrown up his hands and informed her that Caleb's running away was hardly his concern. He could have done so many things other than what he had done — shown her kindness. And yet the way he had strutted about just now as if he owned everything within his view — which, of course, he did — nevertheless irritated her. And there was another cause for prayer. She sometimes suffered from a lack of patience when it came to the quirks of others. Her mother had often suggested that she look on the qualities of others that frustrated her as habits beyond their control. Such people were to be pitied, not scolded, she had advised. But her mother had never met Levi Harmon who did not inspire pity on any level.

She turned the engraved silver knob of the room she was to share with Pleasant and found her sister-in-law staggering about the cabin bumping up against the furnishings as the train rocked from side to side, and yet clearly reluctant to touch anything. Her eyes were clenched tightly shut, fingers knitted together as she murmured prayers in the dialect of Swiss-German they always used in private. She was earnestly beseeching God's mercy and deliverance from this place that was surely the devil's own workshop.

"Pleasant?" Hannah caught her sister-in-law as the train rounded a curve. Although the woman was three years younger than Hannah's age of thirty-two, she looked older. Her face was lined with anxiety. "It's all going to work out," Hannah assured her in their native tongue as she led her to the upholstered bench that was bolted to the floor in front of the dressing table.

They sat together with their backs to the mirror and the array of bottles and jars that filled the insets on top of the ornately curved dressing table. Hannah kept her arm around Pleasant's shoulders as they rocked in rhythm to the train's movement. "I spoke with Mr. Harmon. He's going to do his best to see that we are more comfortable."

"So much temptation," Pleasant muttered, glancing about with wild-eyed worry.

"Not if we refuse to be drawn to it," Hannah said.

There was a soft knock at the door and Hannah got up to answer it.

"Oh, miss," a young woman in a starched uniform exclaimed. "I thought you would be at supper and Hans said that I should . . ." She clutched a large bundle of plain linens to her chest.

"Let me take those," Hannah urged, reverting to English. She engaged in the brief tug-of-war it took to persuade the woman to release them. "These will do just fine. Please thank Mr. Winters for us and thank you, as well. I'll get started and while we're at supper you can finish, all right?"

The maid nodded then bowed her way out of the room, closing the door behind her. Hannah immediately began covering the large full-length mirror with one of the sheets. As if in a trance, Pleasant got up and unfolded another cloth to drape over the dressing table. "I suppose we could use the bench," she said, speaking German once again and looking to Hannah for approval.

"Absolutely," Hannah agreed as she covered the seat's tufted satin with a plain muslin pillow case. "We'll leave these for the maid," she decided as she knelt on the sofa and pulled down the upper berth. It was made up with satin linens and a silk coverlet and Hannah suspected the sofa bed was similarly garbed.

To her surprise, Pleasant giggled. "The maid," she exclaimed with glee.

Hannah saw her point. For two Amish women to be discussing what they could leave for the maid to finish was ludicrous. She started to laugh and soon the two of them were toppled on to the sofa holding their sides as their giggles subsided and then started all over again.

A knock at the door finally sobered them. "Daughters?"

"Yes, Father," Pleasant replied as both women sprang to their feet and Hannah smoothed the covers.

"Mr. Winters tells me that supper is served."

Hannah glanced up at the taller, thinner Pleasant and straightened her sister-in-law's prayer cap that had slipped sideways when they lay on the bed. Pleasant cupped her cheek and within the look the two women exchanged more tenderness and sisterly concern than either had felt for the other in all the years Hannah had been married to Pleasant's brother. "Coming," they answered in unison.

Levi's idea of a simple supper was a three-course meal as opposed to the five-course meal his staff would normally serve. He surveyed the cold cuts, the potato salad, the dark rye bread sliced into thick wedges waiting on the sideboard. They would begin the meal with barley soup and end it with one

50

of his cook's delicious key lime pies. It was the last of those he would enjoy for some time, Levi suspected as he turned to see that Hans was preparing to pour a dark lager into tall glasses.

"Our guests do not indulge," he said.

"But they are of German descent. I thought that this particular lager would . . ."

Levi shrugged. "Start with water and offer tea or milk."

Hans hesitated. "For you, as well, sir?"

"Yes." He turned as he heard the trio coming down the corridor, murmuring to each other in the Swiss-German they'd been raised to speak among their own. He wondered if it would surprise them to realize that he understood every word and decided he would leave them in the dark about that, at least for now. He didn't want to raise their curiosity regarding his past or how he had come to learn their language. "Welcome," he said jovially, indicating that Gunther should take one end of the table and then ushering the two women to the banquette built into the car against the windows.

In German, the woman Pleasant — who seemed to be anything but — murmured a comment about the magenta, tufted-velvet cushioning. She took her seat but did so with an expression she might have worn had she been asked to sit on a hot stove. Hannah gave him an apologetic smile and sat next to her sister-in-law.

Within seconds, a steaming bowl of soup had been served at each place and yet the three of them sat staring down at their bowls. Levi snapped open his white linen napkin and tucked it under his chin into the collar of his pristine white shirt. Still, they made no move, so he picked up his spoon.

"Shall we pray?" Gunther stretched out his hand to Pleasant who in turn took Hannah's hand.

Dumbly, Levi stared down at Hannah's hand extended palm-up to him and Gunther's large work-worn palm stretching to cover the extra space from one end of the small dining table to the other. Levi put down his spoon, stretched to meet Gunther's rough fingers and then placed his palm on top of Hannah's. Her head was bowed but he saw her eyes shift to focus on their joined hands.

Gunther frowned when he observed that connection but then closed his eyes and the four of them sat in silence with heads bowed for several long moments. In spite of the lengthy time allotted for a simple mealtime grace, Levi couldn't complain. He was far too busy analyzing the sensation of touching Hannah's palm. Her skin was smooth and warm and once, when her fingers twitched, he responded automatically by wrapping his fingers around hers. Hannah's breath quickened but she did not glance his way.

Gunther's head remained bowed for so long that Levi could no longer see steam rising from the soup. At last, the older man ended the prayer by looking up and reaching for his napkin. Instantly, Hannah slid her fingers from Levi's. She busied herself unfolding her napkin and placing it across her lap, then waited for her father-in-law to take the first spoonful of soup before dipping her spoon into her bowl.

"My family and I are indebted to you, Mr. Harmon, not only for your assistance in finding my grandson, but also in respecting our ways."

"Not at all. I should have thought about the rooms I offered and their furnishings."

There was a period of silence broken only by the clink of sterling soup spoons on china bowls and the rhythmic churning of the train's wheels on metal tracks.

"How is it you know of our ways?" Gunther asked after a time. "After all, we Amish

53

have not been in Florida for long."

Levi saw Hannah glance at him and understood by her expression that it was a question she had wondered about as well.

"My company travels all over the Midwest and eastern states of America, sir. That includes Pennsylvania where I believe there is a large established community of Amish?"

"Several of them," Gunther agreed and seemed satisfied with the response.

"How did you come to reside in Florida, sir?"

Gunther smiled. "My son was something of an adventurer. He and a friend had traveled to Florida during the time of their *Rumspringa.* That's the time when . . ."

"I'm familiar with the tradition," Levi said. When Hannah gave him a curious glance he added, "Isn't that the time when parents permit — even encourage — their young people to explore the outside world before making their commitment to your faith?"

"That's right," Gunther said.

All three members of the Goodloe family were regarding him with interest, so Levi turned the conversation back to the original topic. "So your son came to Florida and . . ."

"When he returned, he could talk of nothing else. The weather. The possibility of growing crops year-round. The opportunities." Gunther shook his head and smiled at the memory. "Even after he and Hannah had married and he had joined my bakery business, he would bring it up from time to time."

"So you just picked up and moved?" Levi directed this question to Hannah, but it was Gunther who replied.

"As I said, we were in the bakery business and one night there was a fire. We lost everything. A few years earlier his mother had died and I had remarried. My second wife was from another Amish community in another state. They did things differently there and she was having some problems settling in. My son saw it all as God's sign that we should start over someplace else."

"Did you buy land then in Sarasota?"

"No. We did what we knew best. My son and I opened a bakery." Gunther looked a little wistful for a moment and murmured, "It was all seeming to work out until . . ."

"My husband was killed when the wagon he was driving was struck by a motor vehicle," Hannah said softly.

"My only boy," Gunther said, his voice quavering.

Everyone concentrated on finishing their

soup, then Hans directed the removal of the soup bowls and the serving of the cold cuts and side dishes. Levi was well aware that neither of the women had contributed to the limited conversation. It was going to be a long supper. He waited until everyone had been served then turned his attention to Hannah. "Tell me about your son," he said.

Again, the slightest frown of disapproval from the old man, but Hannah appeared not to notice — or perhaps chose to ignore it.

"I have told you that his name is Caleb. He is eleven years old though tall for his age. He has blue eyes and his hair . . ." She paused as she appeared to notice Levi's hair for the first time. "His hair is like corn silk," she murmured and quickly averted her eyes to focus on her food.

"Do you think he might have changed into clothing that is less conspicuous?"

"Perhaps."

"Where would he get such clothing?" Pleasant asked and then immediately glanced at her father and lowered her eyes.

Hannah shrugged. "I am only guessing. I mentioned the English hat. His Amish hat was still on its peg." Her eyes glittered with tears that Levi guessed she would be far too proud to shed in his presence. They were

56

tears of worry and exhaustion and he had to force himself not to cover her hand with his and assure her it would all turn out for the best. For after all, hadn't it turned out that way for him after he'd run away to join the circus when he was only a few years older than Caleb was?

"I'm sure that the boy will turn up," Gunther said as he pushed the last of his potato salad onto his fork with the crust of his bread. "We thank you for your hospitality, sir." He placed his napkin on the table and pushed back his chair.

Levi knew that he should simply permit the supper to end so he could attend to the work he'd brought on board with him and yet he wanted more time. Why? Because of the lovely young widow? Or because he was for the first time seeing the effect that his running away must have had on his grandmother?

"Now that you've told me of your bakery, Mr. Goodloe. I'd be curious to have your opinion of my cook's key lime pie. Would you be so kind as to try it?"

"My daughter is the baker, sir."

Pleasant's cheeks flamed a ruddy brick red as Levi signaled Hans to clear and serve. "And you, Mrs. Goodloe? Do you also contribute to the wares available at your father-in-law's bakery?"

"My daughter-in-law handles the housework for our family," Gunther replied before Hannah could open her mouth. "She is an excellent cook and has been a good influence on my younger daughters."

Levi noticed that Pleasant's scowl deepened. "You have sisters then, Miss Goodloe?"

"Half sisters," she corrected, but said no more.

"Pleasant's mother died when Pleasant was just coming of age. After a time, I remarried so that she would have a mother."

"And these other daughters are the product of that marriage?"

"*Ja.*"

"So they have stayed at home with their mother?" Gathering information from these people was like organizing a menagerie into a parade.

"Sadly, their mother died in childbirth."

"I am doubly sorry for your losses, sir," Levi said.

Gunther smiled at Hannah. "Our Hannah has become like a mother to my younger girls," he said. "God has blessed us."

"I see." Levi would hardly have called the loss of two wives and Hannah's husband a blessing, but he knew better than to debate the point.

"We have indeed been blessed. I only hope God sees fit to bless us yet again by leading us to Caleb," Hannah said in a barely audible voice.

Levi hadn't realized that he had continued to study Hannah far beyond the casual glance her comment might have indicated until Gunther cleared his throat and made a show of tasting his first bite of the pie. The two women followed his lead and all three smiled at Levi as if they had just tasted the best key lime pie ever made.

But Levi had turned his thoughts back to the situation at hand. Here was Gunther, an experienced entrepreneur in his own right, and while Levi did not hold with divine intervention, he had to admit that Gunther had come along at a time when he could use the opinion of a fellow businessman. He needed someone he could trust, someone who had no interest in his business, to review the ledgers for the past season. A fresh set of eyes. But he dismissed the idea as ludicrous. How would an unschooled, Amish baker possibly find what he had not been able to uncover himself?

He looked up and realized that once again Gunther had laid his napkin aside and this time he was standing. The two women had followed suit. Levi scrambled to his feet. "Forgive me," he said. "I'm afraid that at about this time of night my mind often goes to the business of the day past and that to come tomorrow."

"You are worried?" Gunther's eyes narrowed in sympathy.

Levi shrugged. "Always. A great many people rely on me, sir."

"And who do you rely on, Levi Harmon?"

The older man's pale blue eyes were kind and concerned. It struck Levi that if his father had lived, he would be about the same age as this man was now. He felt his throat tighten with the bile of loneliness that he had carried with him from the day his parents had died. Instead of responding to Gunther's question, he motioned for Hans to join them.

"Hans, I believe our guests are ready to retire for the night. Will you show Mr. Goodloe to your quarters?"

"If you don't mind," Gunther added, directing his comment to Hans.

"Not at all, sir. I took the liberty of moving your belongings to my cabin while you were enjoying your supper."

"Then we'll say good night." Gunther waited while the two women nodded to Levi and Hans and walked down the corridor to the guest room. Then he clasped Levi's shoulder. "May God be with you, Levi Harmon."

And as he watched Hans lead the older man to the plainer quarters, Levi understood that Gunther had not missed the fact that Levi had avoided answering his question. The fact was Levi had no response, for since he'd been a boy, there had been no one to watch over him.

CHAPTER FOUR

Hannah found sleep impossible that night. Her mind reeled. Where was her son and had he indeed run off with the circus, or was she on some wild goose chase while Caleb was out there somewhere alone? Every clack of the wheels might be taking her farther from him.

She sat on the edge of the upper berth that she'd insisted on taking. Below her, Pleasant's even breathing seemed to have fallen into a rhythm that matched the rumble of the train. Outside the window, Hannah saw the silhouette of telephone poles standing like sentinels in the fields. As the train rounded a bend, the noise flushed a flock of large blackbirds and they scattered into the night sky. The window faced east and she could see the breaking of dawn on the horizon.

"Please keep him safe until I can come for him," she prayed as she watched the sky turn from black to charcoal and then pink. "He is my life," she added and closed her eyes tight against the memory of the long, lonely years that had passed since her husband's death. Years when her only solace had been Caleb.

Perhaps that was it. Perhaps she and others had put so much pressure on him in the absence of his father. How often had she heard someone remind him that he was now the man of the family? How often had someone suggested that she needed his support and help more than ever because all she had was him? Perhaps his need for freedom wasn't that at all. Perhaps it was more a need to be what he was — a boy. A child.

Oh, how she wished she might talk to someone — a male who might understand the workings of a young boy's mind. Perhaps Mr. Winters, she thought.

Outside the cabin door she heard footsteps. Given the early hour, she assumed it would be Hans Winters, up before dawn to see to the needs of his master and the guests. She eased herself down from the upper berth, taking care not to wake Pleasant and got dressed as quickly as she could, given the need to fumble blindly for the black straight pins that held the skirt and bodice of her dress in place. Once properly dressed, she wrapped her hair — grown now to past her waist — round and round her hand and coiled it into the casing of her prayer cap.

When she slipped into the passageway, she paused for a moment listening for sounds. That way led to Hans's quarters and the kitchen. The opposite way led to the observation room and dining room. She heard the clink of silver and assumed Hans would be setting the dining table for their breakfast.

"May I help you?" she asked as she entered the opulent room. It would be the perfect opportunity to engage the servant in conversation. The two of them working together to prepare the room for breakfast.

But instead of Hans, she found herself facing Levi. He was sitting at a small dropdown desk on one side of the large sideboard, stirring a cup of coffee. "Not unless you've a head for figures," he grumbled.

Actually, I do, Hannah thought but understood instinctively that the circus owner would no doubt laugh at the very idea that she might be able to solve whatever problem that he clearly could not. Still, if the idea brought a smile to his face that would certainly be preferable to the scowl that darkened his deep-set eyes at the moment. "I apologize," she murmured, turning to go. "I assumed that Mr. Winters . . ."

"Kitchen," he grumbled, turning his attention back to the ledger before him.

The table was already set so she turned to go. But she had retreated only two steps before he stopped her. "I'm sorry. Is there a problem, Hannah?"

"Not at all," she said brightly.

"You slept well?" He seemed to be studying her features closely.

"Not really," she admitted, knowing that her face surely showed the effects of her restless night. "But it was not the accommodations," she hastened to assure him. "The berth was quite comfortable and the rhythm of the train's movement was a little like rocking a child."

A smile tugged at the corners of his mouth. "Upper or lower?"

"Upper," she replied and felt her cheeks flush at the impropriety of this particular topic. "Well, I'll leave you to your work," she said.

"Why were you looking for Hans? It's not yet dawn and if there's no problem with your accommodations. . . ."

She took a moment to consider her options. Levi was a man — younger than Hans and perhaps more likely to remember what it had been like to be a boy of eleven. "I am worried about my son," she admitted.

"If he took off with my crew, Hannah, we will find him and until we do, I assure you that he is in good company. No harm will come to him."

"But what if he didn't? What if he just ran away? What if he got to the circus grounds too late and your company had already left and he just decided to go off on his own?" The thoughts that she had successfully held at bay through the long night now came tumbling out. "What if even now with every mile we go I am moving farther and farther from him? Perhaps I was too hasty in my assumption. Perhaps I should . . ."

Levi pushed the ledger aside and indicated that she should take a seat on the end of the tufted settee closest to the dining chair he had pulled over to the desk. "It seems to me that you have ample reason to believe that your son is with my company. From what you have told me, the boy is a planner and as such he would have timed his departure so that he did not run the risk of missing the train."

"But . . ."

"And even if he did miss it, we are going to know that within a matter of hours. We are scheduled to arrive in Jonesville just after breakfast. The company will be doing two shows there today — a matinee and an evening performance. If Caleb is with them we will find him."

"And if not?"

"Then I will see that you and your family are on the next train back to Sarasota and I will personally notify the authorities there to begin the search for your son. One step at a time, Hannah." He stood up and poured a second cup of coffee from the silver coffeepot on the sideboard and handed it to her. "Drink this," he said. "You're running on nerves and you're going to need your strength for the day ahead, whatever it may bring."

"Thank you," she murmured as she took a sip of the hot strong brew. "You've been more than kind to us. I assure you that we'll be out of your way soon." She took a second sip. "Do you recall — I mean, Caleb is a boy of eleven and he's had so much responsibility thrust upon him since the death of his father. It occurred to me that this business isn't really about joining the circus at all."

"It's about finding his way," Levi said. "Testing himself — and you."

"In what way is he testing me?"

Levi shrugged. "He may not realize it but he wants to see if you will come after him and, if you do, whether or not things will be different for the two of you once you find him."

"I love him," Hannah whispered and her voice quaked.

"Enough to one day let him go?"

"He's eleven," she protested.

"I said one day, Hannah. Don't make the mistake of making this boy your reason for living. Don't try to mold him into some kind of replacement for the life you thought you would have with your husband."

"I wouldn't. I don't," she said firmly and stood up. Flustered with irritation at his assumption that he knew anything at all about her or her life, she started to hand him the coffee cup then thought better of it and placed the cup and saucer on the silver tray that held the coffee service on the sideboard. "Thank you for the coffee," she said. "I expect Pleasant will be awake by now — she's used to rising early for the baking. . . ." She started toward the passageway just as the train lurched around a curve.

Surefooted as a tiger, he steadied her before she could fall, his hands grasping her upper arms and remaining there until she regained her balance.

"Thank you," she whispered and pulled away.

Levi stood watching her hurry along the corridor that ran the length of his private car. It wasn't until she opened the door to her cabin and disappeared that he realized he'd been holding his breath and clenching his fists as if somehow that might keep the warmth of touching her from running away as she had.

"It's not the same," he muttered as he turned back to the desk, slammed shut the ledger and then retrieved his suit jacket from the back of the chair. But the picture of Hannah's son striking out in the middle of the night, slipping away from the only house he'd probably ever known as home and heading off into the unknown stirred memories of Levi's own youth that he had thought long since forgotten.

Suddenly, he recalled with graphic clarity the combination of fear and exhilaration he'd felt that night. Equally as strong came the memory of his doubt and regret after he'd been on the road for only a day. "It was different for me," he muttered as he poured himself a second cup of coffee. "I was fourteen."

He heard the sound of conversation in the

passageway, drained his coffee and turned to face whatever this day might bring. Gunther Goodloe was speaking in low tones in his native tongue as he led Hannah and Pleasant to the dining room.

"Good morning, Mr. Goodloe. I trust your accommodations were satisfactory?"

"Yes, thank you for allowing the change." He indicated that the two women should take the places on the settee where they had sat for supper the evening before.

"Please take my place, sir," Levi urged, holding out the chair for the older man. "You'll have a better view of the passing scenery from here," he added, knowing full well that he had decided upon the change in seating abruptly so that he would not have to touch Hannah again during morning prayers.

On cue Hans appeared with a tea cart loaded with covered sterling serving dishes. He lifted the cover on the first and offered a selection of sausages and bacon to the two women, then Mr. Goodloe and finally Levi. He repeated this process with a chafing dish filled with steaming scrambled eggs, then another with a selection of breads and rolls, and finally offered each guest butter and jam. Meanwhile, the maid traveling with them filled glasses with milk and offered coffee and tea.

Through all of this Levi kept up a running conversation about the countryside they were traversing. "I'm afraid the boom times ended for Florida after the hurricane of '26," he said.

"And yet your business seems to be thriving," Gunther replied.

"Even in hard times people need to be entertained," Levi replied. "Perhaps especially in hard times." Knowing it was inevitable, Levi extended his hands to Pleasant and Gunther. "Shall we pray?"

It took a moment before he realized that because he had extended the invitation, the others were waiting for him to bow his head. Forgetting that Amish grace was said in silence, he cleared his throat and murmured thanks for the food and the company and then added, "And may today bring Hannah the news she needs to know that her son is safe. Amen."

When he looked up he was surprised to see Gunther frowning and Hannah blushing. For her part, Pleasant had focused all of her attention on the food before her and he couldn't help but wonder what law of propriety he had just broken. Was it the prayer? He hadn't prayed in years and yet thought he had done a passable job of of-

71

fering grace before a meal. And then he understood his mistake. It was bad enough that he had offered the prayer aloud, but he had also singled Hannah out for special attention and called her by her given name.

"I apologize, sir," he said, refusing to ignore the situation. "It's just that we are all concerned about your grandson and I suppose that has made me feel a particular closeness to your family. Nevertheless, I was too familiar just now. I hope you will forgive my lapse in manners."

"Not at all," Gunther replied. "We are in your world now. I am honored that you have shown such concern for my grandson's well-being. If you are more comfortable calling us by our given names, then that's the least we can do." He drank a long swallow of his milk. "I have noticed that Mr. Winters is distinctly uncomfortable with such formality," he added.

"You are very observant, sir. And very kind."

He saw that Gunther took the compliment in stride without acknowledging it. Instead, he evidently decided that a fresh round of introductions was in order. "And so we are the Goodloe family. I am Gunther and my daughter is Pleasant and as you have observed, Caleb's mother is Hannah."

72

"And I am Levi." He shook hands with Gunther then smiled at Pleasant whose lips were pursed into a worried pucker as if unsure of what to make of all this. Finally, he looked at Hannah who met his gaze directly.

"And my son is Caleb," she said softly. "And today, God willing, we shall find him and not trouble you further, Levi."

As promised, they arrived in the small town of Jonesville an hour later. On the way into town the train slowed and then paused as Levi's private car was moved to a siding next to a large field. From her position on the observation deck at the back of the car, Hannah could see dozens of workers, some hammering in the long stakes that would hold the huge circus tent in place. Other workers performed the same task as a dozen smaller tents went up on the property.

"That one is the cooking tent and next to it the dining tent," Levi told them as Gunther, Pleasant and Hannah leaned out over the scrolled and turned-brass railing of the deck for a better view. "Wardrobe," he continued, "dressing rooms, makeup, props."

"It's like a city in itself," Hannah observed and she was beginning to understand how such activity might have captivated Caleb. "It's so colorful and . . . ."

"Exciting," Pleasant whispered. Then she glanced at her father and added, "If you enjoy that sort of thing."

"So many people," Hannah said as she scanned the throng of workers for any sign of her son.

"We'll find him," Levi said quietly. Then in a more normal tone he added, "Care to watch the unloading of the wagons, Gunther? I promise you it's worth every minute of your time."

"I wouldn't mind getting off this train and stretching my legs on firm ground a bit," Gunther replied.

Levi opened the small gate that led to three steps and disembarked. From the ground he held out a hand to Pleasant. "Ladies," he invited as he escorted them safely to the ground. Then he waited for Gunther to navigate the short flight of steps before beginning the tour.

"There are forty flatcars for transporting the wagons," he said as he headed toward a siding where the line of cars with their cargo of painted and gilded circus wagons waited. "A wagon can weigh as much as six tons," he added, and Hannah saw that her father-in-law was intrigued in spite of his reservations about coming too close to this outside world.

"You use Belgians to do the heavy work," Gunther noted, nodding toward a matched pair of large black horses dragging a ramp into place at the end of one flatcar.

"Belgians, Percherons, Clydesdales," Levi replied. "They serve double duty as both work horses and performance animals. But the men will handle the actual work of taking the wagons off the flatcars."

The four of them watched in silence as the work crew set a ramp in place at one end of the flatcar. Then a crew member took hold of the wagon's tongue and carefully steered the wagon toward the ramp.

"This is where things get tricky," Levi said. "If he loses control and the wagon starts to roll too quickly then we risk injuring a worker. So that man there — a 'snubber' — will control the speed using that network of ropes and capstans."

Hannah held her breath as the unwieldy wagon gained speed and threatened to topple over on its way down the ramp. Safely on the ground another member of the crew hitched it to the team of horses, climbed aboard and drove it across the lot. Then the process began all over again.

"It's a lot of work," Gunther observed.

"Especially when you realize that after tonight's performance we'll simply reverse the process and move on to the next town."

"Are those the tents for housing the animals?" Hannah asked, recalling the notice for a stable boy that she and Caleb had seen on the grounds in Sarasota.

"Yes. Gunther, why don't you and Pleasant go over there to the dining and cook tents and see if there's any sign of the boy while Hannah and I check out the animal tents?"

Before Gunther could object, Levi had started off toward a large tent where Hannah could see horses and elephants stabled. Without a backward look she followed him.

While Levi spoke with the men working the area, she searched for Caleb. Methodically, she checked every stall and gently prodded every pile of hay that looked bulky enough for a boy to be hiding under with the toe of her shoe. Nothing.

She had searched the large open-aired tent from one end to the other and found no sign of her son. Now she stood at the entrance to the tent looking out across the circus grounds, wondering where he might be and praying that she had not made a mistake in guessing that he had left with the circus.

"Mrs. Goodloe?"

She turned at the sound of Levi's call. He was walking toward her with another man. The sun was behind them, streaming in from the far end of the tent and both men were in silhouette, and yet there was something about Levi's confident stride that made her know him at once. The other man was a stranger. She focused on Levi, willing him to break free of the shadows and give her the news she'd prayed to hear — that Caleb had been found.

CHAPTER FIVE

"Mrs. Hannah Goodloe, this is my accountant and business manager, Jake Jenkins."

"Very pleased to make your acquaintance, ma'am," the small wiry man gushed. He was dressed in a business suit and held a bowler hat that he kept tapping against his thigh in a nervous cadence. "I understand your son is missing?"

"Have you seen him?" Hannah was well aware that she had dispensed with the niceties of meeting someone new and gotten directly to the point. But all through the night and especially in the bright light of day, she had felt that time was of the essence. Either she would find Caleb today or . . .

"I may have."

Hannah's heart beat in quick time. "Where is he?"

"Now, ma'am, I said I might have seen

the boy. There was a kid on the grounds in Sarasota yesterday morning as we were loading the last of the wagons. Most everyone was already on board but I saw him hanging around the livestock car."

"Did he board the train, Mr. Jenkins?" Hannah thought that she might scream if the man insisted on stretching out his story any further.

"I'm not sure."

"But back there you said . . ." Levi's voice was tight, as if each word were an effort.

"I said I might have seen the kid, Levi. You know how it is. We get kids hanging around all the time — granted, usually not at that hour of the morning, but still . . ."

"Where did you last see him?" Hannah asked, suddenly unable to swallow around the lump of fear in her throat.

"I hollered at him to get going and he ran off toward the front of the train — up where the sleeping cars are. He could have just kept going or he could have boarded one of those cars."

"Let's go," Levi said, taking Hannah's elbow and ushering her past the dapper little man. "Maybe he's still there — maybe he fell asleep and . . ."

"He could never sleep through all of this," Hannah replied as she practically ran to keep up with his long strides. "Besides, he's an early riser and . . ."

"Let's just be sure."

But after a thorough search of the sleeping, dining and stock cars there was no sign of Caleb. Levi even spoke to the local authorities to see if they might have spotted a boy obviously on his own in town.

"I've alerted the authorities in Sarasota," Levi told the family when they had all returned to his private car where Hans had prepared lunch for them. "And Hans can arrange for your trip home. However, I'm afraid the earliest train is tomorrow."

"It's God's will," Pleasant murmured, and Hannah shivered at the very idea that God would be so cruel as to allow a boy to wander alone over yet a second night while his mother was miles away.

"Or man's failure," Levi added quietly. "I'll question my business manager again, Hannah. Perhaps there's some detail he forgot, something that might offer more information."

"Thank you," Hannah replied and stood up. "Please excuse me," she murmured and did not wait for their permission.

Outside she wandered the circus lot, oblivious to the growing throng surrounding her as people gathered for the matinee

80

performance. But as she found her way around the enormous tent away from the main entrance and the smaller side-show tents and ticket wagon, she began to consider her surroundings through the eyes of her son.

The dining tent was mostly empty now. Only a few of the waiters were left, lounging at one of the tables, cigarettes dangling from their lips as they took a well-deserved break. She followed the sounds of chatter and found herself in what Caleb had described to her as the "backyard" of the circus.

"See, Ma," he'd explained excitedly, "it's not so different from home if they have a backyard."

Hannah watched as a parade of elaborately outfitted animals and performers lined up for their grand entrance into the tent. "The big top, Ma," Caleb had corrected her when she referred to it as a tent on their tour. "Because it's the biggest."

"The big top," she murmured as she trudged on. She had no idea where she was headed. She only knew that she had to find a quiet place where she could think. She had noticed a little creek near the tracks on their way in. Perhaps . . .

"Watch it, honey." Hannah glanced up to

81

find that she'd nearly run straight into a highly made-up woman wearing a skin-tight leotard, tights and a sheer flowing skirt covered in sequins.

Immediately, she averted her eyes. "So sorry," she murmured. "Forgive me, please," she added as she and the woman engaged in a kind of dance as one moved one way and the other moved in unison so that they were still blocking each other.

"Hey," the woman said, "you're the mother of that missing kid, aren't you?"

The mention of Caleb took precedence over anything that might have proved embarrassing about being so close to a woman like this. She met the woman's gaze and saw that beneath the layers of mascara and eye shadow, the woman had eyes that were kind and concerned.

"Yes," she admitted.

"Thought so. Look, honey, you didn't hear it from me but some of us were talking and we're pretty sure we saw the kid. Blond hair, right? Looks like it's been cut by using a bowl as a cap?"

Hannah nodded, unable to breathe for the rush of hope she didn't want to allow herself to feel.

"Skinny kid but taller than most. White shirt, suspenders holding up high-water

82

black pants?"

"What are high-water . . ."

"Too short for him," the woman explained.

"Yes," Hannah said, her excitement building. "Where . . . when . . ."

"All I can tell you is that kid was on the train last night — like a shadow he was." She chuckled. "Now you saw him and now you didn't."

"And now?"

The woman's laughing eyes sobered. "Haven't seen him since we got here, honey," she admitted. "And from the chatter in the dining tent earlier, neither has anyone else. We figured he must have moved on but then I saw you searching this morning and . . . well, I'm a mother myself and when I ran into you just now, it seemed like I was supposed to tell you what I knew even if . . ."

"May I know your name?" Hannah asked.

The woman's eyes narrowed, then she shrugged. "Sure. That's me there." She pointed to the painted side of a large float where the words *Lily Palmer, The Girl in the Gilded Cage* were emblazoned in gold script.

Hannah heard the band sound a fanfare and slowly the parade of people and animals started forward. "Gotta run, honey," Lily shouted as she dashed off to climb aboard her float. Hannah watched as the woman nimbly climbed up the side of a three-tiered scaffolding and into an oversized gilded birdcage. From her perch up high, Lily waved at Hannah. "Keep the faith, honey," she shouted and Hannah realized that she was smiling, and that her breathing was coming in gasps of excitement rather than panic. She waved back to Lily and then headed back to Levi's private car to share the news with the others.

"I thought you said you saw the kid." Levi fumed later that afternoon as he and Jake went over the orders Jake would need to place at each stop on their way north.

"I told you I saw a kid, Levi. Blond hair, Amish looking duds — seemed to match what you described. Don't shoot the messenger, okay?"

Jake and Levi had been friends for years. They had both been stowaways and after spending several months riding the circus train and doing odd jobs, Jake had left to find his fortune in Chicago. A couple of months after Levi inherited the Brody circus from his mentor Jasper Brody, Levi contacted his old friend and the two had worked together ever since. He'd quickly realized that Jake's talents were exactly the right complement to his own. The man had a head for business, plus he was a crowd-pleaser. That meant he was great at negotiating favorable deals for the myriad list of goods and supplies that it took to keep a circus running.

In the process the two of them had become good friends. Jake's naturally outgoing personality was a perfect complement to Levi's reticence and as the years had gone by, Levi had been more than happy to let Jake handle the public and promotional parts of running a circus.

"I just hated to disappoint her," he said by way of apology for snapping at his friend.

Jake shrugged. "You've gone above and beyond the way I see it. It's hardly your concern if the boy decided to take off."

"He's younger than most," Levi said absently.

"Maybe there was trouble at home. Maybe his ma — or maybe his grandpa — were . . ."

"They're good people, Jake."

His friend shrugged. "I'm just saying. A boy doesn't take off for no good reason."

"She thinks he fell for the glamour," Levi said and then both men laughed. For both understood that life on the road with the circus was about as glamorous as shoveling elephant dung at the end of the parade.

"Then there's nothing to worry about," Jake said, clapping Levi on the shoulder. "Give the kid a couple of days — a week at most — and I guarantee you he'll be begging us to send him back — if he's here at all, that is."

"You looked everywhere? Spoke to everyone?"

Jake sighed and nodded. "Lily and some of the gals thought they spotted him on board last night but there was no sign of him. More likely they were all falling asleep when I was chasing the kid and they looked outside, spotted him then dreamed he was running through their sleeping car."

"Why'd you chase him?"

"Because the train was about to move and he was dodging in and out between cars. The last thing we needed was for a kid to get crushed as we were leaving town. Business is bad enough without adding that to the mix."

Levi couldn't debate that point. "I don't get it," he said, his attention now firmly back on the figures he'd been studying for days now. "Our last performances in Sarasota were sold out and yet . . ."

"You gave all those tickets to that charity thing, remember?" Jake reminded him.

"You'll see. Things will start to look better now that we're on the road. Besides, you aren't exactly hurting, Levi."

"You know it's not about my personal fortune," Levi snapped. "We employ so many people, Jake. I'm responsible for their welfare — not to mention the welfare of their families. With the way the economy took a nosedive in Florida these past couple of years, I don't want to have to start letting people go."

"Trust me, my friend. Everyone knows you're going to do the right thing when it comes to taking care of the company. Whatever happens, everybody knows that when Levi Harmon gives you his word, it beats any official piece of paper you might ever hold in your hand." Jake gathered up the orders. "I'll go send these so the supplies are waiting at the next stop. And stop worrying!"

Levi smiled for the first time since he'd sat down with his friend. Somehow Jake had always had a way of putting a new face on things — a more positive face — and Levi was grateful for that.

Supper that evening was a somber affair. Levi was tired from the stresses of the day. Attendance for the matinee had been good but people had not spent the extra money for the sideshows and cotton candy and popcorn that they usually did. Although the wealthy classes were still thriving, these were hard times for ordinary folks and it did not look as if things were going to get much better for some time.

But the real gloom that hung over the gathering was the fact that there had been no sign of the boy. Hannah kept her eyes lowered as she methodically sipped her soup. Levi doubted she was even aware that she was taking in nourishment. Gunther kept glancing at his daughter-in-law and sighing heavily. Only Pleasant seemed to be enjoying the meal.

"Excuse me, sir." Hans entered the dining area with his usual catlike grace. He was holding a piece of yellow paper.

"A telegram?" Levi asked, reaching for it.

"Yes, sir. It's from Miss Ida."

Hannah looked up for the first time, her eyes flickering with some interest.

"Ida Benson," Levi explained to his guests. "She's my personal secretary. She headed straight back to Wisconsin once the company arrived here yesterday."

Levi read the short message. Then read it again. He glanced at Hannah, then handed her the telegram. "It's good news," he said softly.

■ ■ ■ ■

Hannah felt as if everyone must surely be able to see the beat of her heart under her caped dress. It was hammering away so hard that she thought she could actually feel the blood rushing through her veins. Her hand shook slightly as she accepted the telegram.

Amish runaway in my cabin. Stop. Just crossed into Indiana. Stop. Please instruct. Stop. Ida

She read the words again. *Amish runaway.* "It's Caleb," she whispered as if to assure herself, then she turned to her father-in-law and handed him the wire. "It's Caleb," she repeated as relief washed through her like a cleansing dip in the Gulf. She grasped Pleasant's hand as they waited for Gunther to scan the words.

"Could be," he said cautiously.

"Must be," Pleasant said firmly. "Now what?"

All eyes turned to Levi.

"There are several options," he began slowly. "Miss Benson could put the boy on the next train back to Sarasota or she could get him a ticket to meet us tomorrow at our next stop in Georgia."

"She could not accompany him?" Gunther asked.

"Miss Benson has a great deal of work to do once she reaches Wisconsin," Levi explained. "That's why she has traveled back ahead of the rest of us."

"Someone else, then." Pleasant's tone was less a question than a demand.

"There is no one else. Miss Benson is traveling alone."

"You said there were several options," Hannah reminded him. "Allowing Caleb to travel alone seems risky to me."

"And yet, Hannah, he has been traveling alone since the night he ran away."

"That's my point. Caleb ran away and he hates to fail at anything so if he's put on a train alone my concern is that he will decide to make another attempt and that this time we will have no Miss Benson to watch over him."

Levi slowly removed his reading glasses and set them on the pristine, white tablecloth as he leaned back in his chair and ran one large palm over his face. He looked so weary and certainly the last thing he needed right now was this. Hannah hated adding to his worries, but this was her son.

"I suppose," he began, then looked from her to Gunther to Pleasant before continuing. "I suppose that I could instruct Ida to take the boy with her, get him settled with a farm family she knows in Baraboo and keep an eye on him until you can all get there."

"Baraboo?" Pleasant asked, her eyes suddenly alive with interest.

"Yes. It's the town where we have our summer headquarters," Levi replied. "Do you know it?"

To Hannah's shock, Pleasant blushed scarlet and returned her attention to her soup. "I . . . no . . . just a curious name."

"How soon would we get there?" Hannah asked.

"By commercial train, two to three days depending on when we can get you tickets."

Hannah glanced at her father-in-law and saw him frown. She was well aware that he was calculating the expense. "I could go and you and Pleasant could return to Sarasota," she suggested.

"Absolutely not," Gunther thundered. "The very idea of you traveling alone . . ."

"Or you could continue as my guests and arrive back in Wisconsin in two weeks," Levi suggested. "That way you will only encounter the expense of the return trip. In the meantime, I assure you that Caleb will be quite well-provided for and perhaps have the time to consider the error of his actions.

The family I spoke of is Amish. The woman is a close friend of Miss Benson's."

Now all eyes swiveled to Gunther's place at the opposite end of the table from Levi. *Please,* Hannah prayed silently.

Gunther cleared his throat but said nothing.

"We could send word to your people in Sarasota," Levi suggested. "Let them know the trip will take longer than expected."

"I also have a business to run," Gunther reminded him and the women, and Hannah steeled herself to stand her ground. Under no circumstances was she going to allow Caleb to travel alone and risk losing him again.

She was just about to make her case when Pleasant spoke up. "Oh, Father, you know how Bishop Troyer loves taking charge." She turned to Levi, explaining, "He's up in years and has little to occupy him beyond church business these days."

"He's competent?" Levi asked Gunther.

"Exceptionally so," Gunther agreed. "But, daughter, while I agree that he can manage the business itself, who would you suggest do the baking?"

Pleasant opened her mouth then closed it. She clearly had not considered that.

"I will go with Levi to Wisconsin and fetch

the boy. You two girls will return to Sarasota as planned in the morning." He nodded once and flattened both palms against the table as if that made everything final.

Hannah could feel Levi watching her. Well, what did he expect her to do? This was her father-in-law and in the absence of her husband, the head of the family.

But Caleb is your son — your only child.

She closed her eyes tightly against the warring loyalties within her then said quietly, "If you think that best." Then she folded her napkin and pushed away from the table. "Will you excuse me? I'd like to take a walk before bedtime."

To her shock, Pleasant also pushed back from the table. "I'll come with you," she announced.

Hannah sighed. She needed some time to think, but Pleasant was right behind her and as soon as both had stepped off the train, Pleasant took her arm. Her sister-in-law was silent for a bit and then leaned in close, glancing back toward Levi's private car as she whispered, "I think I might know a way Papa will agree to have us all travel to Baraboo."

CHAPTER SIX

Once again the grounds were alive with activity as the company prepared for the evening performance. Levi had explained that the activity would go on long into the night as the crew dismantled the big top, loaded up the animals and wagons and prepared to move on to the next stop. There they would repeat the entire process all over again as they would half a dozen times on the way back to Baraboo. It was so noisy on the circus grounds that Hannah was certain she must have misunderstood Pleasant's astonishing comment.

"Hannah? Did you hear what I said?"

She fought her irritation at Pleasant's sudden and surprising decision to join her in her walk. "No. The noise."

Pleasant pulled Hannah toward the creek, away from the clatter. "I don't mean to pry but . . ."

Hannah steeled herself for what was to

come for when Pleasant said she didn't mean to pry, prying was just what she did. "Go on," she said. *Get it out so we can move past it.*

"Well, of course you're Caleb's mother — his only living parent. I'm just his aunt, but if he were my child, I would want to go and fetch him myself. I would want to be there. I would want to hear what he had to say for himself — why he would put me and the rest of the family in such . . ."

Hannah couldn't help it. She burst into tears. "Of course, I want to go to him," she blubbered. "How could I not? I have been so frightened for him, so very worried that perhaps . . ." She couldn't begin to finish that thought. All of the awful possibilities of what might have happened to her child that had gone through her mind these past two days.

"There, there," Pleasant soothed as she put her arm around Hannah's shoulders. "I didn't mean to upset you so. Of course, you've been worried and of course, you would go to him tonight if you could."

Hannah sniffed back tears and tried to compose herself. They had stopped next to a live oak tree drooping like a willow with Spanish moss. "Then why . . ."

Pleasant pursed her lips and glanced

around as if half expecting someone to be listening in on their conversation. "Do you remember Mr. Noah Yoder from last winter?"

Hannah was so confused by the sudden shift in conversation that she shook her head.

"Of course you do," Pleasant pressed. "He came down to visit his uncle and to see about possibly buying land and starting a produce farm?"

"Vaguely," Hannah said, recalling a small jovial young man who had developed a habit of appearing at the bakery every morning at opening time, and again in the afternoons when Pleasant was cleaning up for the day. "He used to come to the bakery for fresh hot rolls every morning and buy up the leftover rolls at the end of the day."

"That's him," Pleasant said, a smile softening her usually stern features, a look that Hannah had never before witnessed.

"As I recall, he decided against buying land and returned to . . ." Her eyes widened in understanding. "Baraboo, Wisconsin," she whispered.

"Don't you see, Hannah, if we could just persuade Father that it's only right for you to be the one to see Caleb first then he would insist on traveling with you and if he won't let you travel alone then he certainly would not allow me to return home alone and . . ."

"Slow down," Hannah said but she was beginning to see the possibilities in Pleasant's chatter. "So if the three of us traveled on to Wisconsin then you might . . ."

"I could possibly see Mr. Yoder again — I mean Levi said there's an Amish community nearby where Caleb will stay until we can get there and how many Amish communities can there be in such a place and if Mr. Yoder is there, then . . ."

"But what about the bakery?"

"I thought of that and perhaps it's time my half sisters stepped in to help. After all," she continued, "there are two of them to share the baking and the housework and all."

"Lydia is just seventeen," Hannah reminded her, but Pleasant only shrugged.

"Why couldn't she do the work, or perhaps the two of them working together? I mean it would be no different if I suddenly took ill, would it? They'd have to step in then."

"You've thought all this through in just a matter of minutes?" Hannah was impressed. No wonder her sister-in-law had been so quiet when they first started their walk.

"I've been thinking about it — not really daring to hope, of course — since we first boarded the train. And then when Levi mentioned Baraboo earlier it was like a sign. Don't you think so, Hannah? Don't you think that perhaps God has given me this opportunity to travel there and perhaps to . . ." She waved her hand in the air, unwilling to finish her hope aloud.

"But your father has decided," Hannah reminded her, knowing she did not have to add that once he made up his mind Gunther did not like being second-guessed.

Pleasant looked crestfallen, but then brightened. "Perhaps Levi could help. He likes you, Hannah. He would certainly understand how badly you want to see your child. Yes, he's the one I shall speak with and then he can persuade Father. I'll do it right now before I lose my nerve," she announced, and turned on her heels and marched straight back to Levi's private car.

Levi had just learned that the Stravinskys were leaving his employ and staying in Florida. It wasn't that uncommon in his business for people to come and go, but Igor Stravinsky and his wife, Maria, as well as Igor's brother, Ivan, had been with him almost from the beginning. Igor and Ivan had handled the stock of ring or performance horses, grooming the animals and polishing their silver or brass trappings until they glittered. Maria had done everything from mending to designing costumes for the company. Igor had apologized for the inconvenience but pleaded old age even though he was only in his midforties. Maria had admitted that she wanted time to enjoy a home of her own. Together the brothers had pooled their money and bought a small business in central Florida. They had thought the deal would not be finalized for several weeks but the owner of the shop had taken ill and unless they took over immediately the shop would have to be closed until they could.

"I don't like leaving you in the middle of the trip back and all," Igor told him, "but what can we do?"

It was clear to Levi that the decision had not been an easy one for the trio and he was touched by their loyalty. "I wish you well," he said as he walked out onto the observation platform of his railroad car with Igor. "Stay in touch, my friend," he added, and accepted the bear hug the older man gave him before running down the three metal steps and racing off to get ready for his last performance and to tell his wife and brother the news.

Pleased for them in spite of the inconvenience their leaving meant to his business, Levi could not help feeling a little envious. What might it be like to settle down in one place? *You chose your path,* he reminded himself and went back inside to work out the logistics of filling three holes in his company.

He was going over the roster of employees, trying to decide how to shift people around so that they would be covered at least until they got home to Baraboo when Hans cleared his throat.

"Miss Goodloe to see you, sir."

"Hannah?" Levi ignored the quickening of his heart. He'd been worried about her after the conversation at supper was all. He could see that she was upset and why wouldn't she be?

"It's *Miss* Pleasant Goodloe, sir."

Levi stifled a groan. He'd had little contact with Gunther's daughter but her demeanor always set him on edge. "Very well," he said and stood up to put on his suitcoat. "Show her in."

The woman seemed unusually nervous and vulnerable.

"How can I help you, Pleasant? Has something happened?" He suddenly worried that one of the townspeople Jake often hired to help out with the backstage work might have accosted the woman.

She drew in a deep breath, squeezed her eyes closed for a couple of seconds and then blurted out a speech she had apparently been practicing. "Hannah needs your help in convincing my father that it is she who should be the first to reunite with Caleb. After all, she is the parent — the only parent — and if she is not there, well, what does that say to the boy? That she has no authority, that's what it says. So she must be the one to go and fetch him from Wisconsin and since my father is opposed to women traveling alone, I will just have to go along as well because . . ."

Well, well, well, Levi thought as he stifled a smile. *For whatever reason, Miss Pleasant Goodloe was not yet ready to go home. Perhaps young Caleb was not the only member of this family that had entertained dreams of a different life?*

She continued to prattle on making her case, grabbing short breaths between phrases and leaving him no possible entry into the conversation. Finally, completely winded and unable to find the words to add to her plea, she stopped talking and looked

101

at him, her eyebrows raised like question marks.

"And what does Hannah — Mrs. Good-loe — think of your idea?"

"Hannah will not go against my father's decision," she replied. "However, she was sobbing inconsolably before and well, how would you feel if your only son had run away, been found hundreds of miles away and you were going to have to wait for weeks to see him again?"

"I see your point," Levi mused, having only heard the part about Hannah crying. He fingered the papers on his desk, his eyes coming to rest on the place where he had marked through the names of the Stravin-skys and placed blank lines next to their positions. "Do you sew, Pleasant?"

"Of course I sew," she snapped.

"And Hannah?"

"Amish women are well-skilled in the things necessary to run a household, Levi. Cooking, sewing . . ."

"And your father appeared to have a solid knowledge of horses when we toured the grounds," he said more to himself than to her.

Pleasant tapped one foot impatiently. "I fear, sir, that you have lost track of our conversation. Will you help us persuade my father or not?"

Levi looked at her. The woman was speaking to him firmly and yet she was wringing her hands as if her very future depended upon his answer. "I believe I just might be able to be of service, Miss Goodloe. However, my plan involves you and Mrs. Goodloe working for me — in my circus."

Pleasant pressed her fist to her mouth. "Never," she whispered, clearly horrified at the very idea.

"Then I can't help you." He turned his attention to the papers on his desk, stacking them and replacing the cap on his fountain pen.

"What sort of work?"

"Sewing," he replied, still not looking at her. "Mending. The costumes take quite a beating in every performance."

Silence. He tapped the stack of papers against the leather blotter and waited.

"We wouldn't have to . . ."

"If you like, you could do the work in your cabin. You wouldn't have to have any contact at all with the performers if that's what worries you."

"I see. It might work."

"Is that a 'yes,' Miss Goodloe?" he asked as he turned to face her.

She hesitated only a second, again closed

her eyes tightly as if entreating God to show her the way, then nodded. "Yes," she whispered. "If you can convince my father to let us come to Wisconsin with you, then yes."

Levi smiled. "Very well. I'll speak to your father right away. Good night, Miss Goodloe."

Pleasant practically curtsied she was so happy with the news. "Thank you," she repeated as she backed her way down the hall. "Oh, thank you so much."

Levi was well aware that whatever Pleasant's reasons for coming to him, they had less to do with helping her sister-in-law than they did with facilitating a visit to Wisconsin for herself. Whatever her purpose, if he could convince Gunther to let the two women stay on, it meant he would see more of Hannah and, surprisingly, that thought made him feel an emotion he had long ago abandoned. Levi felt happiness.

When Pleasant had taken off to talk to Levi, Hannah had hurried to catch up with her. But then she had seen Lily outside the women's dressing tent having a cigarette. Lily had shown her a kindness and Hannah felt it only fair to let her in on the good news that Caleb had been found. To her surprise, Lily had hugged her hard as tears streamed down her cheeks.

"Oh, honey, that is just grand — just fabulous news. I am so happy for you." Then she'd brushed away her tears and asked about the plans for a reunion, frowning when Hannah told her of the current plan for Gunther to travel to Wisconsin while she and Pleasant returned home.

"But it should be you he sees first," Lily had protested.

Hannah had to admit that she agreed but what was she to do? In her world the men were the heads of households and in the absence of her husband, her father-in-law had every right to make the decision. Then she remembered Pleasant's idea and glanced toward the railroad car where she could see Levi pacing as Pleasant laid out her case, hands aflutter and voice rising enough that the sound carried out to the grounds.

"I should go," she told Lily. "Thank you again for your concern."

"We mothers have to stick together," Lily said as she hugged Hannah again and then hurried away, wiping away tears.

By the time Hannah reached Levi's private car, Pleasant had left the room and he was standing at his desk studying a typed sheet of names.

"Levi?" She was stunned when he turned

to her with a smile that lit up his handsome but usually brooding features.

"Ah, Hannah. I've just had a most interesting conversation with your sister-in-law. It seems that we may have come up with a plan that will be mutually beneficial to all parties concerned."

"I don't understand."

He chuckled. "No, I suppose not. Give me time to speak privately with Gunther and then I can explain everything."

"My father-in-law does not take kindly to having his decisions questioned once he's made up his mind," Hannah cautioned.

"Nor do I. But I believe I may be about to offer a proposition — a business proposition that may interest him." He shrugged. "If the result of that is that the three of you continue to travel with the show all the way to Wisconsin, then I can understand where that would be a bonus for you."

The man actually winked at her.

"I . . . we . . ."

"By the way," Levi continued, "I fully understand why you would want to go on to Wisconsin and be reunited with your son. What's Pleasant's agenda?"

"Agenda?"

"What's in it for her?"

"She . . ." Hannah felt her irritation at the

twists and turns of this conversation getting the better of her. "Can't she just want the best for me?"

Levi nodded. "She might but that's not her main goal. Pleasant is a woman who looks out for herself."

"In our culture we look out for each other," Hannah snapped.

His features darkened once again to the more familiar solemn demeanor she had come to expect from him. "Not always, Hannah," he murmured. "Not always."

In the silence that fell like a curtain between them, she could hear the brass trumpets of the circus band announcing the grand march that opened the evening show. "If you'll excuse me, Hannah, I want to be sure everything is going well with the opening," he said, moving toward the observation platform. "After that I'll speak with Gunther. Have a good evening."

Upon returning to their shared cabin, Hannah had insisted that she and Pleasant prepare for the journey back to Sarasota the following morning. The plan was that the two women would be taken to the public train station before dawn to await the southbound train while the circus train — this time pulling Levi's private car — moved north into Georgia.

But Pleasant refused to give up. She sat on the edge of her berth, gripping the muslin coverlet and murmuring prayers in the language they had learned as children.

An hour passed, and through the open window they could hear the laughter and oohs and ahs of the audience at the big top as the show moved from act to act. Another hour passed, and they could hear the finale and the applause and the excited chatter of the patrons as they left the show and headed home. And with every passing moment, Pleasant's assurance faded and Hannah released the kernel of hope that she had dared to plant.

"We should get some sleep," she said.

Pleasant nodded and pushed herself to her feet.

The knock at their cabin door startled them both.

"Daughters?"

Pleasant pressed her fist to her mouth to stem the flood of giggles that threatened to escape. Clearly, she thought her prayers had been answered.

Hannah was not so sure and when she opened the cabin door and saw her father-in-law standing in the narrow passageway, his brow knitted into a frown, she was positive that Levi's conversation with him had

108

not gone well.

"We have a dilemma," he said. "Please come so we may discuss this." Without another word he headed for the sitting room.

Pleasant practically pushed Hannah down the hallway in her eagerness to follow.

"Sit down, please," Gunther said as he remained standing — and pacing. Levi was nowhere in sight.

"What is it?" Hannah asked softly.

"Our friend, Levi, has a problem. One that he has asked for our help in addressing." As he told them the story of the Stravinskys leaving Levi's employ, Hannah could barely concentrate because Pleasant was squeezing her hand so tightly that she thought her fingers must surely crack and break.

"So we will help our friend who has shown us such kindness. We will all travel the rest of the way to Wisconsin and during the trip, Pleasant, you will mend and sew as needed and I will see to the ring horses. It is only right," he added, as if trying to assure himself that he had not gone back on a decision. Rather, he had made a new plan — one that served a fellow man.

"And what shall I do to help?" Hannah asked.

"Levi had thought to have you both tend

to the costumes although he only needs one. He asked if I could think of some other task for you, Hannah. I told him that you had taken charge of the office duties and accounting in the bakery back home. He seemed both surprised and pleased at that news. He wants you to serve as his secretary while Miss Benson is in Wisconsin."

Hannah let out a squeak of protest. "But . . ."

"It's only right that we should do whatever we can to help Levi now that he is the one in need," Gunther continued.

But as his secretary I will be called upon to spend time with him — time alone without the buffer of you and Pleasant. Hannah could not seem to find the words to convey these thoughts to Gunther. Instead, she said nothing, wondering why the idea of spending time alone with Levi was so upsetting to her when clearly it was not an issue for her father-in-law.

CHAPTER SEVEN

Hannah spent yet another sleepless night as she lay awake listening to the sounds of the workers dismantling the tents and loading the wagons and livestock. Sometime well after midnight, she felt the train begin to move and in minutes faced the fact that instead of boarding a public train for the trip back home, she was heading north to be reunited with her wayward son. The idea of seeing Caleb again cheered her, but she could not seem to control her anxiety at what working with Levi might mean.

What would he expect of her? And more to the point, was she up to the job? Keeping books for her father-in-law was one thing. His business was relatively simple. Over the past couple of days, she had been amazed at the complexities of running a circus. Levi employed so many people, some salaried and some paid by the hour. Still, they all needed to be paid. And then there was feeding them — not to mention feeding and caring for the animals and . . .

What did lions and tigers and elephants eat? she wondered. "And where does one purchase such items?" she muttered aloud. She imagined herself filling out orders for tons of wild animal food which led to imagining herself writing up correspondence as Levi dictated. She bolted upright. What if Levi expected her to use the typing machine that she'd seen Jake Jenkins pecking away on when she'd walked past the railroad car that served as the traveling circus's office?

But remembering Jake in that other car — in that more public place — was reassuring. Surely she would carry out her work as Levi's secretary from a desk there. She even recalled seeing an empty desk when she'd returned Jake's jovial greeting the previous afternoon.

She lay down again and this time she slept. It might not be so bad after all, she decided. At least it would make the time go more quickly and before she knew it, they would arrive in Wisconsin and she would see Caleb.

Levi sat on the private observation platform at the very rear of the train watching the shadowy scenery fly by. What had he been thinking suggesting that Hannah work as his secretary? Gunther had suggested both women take Maria's place in the costume shop and surely that would have been the wisest choice. After all, Maria was an experienced and talented circus seamstress. Sewing sequins back onto velvet or satin costumes was a far cry from what he imagined the usual sewing tasks might be for an Amish woman. Surely between the two of them they could muddle through until the company reached Baraboo and he could start interviewing potential replacements for Maria.

But, no, almost the minute Gunther had suggested the idea, Levi had rejected it. "I wonder if Mrs. Goodloe might not be qualified to assist me in the absence of my secretary, Miss Benson. I find that I have a great deal of work to get done before we get home to Wisconsin and while I can certainly instruct Miss Benson by way of letters and telegrams, it would be so much more efficient if I could simply handle things from here."

In his eagerness to repay Levi's kindness to his family, Gunther had readily agreed. He'd spent the next several minutes singing Hannah's praises. "The woman is remarkable with figures," he told Levi. "And she

113

writes a fine hand as well. I'm sure she could be a great help to you, Levi." Then he had smiled and added, "Frankly, her handiwork with a needle leaves something to be desired according to my daughter. Not that she can't sew a seam or mend a tear — it's just her stitches are not as small and tight as Pleasant's are."

What were you thinking? Levi wondered, propping his feet on the brass railing and closing his eyes as the warm May breeze rushed over his face. But instead of the blackness he sought in shutting out the passing world, he found himself visualizing Hannah.

Plain or not, she was one of the most beautiful women he'd ever seen. Her competitors had the advantage of enhancing their best features and concealing their lesser ones with cosmetics. Lily, for example, was by any man's standards, a beauty. But then he had never seen Lily without rouged lips and cheeks highlighted with fake color and eyelashes that had been artificially embellished.

Hannah wore no makeup and yet her lashes fanned her cheeks when she looked down — as she did far too often — and her cheeks glowed pink with the natural brush of the sun's kiss. Her lips were full and a soft rosy pink and every feature was set off perfectly by her skin — a soft golden color that was, no doubt, the result of days spent coming and going in the Florida sun.

He tried to imagine her hair and thought of the gold satin gown that Lily always wore for her entrance. Hannah's hair reminded him of that luxurious satin. She wore it in the traditional Amish style, pulled tight away from her face and wound into a bun under her prayer cap. What might it be like to see that hair falling freely down her back? he wondered. Would it come to her waist? Would it fall straight like a waterfall, or cascade its way down her back with natural curls and ringlets like a brook thawed after the winter, finding its way over rocks?

Levi pushed himself to a standing position, adjusting to the sway of the train as naturally as a ship's captain might adjust to the pitch and fall of a ship's deck. "Enough," he muttered, banishing the thought of Hannah Goodloe from his thoughts. "She's not for you so get some sleep."

But that night Levi did not enjoy the kind of dreamless sleep that comes from sheer exhaustion. That night he dreamed of Hannah Goodloe and by morning, he had made up his mind that she would be reassigned immediately to the costume department.

■ ■ ■ ■

But Hannah had been dressed before the train pulled on to the siding near the field where the circus would set up. The instant she felt it roll to a stop, she quietly left the cabin and hurried along the passageway to the rear exit from Levi's private car. The morning was cool so she wrapped her head and shoulders in a shawl as she walked quickly along the length of the train.

All around her people had already sprung into action, unloading wagons and hitching them to teams so they could be pulled to the circus grounds several blocks away. The dining and cooking tents were already up, having arrived on a separate train that had left Jonesville even as the evening performance was going on. Hannah could smell eggs and bacon frying and gallons of coffee brewing in anticipation of feeding the cast and crew. Several dozen local people had already gathered at the site — some to watch and some hoping to help out and perhaps pick up some extra money. Automatically, Hannah scanned their faces for any sign of Caleb. Although she knew he was safe in Wisconsin, somehow she couldn't help looking for him.

116

Finally, she reached the steps leading into the car reserved for the female performers. She wanted some advice and she thought she knew exactly who would be her wisest choice as a counselor and confidante. A woman on her way back to her berth pointed to a private cabin at the opposite end of the car near the galley kitchen.

Hannah tapped lightly on the frosted glass of the narrow door. "Lily?" she whispered so as not to disturb others who were still sleeping. "Are you awake?" She opened the door a crack.

"Coasting," Lily grumbled. "Who's that?" She rolled over and blinked several times as she adjusted her eyes to the light and to the unexpected sight of Hannah standing next to her. "What's happened?" she demanded as she rolled to a sitting position and reached for her robe.

"Nothing," Hannah assured her. "I'm sorry I woke you. It's just that . . . I mean if you could spare me a few minutes . . ."

"It isn't your son, is it? I mean, nothing's happened to the kid?"

"No. As far as I know he's fine — safe in Baraboo."

"Could you keep it down?" a voice from down the way grumbled. "I'm trying to sleep."

Lily thrust her feet into feathered slippers as she wrapped her robe tightly around her and tied the sash, then motioned for Hannah to follow her. In the small galley kitchen she filled two stained mugs with coffee and handed one to Hannah. "Speak," she commanded as she took a long swallow of the hot liquid and closed her eyes as it made its way down her throat.

Hannah told her of the plan for her to work for Levi while her in-laws also worked, but in other parts of the circus.

"Sounds like you got the better end of that deal," Lily said. "What's the problem?"

And suddenly Hannah was completely at a loss for words. What was she going to say? That she couldn't work so closely with Levi because . . . *Because why?*

Because you are drawn to him. Because there is an attraction there that you recognize because it's what you once felt for your husband when you first met him. Because . . .

"Hannah?" Lily had set her mug aside and was patting Hannah's shoulder and peering at her with curiosity. "Is it because Levi — I mean he hasn't made any — you know — advances or anything, has he?"

"Oh, no," Hannah rushed to reassure her and when she saw the relief in Lily's eyes, she realized for the first time what a fool

118

she was being. Levi would hardly be interested in someone like her when there were women as beautiful as Lily around. After all, he could have his pick of any number of women — not just the performers, but women in the towns where the circus traveled, high-society women in Sarasota. What had she been thinking?

She smiled at Lily. "I'm just having a case of nerves," she said. "I've never worked for anyone but my husband and father-in-law. This is going to be so different and . . ."

"Levi is a good and patient man. If he's asked for you to step in for Ida while we're on the road, then take that as a compliment. Ida is like his right arm. She does everything for him, knows where everything is, can almost do what he wants before he even knows he wants it. Ida and Hans keep Levi on track."

Hannah blurted the first thing that came to mind, "Sounds like a wife."

Lily burst into laughter so raucous that several sleepy-eyed women poked their heads out of their berths and shouted at her to keep it down. "Ida might be like his wife, but I think Levi's taste in women runs to someone a lot younger and prettier — like you, honey." She pinched Hannah's cheek and drained the last of her coffee. "You'll be fine. The boss is way too much of a gentleman to cause you any problems, okay?"

"Thank you."

Lily yawned and stretched. "Let me throw on some clothes and let's go see what the cook's fried up for breakfast."

"I should . . ." Hannah started to say that she should get back to Levi's private car for breakfast with her in-laws and Levi, but then thought better of it. If they were going to work for Levi then why should they receive special treatment? "Lily, are there any extra berths in this car?"

"A couple of third berths," she replied, pointing to a row of top berths where even lying down a person's nose would be only inches from the ceiling. "Why?"

"I was just thinking that maybe Pleasant and I should move in here — I mean now that we're working for the circus."

Lily stopped midstride. "Okay, let me get this straight. You have your own private quarters in Levi's luxuriously appointed car, your meals served up by his personal cook, your needs attended to by Hans and you want to trade that for this?" She swept her arm in an arch to take in the cramped, stuffy surroundings.

Hannah shrugged. "It only seems fair."

"Well, I'd pay to be a fly on the wall when you have that conversation with Levi, honey."

Once Levi Harmon made up his mind about something he liked to take action and move on. The problem was that he could not seem to locate Hannah to tell her of his decision to put her to work with Pleasant in the costume shop.

She had not appeared for breakfast and neither Pleasant nor Gunther had seen her. Pleasant remembered hearing her go out quite early and surmised that she had gone for one of her usual walks. "She starts every morning that way," Pleasant told him. "And more often than not ends the day with a walk as well. Of course, since we've been traveling with you, she's had that schedule disrupted a bit, but my guess is that if there's a stream or river nearby you'll find her there."

Gunther had offered to go looking for his daughter-in-law, but Levi needed the older man to get started working with the rest of the crew. He would be checking the horses, replacing a shoe if necessary and making sure the horses and their harnesses were in perfect order for the day's parade and two performances. "I'll go," Levi said as he

121

dabbed the corners of his mouth with his linen napkin and laid it aside. "Pleasant, if you would be so kind as to report to the costume tent. The head seamstress, now that Mrs. Stravinsky is gone, is Ruth Davis. She can show you what needs to be done before this afternoon's matinee."

He'd looked everywhere when he saw Hannah talking to the box-office manager. She glanced up as if she had somehow sensed his nearness, said a few words to the box-office manager and hurried toward him.

"Good morning," she said a little out of breath. "I think I lost track of time. I was talking to some of the cast and crew, wanting to learn as much as possible about how things work. I mean, Levi, it's actually quite exciting, isn't it? It's like a small community in and of itself but one that moves around."

Her cheeks were flushed and her smile radiated the excitement of her discovery.

"And so perhaps you begin to understand the appeal for young Caleb," he said, and knew in that instant that he would not forbid himself the opportunity — however brief — to be closer to her by working with her. There was something about her that made him look forward to the day. Perhaps it was her innocence, that naiveté that came with discovering a world you never knew existed. He'd been living in the midst of it for so many years that in spite of his wealth and material comforts, life had lost all of its freshness for him.

Her expression sobered. "What I know is that I have suffered the sin of prejudice, Levi. I had judged these people and their lifestyle without once taking the time to understand. It's not a life I would choose, but I see now that these are good people whose hopes for themselves and their families are not so very different from my own."

He started to walk back to the outside of the big top toward the backyard of the circus and she fell into step with him. "And what will you do if your son's infatuation with the life has not yet been satisfied?" he asked.

"I don't know," she admitted.

"I mean Caleb is what? Eleven, you said?"

"Almost twelve."

"Then he has some time."

He saw her peer up at him curiously. "Time?"

"Well, as I understand it, a boy does not make a final decision to follow the ways of the Amish until he's maybe fourteen?" He had taken this conversation too far and soon she would start to raise questions he wasn't prepared to answer. Questions like how it was that he knew so much about the Amish life. He cast about for some way to change the subject. "Ah, there's Jake. Good. You can go over the accounting procedures with him while I see how your father-in-law is adjusting to his new duties." He walked ahead of her, hailing his friend. He had almost said too much. He had almost opened the door to the past. What was it about this woman that made him want to do that? He'd had dealings with other Amish before — trading with them as the circus traveled from town to town. But of course, he had never actually had members of that faith traveling with him. He had never had to face the daily reminder of what he had run away from all those years ago. Not until Hannah Goodloe had walked up to his front door and into his life.

CHAPTER EIGHT

The business office was housed in a converted passenger car, although any resemblance between that space and Levi's private car ended there. The seats and overhead berths had been removed and in their place were three large oak desks on the window side of the car, and behind them a wall of enclosed shelving filled with files and ledgers and office supplies.

"That's Ida's desk there," Jake Jenkins said. "The middle one is for our twenty-four-hour guy, Chester Tuck, and that last one near the payroll window is mine."

"Mr. Tuck really works twenty-four hours a day?" Hannah asked.

Jake scratched his slicked-back hair and frowned. Then he exploded into laughter. "No, not at all. It's a circus term for the lead guy. Chester is the one member of the staff who travels ahead of the rest of the company to make sure everything's ready for us when we arrive. Usually, that's a day ahead, like he got here yesterday while our first train section arrived this morning. See?"

"It's confusing but yes, I think I understand. Mr. Tuck works with the townspeople but always in the next town on the schedule."

"That's pretty much the idea. He's hardly ever here. Or if he is, he tends to be here at night while the show's going on, catching up before he heads out to the next town," Jake said as he sat down in a scarred wooden swivel chair and plopped both of his feet on top of his desk. "So, what's Levi got in mind for you?"

Hannah didn't like his tone or the way one of his eyebrows arched suggestively. "Filing. Correspondence," she replied as she considered the items on Ida Benson's desk. A compartment filled with pencils, a stack of unused paper, a spiral-bound notebook, two bottles of ink — one black and one red — and two fountain pens resting on an onyx stand. The typewriter sat on a separate metal stand to one side of Ida's desk chair.

"You know how to type?" Jake asked as Hannah ran her fingers over the keys.

"No," she admitted, noticing for the first

time that the letters were not in alphabetical order as she might have expected. The squeal of Jake's chair as he stood and came toward her startled her and she jumped as if she'd just had a terrible fright.

"Sorry. Didn't mean to scare you." He reached around her and took down a straw hat from the brass hook behind her. The hat looked brand new. Jake was definitely a man who took pride in his looks, she thought. "I have to go out for a while. In the meantim —" he plopped a wire basket piled high with papers on the desk "— you can start filing these." Near the doorway he pulled open a file drawer and pointed. "Each invoice goes into a folder in here — these are paid," he said. "So animal food goes under 'feed,' people food goes under 'kitchen' and so on. Pretty straightforward," he assured her as he put on the hat, checked his appearance in a small mirror hanging by the door and left.

"When do you think Levi . . . that is, Mr. Harmon will return?"

Jake shrugged. "He'll be back soon enough. If you want to impress him, get that filing done." He waved then turned a corner and was gone.

Hannah stood at the door for a minute longer scanning the grounds for any sign of

Levi. After all, supposedly she was working for him. Shouldn't he be the one giving her tasks to complete?

But there was no sign of him. Outside the railroad car, the grounds teemed with activity and Hannah was struck once again with how very much the circus was like its own little neighborhood. People coming and going, attending to their work, calling out greetings to each other. It felt like . . . home. It was nothing like she had imagined, and the idea that Caleb had traveled that first night with these good people gave her such a sense of relief that she found herself humming an old hymn as she turned to attend to her work.

Levi had made his escape so abruptly that he realized now that he had failed to give Hannah any proper instructions. Well, Jake could show her the ropes. His friend and business manager certainly knew as much about what Ida did day-to-day as Levi knew.

But that really wasn't the point. There was something about the Amish woman that made him want to run as far and fast away from her as possible and yet at the same time, he was drawn to her like the moths that fluttered around the spotlights at the evening performances.

True to his nature, Levi was determined to solve the mystery of his attraction to Hannah Goodloe — an attraction that he suspected she would agree was impossible. Okay, so she was a natural beauty. That much he'd already determined. And she was a person of conviction and strength — two traits he had always respected in others. But there were plenty of beautiful women and most of his friends and employees had been chosen on the basis of their strength of character. So what was it?

Her unavailability? Was that the attraction? For some men — like Jake Jenkins — that would have been the draw. The sheer challenge of the chase. But Levi wasn't like that. Men like Jake tended to view women as objects set before them for their personal pleasure — objects that could be replaced. The one thing that was missing in Levi's life was a woman with whom he could share the fortune and lavish lifestyle that he'd worked so hard to build. Someone whose eyes would light up with delight as he showered her with jewels and gifts and showed her places she had only read about in books.

Hannah Goodloe was not that woman. She was of the "plain" tradition — a tradition that set no value on material things.

And suddenly it clicked. Hannah Goodloe's attraction for him was that she had found contentment in the very life that he had cast aside all those year earlier. A life that he had cavalierly rejected as too boring and restricting.

Relieved that he finally understood why he was drawn to the woman and could safely dismiss the idea of any romantic attraction, Levi headed back across the circus grounds to the payroll car. He could work with her now that he understood her and he would simply ignore the obvious question of why Gunther and Pleasant Goodloe did not stir the same fascination within him that Hannah did.

Hannah made quick work of the filing project then looked around for other ways to make herself useful. She found cleaning supplies in a corner of the car near the sink. Using a feather duster, she went over Ida's desk — now hers, she supposed — and then Chester's desk, which was bare except for a wire basket attached to one corner and filled with papers similar to those she had just filed.

The basket was labeled "Invoices to be paid" so she carefully dusted around them so as not to disturb the order. But the top invoice caught her eye. It was from a feed company in Jonesville, Florida — the town they had just left. She had filed a similar invoice in the paid drawer — similar in more than just the letterhead it was printed on. The amount for the bill struck her as odd.

"Seventy-nine dollars and ninety-seven cents," she murmured, remembering that she had noted the same reversal of numbers on the filed invoice. She carried the invoice from Chester's desk over to the file cabinet and compared it to the one marked "paid." They were identical — date, list of items ordered, amount — everything. "Why would there be two . . . ?"

"I apologize for being away so long," Levi said as he climbed the two metal steps to the entrance and filled the car with his presence.

Unnerved that she'd been caught snooping into matters that were certainly none of her business, Hannah slammed the file drawer shut as soon as she heard his voice, and by the time he'd entered the car, she was back dusting Chester's desk.

"I see you found something to occupy yourself," Levi said, nodding toward the feather duster. "Where's Jake?"

"He said something about an errand. I did the filing he gave me and then — well, I found the duster and broom and thought . . ."

"Hannah, I don't expect you to clean," Levi said.

"I don't mind," she replied. "In fact, I find it soothing. Besides, you keep money in here for the payroll, right?" She had noticed the large heavy safe that practically filled one end of the long car.

Levi's eyes widened. "We do. I don't see . . ."

"It just occurs to me that if only you and I and Mr. Tuck and Mr. Jenkins have access to this car, it would be a kind of safety measure. If it's just the three of us — and you, of course — then there's no temptation for someone coming in."

To her surprise, Levi grinned and then laughed out loud. Oh, the things laughter did for his features. It took her breath away how handsome he was when he smiled.

"It's just a suggestion," she huffed, offended that she had been the cause of his laughter.

"And a good one it is," he agreed. "I didn't mean to laugh, Hannah. It's just that you're the last person I would have thought might imagine anyone trying to steal something."

"Why?"

He shrugged. "You're Amish."

"We are Amish, Levi, not angels. As among any people, there are those who lose their way. Some young men broke into the bakery just last fall. They nearly tore the place apart looking for money, not knowing that Gunther always carried the day's receipts home with him after closing."

"Were they arrested?"

"It is not our way to turn our own transgressors over to outside authorities. The two young men were brought to the bishop by their families and it was handled within our community."

"They were shunned," Levi guessed, and she could not help but notice that it was not a question.

"They were banned and when they saw and admitted the error of their ways and promised to change, they were forgiven."

"And where are they now?"

"One of them works for my father-in-law and the other works on his family's celery farm."

"They came back even though . . . ?"

"Everyone deserves a second chance, Levi," she said softly. "Our ways offer that."

He took the feather duster from her and placed it and the broom back on their hooks. "Either way, I do not expect you to

133

clean, Hannah. If you feel the urge to do so in order to think through some issue you may be dealing with, then I suppose it would be cruel to stop you. But you are here in the capacity of interim secretary, and I suspect you will have plenty to do between now and when we reach Wisconsin in a few weeks."

"I don't know how to use that contraption," she blurted nervously, pointing to the typewriter.

"I prefer letters written in longhand for my correspondence. Anything else can wait until we reach Baraboo," Levi replied. "What else?"

Hannah glanced around the space. "I don't know — not until you tell me what you expect."

"Hannah, this is not a test. Gunther wants — no, he needs to feel as if the three of you are somehow making a contribution in repayment for the journey to collect your son. I am just trying to honor that."

"Then why not put me to work with Pleasant in the wardrobe department?"

To her surprise, another smile tugged at the corners of his mouth. "The fact is that I was told that your sewing skills are not exactly . . . that you are far better at figures and filing and the like."

"It's true," she admitted. "I mean, Pleasant's stitches are tiny and so wonderfully straight and mine . . ." She shrugged and risked a glance up at him.

"Actually, I'm relieved," Levi said. "I find that at the moment, I need the services of a good and efficient secretary far more desperately than I need another pair of sewing hands. So, will you help me?"

It occurred to Hannah that he was very good at his work. For what was the circus business after all, except one of persuading others to part with their hard-earned money to experience something that would be over in a couple of hours with nothing to show for it but memories? That kind of persuasion came so naturally to him that it no doubt took very little to turn those talents of persuasion into talents for making others feel needed. She studied his expression for any sign that he was trying to trick her. But instead, she saw that his eyes were almost pleading. She didn't know why, but Levi Harmon was counting on her, beseeching her to accept his offer.

"Very well," she said, and was quite positive that his expression shifted at once to one of relief and then as quickly to one of business.

"Excellent. Now let me show you the basic

routine. Every morning, there will be several messages that have come in during the night. I'll need you to sort through . . ."

And so it went for the better part of an hour. As Levi instructed, Hannah made notes in the spiral-bound notebook. These files were kept separate. Those were ready to be disposed of as soon as she had updated the ledger. Jake would give her this. Chester would need her to see to something else. She began to have a deep respect for Ida Benson's ability to keep it all running smoothly.

Still, it was invigorating. For one thing, it took her mind off Caleb and her worries about the boy. For it had occurred to her that bringing him home to Florida would not solve the problem. He had run away — more to the point he had run toward another lifestyle. And now having experienced a bit of that lifestyle herself, she could understand why circus life had been attractive to her son. How was she going to make sure that he didn't resent returning to the community and culture that he had abandoned?

"What is it, Hannah?"

She'd allowed her thoughts to wander and failed to notice that Levi had stopped talking.

"Nothi . . ." But she was incapable of lying. "I was just thinking about my son," she admitted. "I apologize. It seems that even though I know he is safe, I can't stop worrying about him. I'm sure you never gave your mother cause for such concern, Levi." She was trying to lighten the moment, but the dark shadow that crossed his eyes told her she'd failed.

"My parents died when I was just a little older than Caleb is now," he said.

"I'm so sorry. That must have been so very painful. Both of them?"

He nodded. "There was a tornado. My grandfather had insisted that my father go out to the barn and secure the animals. When he didn't come back, Ma made all us kids go into the cellar and then she went after him. The tornado hit the barn and it collapsed, killing them both."

"Oh, Levi, how awful for you — for all of you."

He picked up the story as if she hadn't spoken, as if he needed to tell it all and be done with it. "My sisters went to live with an aunt and uncle in Iowa. My younger brother and I went to live with our grand parents." He studied her for a long moment as if trying to decide whether or not to tell her more. "And then," he said softly, using his forefinger to push a wisp of her hair back into place, "the circus came to town and when it left — just like Caleb — I went with it."

CHAPTER NINE

Levi watched her incredible blue eyes grow large with shock. "You?"

He nodded.

"But your grandparents — your siblings . . ."

"They were all happy with the life they had. Three of them were too young to truly miss our parents. My eldest sister was being courted by a boy she'd met in Iowa. I had never really taken to life on the farm even when my parents were alive. But Matthew was a natural. He followed our grandfather around like a puppy, soaking up every facet of the farm life."

"How old were you when you left and what did your grandparents say when they found out where you'd gone and didn't anyone try and find you or bring you home?"

The questions poured out of her and he knew that in place of him she was seeing her own son. Instead of comforting her, he had only added to her worries. "It's not the same, Hannah. My situation and Caleb's are completely different."

"I don't see how. You were what — twelve?"

"Fourteen — old enough to begin to think of being out on my own. Old enough that others expected me to take an interest in the farm that I would one day inherit."

"Even so," she conceded reluctantly, "it was circus life that drew your interest and made you decide to leave."

He really couldn't argue that point, but he had to try. "Look, there's more to the story than just a boy out for an adventure. Just take my word for it. My circumstances were nothing like Caleb's."

"I don't see so much difference. Caleb's father is dead and . . ."

"But he has you and he has Gunther."

"And you had your grandparents," she pointed out.

"Not the same," he said, and gazed out the open door of the payroll car. "Ah, here's Jake." Relieved to have a buffer that would prevent Hannah from questioning him further, Levi did not even think of wondering where his friend had disappeared to, or what might lie behind the scowl he wore in

140

place of his usual hearty smile.

"I was just going through the routine with Hannah," Levi explained. "I think we're going to have to keep her busy with filing and correspondence, Jake. I found her cleaning the place when I got back."

"Oh, that won't do, Mrs. Goodloe," Jake said. "Miss Benson is quite dedicated to the cause of making sure women hold what she likes to refer to as 'their rightful place in the world.' And that means if you have been given the post of secretary, you have not — at least in Ida's world — been handed the position of cleaning lady along with it."

"But . . ."

Levi held up one professorial finger to Jake, interrupting her. "I'm afraid we may have to remind Ida that in Mrs. Goodloe's world, the role of women first and foremost is that of making a home for others."

"Ida will try and change your mind on that one," Jake told Hannah. "Trust me, she thinks the world would be a good sight better run if women handled business and politics and men were relegated to cleaning and cooking."

Levi saw that Hannah was becoming alarmed at this discussion, but he was also relieved that it had at least taken her mind off her son. "Don't pay too much attention to what my friend here says. He does tend to embellish the situation."

Jake grinned. "You meet Ida," he instructed Hannah, "and then decide if every word I just spoke isn't the truth." He walked the length of the car and settled into his desk chair as he pulled a stack of papers toward him.

"That reminds me," Hannah said. She picked up the top paper from the basket on Chester's desk and showed it to Jake. "When I was dusting I saw this. It's a duplicate of the one you had me file earlier and I was just wondering . . ."

Levi watched as Jake snatched the invoice from Hannah's outstretched hand and studied it. "No, I paid this," he muttered as he rifled through the pages of an oversized ledger. "Yep, here it is right here." He pounded the notation several times with his forefinger, then glanced up at Levi.

"I'm sure you did," Levi said. "Chester might just like to keep his own copies of each invoice. I think he told me once that it helps when he's negotiating with a new vendor to be able to show what price we've gotten from others."

Jake seemed unconvinced. "I guess. Anyway it's paid — says so right here." He tapped the ledger page again and then closed the book and smiled up at them. "Well, getting close to matinee time. You should come see the show, Hannah. I mean if you're going to work here, shouldn't you know how the folks we're paying earn their money?"

Hannah smiled. "It is not . . ."

". . . Your way," Jake finished for her. "Got it."

Levi frowned. He didn't like Jake making light of Hannah's lifestyle. And although she seemed unperturbed by the comment, Levi felt keenly protective toward her, wanting to be sure that she was not offended. "What Jake means is . . ."

"It's all right," she assured both men. And then with a twinkle in her eye added, "It is our way to have very thick skins when dealing with the outside world."

Jake exploded into laughter and nearly tipped his chair over backward. "She's a winner, this one, Levi. Can we keep her and get rid of Ida? I think she's going to be like a ray of sunshine around here."

Levi saw that Hannah was about to protest such an idea. "He's kidding," he told her. "Better get used to it. Jake is a great kidder, especially with anyone prone to taking his outrageous comments seriously."

"Does Miss Benson take you seriously?"

143

Hannah asked.

"Extremely," Jake assured her.

"Well, if someone who is seemingly so well-educated can be fooled by your humor, I can see that I will have to watch myself."

"Wise move," Levi said.

"But no fun at all," Jake added as he pushed himself away from the desk and headed for the exit. "Showtime," he said. "You kids have a good evening now." And he was gone.

"He makes you smile," Hannah noted.

And it was true. Levi's usually somber mood could always be relieved by an encounter with Jake. "He's my best friend — almost like a brother to me."

"You've known each other for some time, then?"

Levi smiled. "We were stowaways together on the circus train."

"Jake ran away as well?"

"There I was thinking I was so smart, hiding out in one of the baggage cars when all of a sudden a voice grumbles, 'This is my hiding place, kid. Find your own.' "

"You must have been frightened," Hannah guessed.

Levi chuckled. "I was. I mean, the voice was deep like a grown man's would be but my choice was to stay put or jump from a moving train. So I decided to stay put and before I knew it, I fell asleep."

"What happened?"

"When I woke up, Jake was sitting next to me chewing on a piece of jerky. It wasn't until he offered me a piece and muttered something about how he expected to be paid for the food that I put it together. That deep voice from the night before belonged to this skinny little kid who had to be at least a couple of years younger than I was."

"And the two of you became the best of friends," Hannah said, her smile radiant. "That's lovely, Levi."

"Friends and coworkers."

"So when you bought the circus . . ."

"Actually, I inherited it from the former owner. By that time Jake had gone his own way again — staying in Chicago for a time. The first thing I did once I took over was get in touch with him and ask him to come work with me."

"And neither of you ever married?" She blushed after asking the question. "I apologize. That is really none of my business."

"Jake came close. Me? I never even got close."

"I imagine it's difficult to maintain a relationship if one travels so much of the time," she said.

I could make it work with the right woman, he thought as he looked down at her. She was standing near the desk she would occupy and suddenly busied herself with rearranging the pens and other supplies Ida had left there.

"Hannah," he murmured more to test the feel of her name on his lips than to say anything.

She glanced up.

He reached over and twisted one string of her prayer cap around his forefinger. She did not waver from meeting his gaze. He leaned forward slightly and she remained as still as a flower on a windless day.

"Hannah," he whispered and her eyes drifted closed.

Levi was going to kiss her, Hannah thought and realized the greater surprise was that she was going to permit him to do so. *What's happening to me?*

"Hannah," he said softly. "Open your eyes and look at me."

She did as he asked and almost had to look away when she saw that the indecision she felt was mirrored in his gaze. "This is impossible, you know."

"Yes," she whispered and bowed her head.

He placed his forefinger under her chin

146

and gently lifted her face to meet his. "You are so very beautiful," he said, his voice husky and completely lacking in the self-assurance she had come to expect from him.

Her heartbeat quickened and she prayed for forgiveness that his compliment had meant so much to her, had made her think of ways that a kiss shared with him might not be impossible after all.

With determination she took a step back so that his finger slipped free of contact with her skin. "It is not our way to speak of such things," she said.

"Ah, but it is your way to speak the truth and that was all that I was doing." He picked up his hat and moved past her to the doorway. "Did Jake show you how to lock up?"

Confused by the abrupt shift in his demeanor, she nodded and showed him the keys that Jake had given her. The music coming from the big top told her that the matinee was already half over. During dinner the night before, he had told them that he liked to be at the back entrance to the big top when the show ended so that every performer passed by him as they exited the tent.

"Was there anything you wanted me to do yet this afternoon?" she asked, forcing her voice to reflect his professional business tone.

"No. Just take your time getting to know the files and procedures we went over. If Jake isn't back by the time you finish, be sure to lock up. I'll see you at dinner."

"Yes," she murmured, but he was already gone. She watched as he strode quickly across the large circus lot and it wasn't until he had disappeared around the side of the ticket wagon that she realized that all the while she had been gently stroking the place where he had touched her chin.

Levi could not believe that he had almost allowed himself to surrender to the feelings for Hannah Goodloe that he now realized had been planted that first day she'd come to his home in Sarasota. What was he thinking? Any real relationship between them was impossible.

He watched as Lily mesmerized the crowd with her acrobatics on the swing high above them. He and Lily had had a brief romance a few years earlier when he'd first hired her, but both had admitted that they were not well-matched for anything long lasting. They had ended the romance amicably and remained good friends. It was obvious to Levi that Lily's heart belonged to Jake. Too bad his friend was too much of a ladies' man to realize what he was missing.

All around him, performers and exotic animals lined up for the grand finale where they would enter the tent one last time and parade around the perimeter of the ring to thunderous applause, whistles and stamping feet. It was a moment that never grew old for Levi and whenever he was traveling with the company, it was a moment he tried not to miss.

But you would gladly have missed it today and every day from now on if Hannah had not stepped away.

The truth of that thought struck him like a thunderbolt. Behind him, elephants trumpeted their impatience to get moving while lions roared in agreement. But Levi barely heard them as he considered the idea of what he might be willing to sacrifice to win Hannah's affections.

"Hey, boss man!"

Levi turned to see Fred Stone waddling toward him. Fred was the lead clown for the company and at the moment he was in full costume — baggy pants and oversized clown shoes that slapped the ground with each step. His red hair had been frizzed into a halo and he was wearing his whiteface makeup with the exaggerated red lips turned

149

down. Fred was one of the most cheerful people Levi knew, but his act was that of the sad clown and it won the hearts and cheers of audience members every performance.

"Heard the Amish kid turned up in Baraboo," Fred continued. "Good news for the pretty little widow I'd say."

"She's very relieved," Levi agreed.

"So, you gonna have Ida ship the kid back down to meet us on the route or what?"

"His mother is going with us to Baraboo," Levi replied.

Fred nodded slowly. "Makes sense but I'd think she'd want the fastest way possible to get the boy back in the fold."

"I'm sure she does, but we have commitments along the way and her father-in-law is against her traveling alone so this seemed the best option under the circumstances. Ida's watching over the boy."

"Did she take him out to the farm?"

Only four people in the company were aware that Levi stayed in close touch with his younger brother. Fred, Hans, Ida and Jake. Matthew had inherited their grandfather's farm and lived there with his wife and five children. "The door's always open," he had told Levi more than once. "As Ma used to say, 'you can always come home.' "

"Levi?" Fred was looking at him curiously.

"Yeah. The boy's with Matt," Levi said. "Better get in there," he added with a nod toward the parade that had begun to move into the tent for the finale.

"Going," Fred said as he slap-footed his way to the rear of the line. "She's a nice lady," he called. "The Amish widow. Lily and the girls say she's top drawer."

Too good for the likes of me, Levi thought and mentally vowed to keep his association with Hannah on a strictly business level now that she was technically working for him.

But later, after he was delayed by a vendor insisting that he had not been paid for the goods delivered earlier that day, Levi arrived at the dinner table to see that the only available seat was next to Hannah.

"Ah, Levi, Hans had suggested we start without you," Gunther said. "We were just about to say grace."

Gunther was holding Pleasant's hand who in turn was holding Hannah's. In order to complete the circle he needed to take Gunther's free hand as well as Hannah's. He grasped Gunther's calloused hand but then hesitated.

Slowly and without meeting his eyes, Hannah slipped her fingers over the back of his hand. She was barely touching him and yet

151

he felt a warmth radiating from that contact that made it impossible not to want to turn his palm face up and entwine his fingers with hers.

"Shall we pray?" Gunther intoned and as he and Pleasant closed their eyes, Levi risked a look at Hannah. Her eyes were as wide open as his were and did not waver as she met his gaze. To his surprise, she seemed to be trying to come to some decision about him.

Levi was not used to being judged by others. With his wealth and position in the community, more often than not, others sought to get something from him. But Hannah was different. When Hannah looked at him it was not for the purpose of trying to find the best way to curry his favor. No. Levi knew that expression because he'd seen it often enough staring back at him from his shaving mirror. Hannah Goodloe was trying to figure him out.

CHAPTER TEN

Gunther was not pleased. And Hannah was surprised to realize that Pleasant was no more anxious to move out of Levi's luxurious private car than Gunther was to approve the idea of the two women traveling with the other women of the company.

"But now that we are employees," she argued, "it seems only fair that we have no better accommodations than the others. You were right to ask to stay with Hans when we first arrived, Gunther. Pleasant and I should have done the same."

"But Hans is different," Pleasant protested.

"How so?" Hannah asked, genuinely perplexed by the idea.

"He's — well, that is, his work is more . . ."

"These people are good people, Hannah," Gunther interrupted. "I realize that. But they have chosen a profession that does not fit with our ways. They don't mean to, I'm sure, but their ways could pose unnecessary temptations before you and Pleasant."

"I don't see how."

"As one example there's the issue of making themselves up every day. Taking great pride in how they look to others."

"They are performers," Hannah argued.

"And yet I see the women continuing to wear their makeup when not performing. And the way they dress . . ." Gunther shook his head.

"And what does it say for us that we continue to live here? Is that not also prideful?" She saw that Gunther was wavering and pressed her point. "It's only for a week," she said. "Then we'll be in Wisconsin."

"Your daughter-in-law makes a good point," Levi said as he stepped out onto the observation platform where the Goodloes had been holding their conversation.

Hannah could not believe what she was hearing. Levi confused her so — the way he looked at her when he thought she wasn't aware and the ways he seemed to find to be near her. Jake had commented twice on how much more often Levi was showing up unannounced in the payroll car during the day. Now this. As if he couldn't wait to be rid of them — of her.

"It would be a great help to me if you

154

would agree to the new arrangements, sir," Levi continued. "When people are living in such close quarters as this company does and when the stresses of the daily schedule begin to wear on them, there can be problems. Right now I just need to keep a lid on everything until we can reach Wisconsin and folks can spread out a bit for the next few months."

"I cannot see how my daughters moving in with the women of the company will make much difference," Gunther said.

"Oh, but it will. It will also help to have the three of you take meals with the rest of the company. You see, while it is not your way to give in to petty jealousies, that particular malady runs rampant in a situation like this. If your daughter and daughter-in-law were to show that they expect no special treatment, it would calm the rumblings of several ladies who are beginning to think they deserve more."

"I suppose there's no real harm," Gunther said more to himself than to the others. "There's no fraternizing between the sleeping cars?"

"I don't allow that," Levi assured him. "In fact, it's grounds for dismissal and believe me, Lily Palmer would be the first to raise the alarm."

All eyes were riveted on Gunther as he wrestled with his decision. "And we'll reach Wisconsin in a week?"

"Ten days," Levi corrected.

"We're still going to offer grace before meals," Gunther said in a tone that showed he was daring Levi to cross him on that point.

"I would expect so, sir."

Hannah saw that her father-in-law had run out of arguing points and yet she held her breath waiting for his final answer.

"All right then," Gunther said. "Let's get you two women packed up and moved in while the others are doing the matinee. The less fuss there is surrounding this, the better."

"Very wise," Levi said. "I'll leave you to your packing, then." He extended a hand to Gunther. "Thank you, sir."

Solemnly, the two men shook hands while Pleasant practically fled down the passageway to their cabin and Hannah wondered why she felt such sadness that she would no longer be sharing her meals with Levi. After all, hadn't she begun this campaign for the real purpose of distancing herself from him?

"Yes, thank you, Levi," she said, determined to put her regrets behind her. She had no clue why he had been so supportive. Perhaps she had misread his interest in them — in her. *Sheer vanity,* she thought, and prayed silently for the will to resist such worldly ways in the future.

It was done. The solution to his problem with Hannah Goodloe had been provided by the woman herself. Probably an indication that she was alarmed at the growing attention he paid her. Levi could not believe it when he overheard her making a case to move with Pleasant to the women's sleeping car.

He hadn't intentionally listened in on the family discussion, but after all, this was his private car — his residence when traveling. They were his guests and also his employees now. Yes, he had every right to eavesdrop on such a conversation. And when it had looked as if Gunther would stand firm against the idea, he had stepped in.

Relieved to have spent his last sleepless night thinking of Hannah just two doors away from his own cabin, he left the Goodloe women to their packing and headed over to the resting tent where performers waited for their act to be called. Lily was there as he had expected.

"The Goodloe women are moving into the

women's dorm car," he said, grateful that for the moment, Lily was the only performer in the tent.

Lily paused in the series of stretches she routinely performed as a warm-up for her act and glanced up at him. "And hello to you, too, Levi."

He ignored her sarcasm. "You'll make sure they have what they need?"

"That depends."

"On what?" he snapped impatiently.

"On whether you want them to be settled in as one of the gang or as special."

"You know what I mean. They are different — their ways are different and I just don't want . . ."

"We're not going to embarrass them, Levi," Lily interrupted. "Or you."

"That's not . . ."

"Then stop acting like it is. If you want us to put on a show for Hannah and Pleasant then I'm afraid you're going to be disappointed. We're all tired and anxious to get back home to Wisconsin. I'm pretty sure Hannah understands *our ways*."

"Are you mocking me?"

"A little bit. Sometimes you need to get down off your high horse."

Levi smiled. "All right, I deserved that."

Lily went back to her stretching. "Jake tells

158

me that Hannah's caught on to stuff real quick over in the office."

"He's right. In just a couple of days she's already done all the filing and caught up with the ledger entries. I may have to start looking for things to keep her busy over the next ten days."

"Don't be too hard on her, Levi. You're the one who's gone sweet on her, not the other way around." He opened his mouth to protest but Lily wasn't done. "Oh, don't give me that look. You're as transparent as a pane of glass when it comes to trying to hide your feelings."

Levi perched on the edge of a chair, his hands hanging between his knees as he watched her finish her warm-up exercises. "It's that obvious?"

"To me," Lily said. "I doubt others have noticed. Everybody's pretty single-minded about getting through each day and getting home right now, so they're fairly wrapped up in themselves."

"It's an impossible situation," he muttered.

"You like her. She likes you. Pretty simple, really."

"She's Amish."

Lily sat up and wrapped a towel around her neck. "So were you once upon a time."

If she had suddenly announced that she was off to join a nunnery, Levi could not have been more shocked. "How do you . . ."

"Everybody knows, Levi. You're hardly immune to gossip and speculation. People talk and when you showed up in Jonesville with three Amish people along with you, tongues really started to wag."

"Well, I'm not Amish anymore — haven't been since I was a kid."

"But your brother and sisters are and you could go back to it, right?"

Levi looked at her incredulously. "Oh, yeah, sure. I could just say I took a little time off to build a fortune by doing circus shows around the country — a profession that would not exactly endear me to the clan. Oh, and I could tell them that by the way, I would be heading back to Florida in October for the next season of performances. Yeah, that would work."

Lily shrugged and sprang nimbly to her feet. "Just a thought. Got to run. Almost time for my entrance." She gave him a platonic peck on the cheek as she left. "Think about it," she whispered. "I think Hannah might be worth it."

It was hard not to share Pleasant's doubts about the idea of living with the other women. The matinee was still going on as they carried their few belongings from Levi's car to the women's sleeping car. Hannah led the way down the narrow and shadowy center aisle to the far end of the coach.

Along the way she could not help but take note of the berths they passed. Far more than a place to sleep, many of them seemed to be like a small house. There were makeshift shelves that held dog-eared novels, framed family photos and other memorabilia. There were curtains and coverlets of different fabrics and colors. There were canvas shoe bags, the pockets holding not shoes but personal items such as lotions and reading glasses and letters from home.

When they reached the far end of the car, Hannah pointed to two top berths across the aisle from one another. "These two," she said. "You choose."

Pleasant looked at the bunk hung just inches from the ceiling of the car and then back at Hannah. "But . . ."

"We're the new girls," Hannah explained, using the lingo Lily had used to explain things to her. "If someone leaves then we get to move down to the second tier of bunks."

"And that's so likely to happen over the

next ten days," Pleasant grumbled as she ripped a threadbare blanket off one bunk and held it up with two fingers. "Where can I dispose of this?"

"I'll take care of it," Hannah said, laying it on top of her bunk before turning back to Pleasant. "Here, let me help you get settled."

But Pleasant had already climbed up the wooden ladder and started making up her bunk. Within minutes, she had transformed the space from dreary to cheery with the use of a quilt she'd made and her very pristine organization of her clothing on the shallow shelf at the foot of the bunk. Hannah watched as wordlessly her sister-in-law leaned back on the ladder to inspect her work, and then catapulted herself into the space. She lay flat on her back, her arms folded over her stomach, her legs straight.

And then Hannah noticed that the bunk had begun to shake and realized that Pleasant was laughing, tears running down her cheeks.

"What is it?" Hannah asked, fearing Pleasant might be having an attack of hysteria.

"It's . . . it's like . . . I can't . . . ." The more she tried to speak, the harder she laughed until Hannah could no longer contain her own laughter. "You try it," Pleasant managed to get out before setting off on a fresh round of giggles.

Hannah quickly spread out her own quilt and climbed in. Just trying to maneuver so she could lie down she bumped her head twice and her knees and elbows several times. Finally, she plopped onto her back. "It's a little cramped," she said, which set the two of them off again laughing so hard that they were unaware that the matinee had ended and the women were slowly coming back to the sleeping car.

Moments later, they looked down to see several of the female performers gathered below them watching them. Both struck their heads as they tried to sit up, setting off a chorus of sympathetic murmurs from the women below.

"It gets easier," one said. "Took me a week but . . ."

"The trick is to . . ." another offered and was interrupted by two others with different advice.

Outside they heard the clang of the dinner bell. "Supper time," one woman bellowed as she turned and hurried back down the aisle. And like a herd of sheep the others followed.

"You coming?"

Pleasant glanced over and Hannah was relieved to see that she was still smiling.

The two of them wrestled with the acrobatics of getting out of the bunks they had thought were so difficult to get into, and followed their dozens of roommates out into the late afternoon sun and on to the dining tent.

Time was so short between the matinee and evening performances that most of the company ate with their costumes and makeup on. So when Levi stopped by, telling himself that he just wanted to be sure things were running smoothly, he had some trouble locating Hannah among the throng of performers.

Then he saw the white prayer cap. She was sitting at a table with Pleasant, Lily and Fred and three other performers. He positioned himself next to one of the large tent poles, glad to have this opportunity to watch her without her being aware he was anywhere nearby.

He knew Fred well enough to know that the clown was in rare form, keeping Lily and Hannah so consumed with giggles at his antics and tricks that they had barely touched their food. Even Pleasant was smiling. He couldn't help but wonder if Hannah and her sister-in-law had insisted on saying grace before taking their supper, or had been intimidated by the throng of performers and stagehands and decided against it.

And then to his amazement, she said something to the others. Lily looked over at Fred, who had a fork filled with mashed potatoes halfway to his lips and he stared back at her for an instant and then slowly lowered the fork to his plate and took Lily's hand. One by one the occupants of the table completed the circle of linked hands and bowed their heads. Like a wave, silence settled over the tent as those at nearby tables observed the action and grew still. And while no one else repeated the practice, everyone waited respectfully for Hannah and Pleasant to complete their prayer and raise their heads.

If he hadn't seen it with his own eyes, Levi would have thought it impossible for two Amish women to quiet a tent filled with rowdy circus people. Not that there weren't some among the company who were religious. Long ago, he'd hired a retired minister to travel with the company and offer Sunday services. But those services were poorly attended, his employees preferring to take their day off and use it for much-needed sleep or to catch up on chores such as laundry or letter writing.

And as suddenly as the silence had descended, it was gone and the usual chatter and clang of utensils against tin plates prevailed. *As if it had never been,* Levi thought, and suddenly remembered the way the tornado had roared across the plains, straight for his father's farm and just as quickly been gone, leaving death and destruction in its wake and changing Levi's life forever.

"Hey there, boss man," Fred bellowed, spotting Levi from across the room. "Come join us."

It wasn't unusual for Levi to take meals with the company. It got pretty lonely eating alone in his private car and now that Hannah and Pleasant had moved out, Gunther had insisted on taking his meals with Hans and the rest of Levi's personal staff.

Lily and Fred scooted closer together on the narrow wooden bench making room for him and he had no choice but to sit across from Hannah. Someone set a plate of food in front of him and filled his glass with fresh milk that he knew had been bought from a local farm.

"You missed saying grace," Fred said.

"I was here," Levi replied, unfolding his napkin and laying it across his lap.

166

"What a lovely tradition," Lily said. "I was thinking, Levi . . ."

"Always a danger sign," Levi teased, glad to be able to focus on his star rather than have to deal with the fact that keeping his knee from brushing Hannah's skirt under the table was becoming a problem.

"I'm serious. We should have a prayer circle before every performance — nothing too formal. Just all gather round and take a moment to pray for safety and a good performance."

"Then afterward we could do it again," Fred agreed. "Then it would be a prayer of thanksgiving that we all made it safely through another show."

"I don't know," Levi hedged. "Some folks . . ."

"Well, let's ask them," Fred said and before Levi could stop him, he had leaped onto the bench and was banging his fork and knife against an empty metal tray that one of the waiters had been taking back to the kitchen. "Hey, everybody listen up," he bellowed.

And because this was Fred and because in many ways the employees saw him as their spokesperson, everyone stopped talking and turned to hear what the clown had to say. In less than three minutes Fred had laid out the idea, allowed time for people to object and called for a motion, a second and then a vote.

It was unanimous and the company chaplain stood and volunteered to lead the first prayer circle that very evening before and after the performance.

Slowly, Levi got to his feet. He did not need to stand on the bench for he knew that every eye was riveted on him. He was, after all, the boss.

"One thing," he said. "This is a voluntary activity. Anyone who chooses not to participate has that right and anyone who shames or intimidates such a person will be reprimanded. Understood?"

There was a general murmur of agreement and Levi saw that a few of those assembled look relieved. It occurred to him that he should feel comforted by the idea that he was not the only one around who had long ago turned away from the faith of his father. Instead, he looked at those individuals and wondered what kind of pain had damaged their belief in a higher being, a loving God.

"Father will be so pleased," Levi heard Pleasant whisper excitedly to Hannah as he sat down again and everyone resumed eating, and the conversations they'd been enjoying before Fred made his announcement.

"Yes," Hannah replied, but she was watching Levi and the tiniest of frowns marred her perfect face. "If you'll all excuse me," she added, dabbing at the corners of her mouth with her napkin. "I want to finish those ledger entries," she said as if Levi had asked for some explanation.

"And I've got mending to complete before the next performance," Pleasant said, hurrying to add as she swallowed a bite of chocolate cake and finished her milk. It was clear that it was one thing to sit with the circus folks in the company of her sister-in-law, but Pleasant was not yet comfortable being alone with them.

Lily and Fred and the others followed the Goodloe women's lead. Before he knew it, Levi was finishing his dinner alone after all as everyone left the long tables and headed off to prepare for their next show.

For the remainder of the week they followed the same routine. Arrive in town, unload the train, set up the circus, perform two shows and move on. All within twenty-four hours. Each night, Hannah wrote a long letter to Caleb and gave it to Hans to post the following morning.

She took great care not to talk too much about the circus and the friends she was making there. How could she deny her son this life if she admitted that she found the people and the adventure of the travel every bit as exciting as he must have? Instead, she wrote about Gunther and Pleasant and how much they were all missing the rest of the family back in Sarasota. She reminded him to say his prayers and to help with the chores and to be respectful of the people who had taken him in.

After a week, she had had no letter from her son. Instead, there had been daily wires from Miss Benson assuring her that Caleb continued to be well cared for and in good health and that he was anxious to see her. Hannah would carry the day's telegram in the pocket of her apron and take it out several times in the course of the day, hoping to find some turn of phrase that would give her more information.

To overcome her sadness and worry, she buried herself in work. Jake marveled at her ability to get through what to him seemed a full day's filing and correspondence before noon. "Ida had best watch out," he told Hannah. "You'll have her job."

"Oh, no," she protested. "I'm just doing this until we reach Baraboo. Then my son and I will return to Florida."

"And Miss Pleasant as well?" Jake asked, not looking up from his newspaper.

"Of course, Pleasant and my father-in-law — the four of us."

"And do you think the boy will try again?"

It was the single thought that haunted Hannah's dreams every night. "I don't know," she admitted. "I hope not, but then Levi . . ."

"You know his story then?"

"He told me that he ran away when he was only a few years older than Caleb."

"It's completely different," Jake assured her. "Levi had lost both his parents, not just the one, and he'd been farmed out to his grandparents and I take it he and his grandpa didn't see eye to eye on his future."

"So he ran away — and stayed away," Hannah said.

Jake folded his newspaper, uncrossed his legs and stood up. "Ah, now, don't go down that road. You can't know how things will go with your boy. My advice? Look for some way that you might offer him what he was looking for in the first place."

"He wanted to join the circus," she reminded him.

"Nope. He wanted a change — something out of the ordinary. The circus just happened to come to town about that same time."

"Our life is pretty . . . plain," she said, faltering for the right words.

"And yet from what you've told me, you and your husband and your father-in-law all left the farms of the Midwest and started over in Florida. I'd call that adventure. Maybe the boy doesn't know that whole story?"

Hannah felt a glimmer of hope. Jake was right. By the time Caleb was born, the family was settled in Florida. He'd never known any other life. And then his father had died and there had been pressure on him to assume the role of man of the house.

"Show him his roots," Jake advised, "and the kid might just find his wings right there at home." As was his habit, he headed for the door citing some appointment that he was late for. "He'll be all right," he said as he left. "He's got a good mother who will see to that."

Hannah had gotten so caught up in the personal conversation with Jake that she had completely forgotten to show him some things she'd noticed while attending to the filings and bookkeeping assignments he left for her each day.

"Jake!" she shouted, but he just raised one

hand and kept walking.

"Never mind," she mumbled to herself as she watched him go. "I'll take care of it."

She spotted the ledgers on Jake's desk. She could take care of it. She could look up the answers as easily as Jake could. She carried the heavy oversized ledger to her desk and set to work.

CHAPTER ELEVEN

On his way back to his private car after seeing the grand finale and congratulating the performers on yet another stellar performance, Levi noticed a single lamp still burning in the payroll car. He knew that Chester had left early that morning for the next town to make sure everything was ready for their arrival, and Jake had headed off to town as was his habit. His friend was quite the ladies' man and something of a legend within the company for his ability to balance multiple romantic relationships. Lily called him "The Juggler" and Jake smiled every time he heard her say it.

Truth was, Levi had been wary of having Hannah work in such close quarters with Jake, but he trusted his friend to know that trying to romance an Amish widow would be way out of line. Instead, it appeared that Hannah and Jake had become good friends. More than once he had heard Hannah laughing at something Jake said or inviting him to join the group she was sitting with in the dining tent.

Truth was, Levi was jealous of his friend's easy way with the ladies. No, he was jealous of Jake's friendship with Hannah. Jake had mentioned some things to Levi — things about the runaway boy and about the dead husband that Levi hadn't known. Things that Hannah must have felt comfortable confiding to Jake — but not to him.

He brushed the thought aside and headed for the payroll car. Most likely Chester had been in a rush to leave and left the lamp burning. Levi would have to speak to him about that — unnecessary lights cost money and these days the company could not afford waste.

Digging the keys from his pocket as he climbed the three steps to the platform outside the payroll door, Levi didn't see Hannah at first. But when he found the door unlocked, he peered in through the barred window and saw her, head down on her desk, a pencil in one hand. Not wanting to startle her, he turned the brass doorknob and stepped inside the car.

Her desk was at the far end of the car so he turned on the lamp on Jake's desk, then the one on Chester's as he made his way

175

toward her. He didn't want her to wake up and see someone lurking in the shadows, and at the same time he realized he was making as little noise as possible, reluctant to disturb her sleep.

She slept with one cheek resting on a bent arm. Her breath came in even rhythmic sighs and her prayer cap had fallen a little to one side revealing the bun of hair that she kept hidden beneath it. Levi studied her hair for a long moment, recalling the Amish habit of a woman never cutting her hair — her crowning glory. And yet the only man who ever saw it down would have been her husband.

He imagined her sitting in her berth at night, releasing the golden strands from their bonds, shaking it free and then brushing the length of it until it shone. He reached out to touch it — just one touch to know the reality of its silkiness. But instead, he lowered his hand to her shoulder and shook her gently.

"Hannah?"

She stirred and blinked up at him and in the amber of the lamplight, he thought she had never been lovelier. Her lips were full and soft from the relaxation that came with sleep and he could not remember ever wanting to kiss a woman more. For one mad

instant he thought of pulling Hannah Goodloe to her feet, wrapping his arms around
her and kissing those sleep-heavy eyelids,
the flushed cheeks and those lips that had
haunted his dreams for days now.

Instead, he turned his attention to the
ledger. "What's this?" he asked and was well
aware that the desire he felt for her came
out as gruffness in his tone.

Hannah sat up and righted her prayer cap
in the same motion. "I was . . . I had some
questions about some of the invoices and
Jake had to leave and I thought that perhaps . . ."

"What questions?"

"It's nothing, really," she stammered,
clearly unnerved by his irritable tone. "Have
I done something wrong, Levi? I thought
perhaps . . ."

He closed the ledger and placed it back
on Jake's desk. "The ledgers are none of
your concern," he said, his back to her as
he tried to regain control of emotions that
had, in a matter of minutes, gone from long-
ing for her to annoyance that she had taken
it upon herself to go snooping into his business affairs. "It's late," he said, still not looking at her. "The train will be pulling out
soon. I'll see you back to your sleeping car."

Behind him, he heard her stacking papers

177

and putting them away so that they would not scatter with the movement of the train. He heard the click of locks on the file cabinets and then she was beside him holding out the ring of keys he'd given her when she first started to work in the office.

"What's this?" he asked, automatically holding out his hand as she dropped the keys into his palm.

"I do not wish you to question my trustworthiness," she said. "I will work here only when either Jake or Chester are also here and they can unlock the files and such as I need them." Without another word she started for the door. "I can see myself out," she said. "Good night, Levi."

Warring with his frustration that she'd made too much of this and his admiration of her spunk, he allowed her to make it past Chester's desk before he overtook her. He spun her around and cupped her face in his palm. She met his gaze defiantly but did not pull away.

"You're angry with me," he said softly, his eyes roving over her features, memorizing each tiny frown line. He felt a smile pull at his lips.

"Was that your purpose then? To provoke me?"

"No," he admitted. "My purpose was to

avoid what I can no longer avoid, Hannah." And he lowered his face to her, allowing his lips to rest lightly against her forehead and then move across to her temple, her now-closed eyes, her cheek and finally . . .

"No," she whispered and the sweetness of her breath against his lips was like a warm spring breeze.

He hesitated, not moving. Waiting.

"Yes." She raised onto her toes to meet his kiss.

Hannah fought against the guilt she felt in taking such joy in being in Levi's arms.

But when he lifted his lips from hers but did not release her from his embrace all she could think was, *How can such feelings shared be wrong?*

And yet she knew they were and she pulled away. "I must go," she said, her voice trembling as she made her way past Jake's desk to reach the door. To her relief, Levi did not try and stop her.

What could I have been thinking to allow such a thing? To invite such a thing? she thought as she ran alongside the unmoving train on her way to the sleeping car. Up and down the track she could hear men's voices calling out directions as they hooked the cars together and loaded the wagons and animals.

"Help me make this right," she prayed. "Show me Your way and guide my steps, my words and my actions until I can reunite with my son and both of us can return safely home again."

"Late date?" one of the women teased good-naturedly as Hannah boarded the car and climbed into her upper berth. She glanced over and saw Pleasant watching her curiously. "I was working and fell asleep," she offered and was relieved when Pleasant nodded and went back to reading her Bible.

Hannah hated the half truth of her statement. Surely this could only lead to more trouble for her. She had allowed herself to believe that she could befriend these people and maintain her Amish decorum. She had believed that she could look upon Levi as a man who had done a good deed for her family, a kind man in spite of his brooding and sometimes cantankerous exterior. She had believed that what she felt for him was gratitude.

She had been fooling herself.

She had fallen in love with Levi Harmon, and in his arms she had permitted herself to forget everything and everyone else and surrender to what she had wanted for so many days now. Not his kindness or his polite hospitality, but his tenderness and affection. She had wanted what she'd seen in his eyes as he bent to kiss her — attraction that comes only between a man and a woman who believe they are destined to be together.

And yet the very idea was impossible. Levi was an outsider — a man of the world in ways that she couldn't begin to understand. He had wealth and power. His life was complex, wrapped up in the kingdom he had built and chosen to inhabit. His faith was shaky at best, maybe even nonexistent other than on the level of a polite respect for the faith of others.

No, she thought as she went through the necessary contortions to undress and get into her nightgown. She had lost her way just as Caleb had. She had permitted herself to be enticed by the colorful and exciting culture of life in the circus — just as Caleb had. But she was the adult here. Caleb could be forgiven for such transgressions against the ways of his people. Hannah would surely be shunned if anyone learned of this indiscretion.

"Only three days more," Pleasant said. She stretched and yawned then carefully lay the ribbon bookmark on the parchment pages of her Bible and turned out the little light she used for reading.

Three days until they reach Baraboo. Three days until Hannah was reunited with Caleb. Three days to be gotten through and then they would take Caleb and go home. And by the time Levi Harmon returned to his fine mansion in Sarasota, Hannah would have found her bearings and there would be no reason for them to have contact ever again.

"Hannah," Pleasant whispered leaning out her berth to tap Hannah's shoulder.

Hannah thought of pretending to be asleep but she had told enough half truths for one day. "Yes?"

"Do you think there's any possibility that Noah will live near Baraboo? That I might see him?"

Hannah was well aware that Noah was the young man who had come to Florida during the winter to visit his uncle and aunt. The man who had also developed the habit of stopping at the bakery every day that he was in town.

"I don't know, Pleasant. What if you do see him?"

There was a long silence punctuated by snores and coughs and grumblings up and down the car. "I might stay," Pleasant said softly, and Hannah sat up so suddenly that

182

she cracked her head against the ceiling as the train car jolted into place and started to move.

The train had just started to move when Levi heard Lily shouting his name. "Levi, come quick! Hannah's been hurt!"

His heart skipped several beats but somehow his brain remained active and he followed his star through several cars on their way to the women's sleeping car.

"She cracked her head pretty hard," Lily was explaining as they moved from one car to the next, the rush of air catching her words and flinging them back at him. "There's quite a bump on top and she's dizzy and . . ."

"Did somebody send for Doc?"

Doc Jones was the veterinarian on staff but he knew enough human medicine to keep the company rolling. If one of the cast or crew needed something more, then Levi would call for the doctor in the next town.

"He's with her now along with her father-in-law," Lily said. "I also saw Hans and he's wiring Chester to make sure the town doctor is available in case we need him. I'm afraid she might have a concussion," Lily said, wringing her hands nervously.

The scene inside the women's sleeping car

might have been comical under other circumstances. Pleasant was standing guard over Hannah laid out on Lily's private bunk in the front of the car. Doc was peering in over Gunther's shoulder as several of the other women pressed in for a better look. But Gunther was barring the entrance and wore an expression that dared anyone to try and get past him.

"I can't examine her, Gunther, unless you let me in there," Doc protested.

"It's not proper," Gunther argued. "Tell my daughter what to do and look for and she'll report."

Doc rolled his eyes and then saw Levi. "Maybe you can talk some sense into him," he muttered as he made way for Levi and Lily.

"Is she conscious?" Levi asked the vet.

"Far as I can tell."

"Gunther, we need to be sure she's all right. Doc doesn't need to touch her other than on her face and head."

Lily pulled a blanket from a nearby berth. "Maybe cover her with this," she suggested. "It's plain," she said, meeting Gunther's eyes.

"We should not have . . . I should never have agreed . . ." Gunther muttered to himself as he took the blanket.

"Here, Papa," Pleasant said and Levi thought he had never heard the woman speak with such gentleness. "Let me." She took the blanket from her father and covered Hannah from her chin to her toes, then stood aside to make room for Doc.

"How did this happen?" Doc asked as he peered into Hannah's eyes and cradled her head in both hands.

"Oh, come now, Doc," Lily protested. "You know what those third berths are like. There's barely enough room to turn over much less sit up."

"I sat up," Hannah replied in answer to the vet's question. "I forgot," she added with a smile at Lily.

Levi could not help noticing that Pleasant seemed inordinately distressed, near tears. "Will she be all right?" she demanded, in what was her more usual no-nonsense voice.

"She will have a headache and a lump," Doc announced as he instructed Hannah to follow his finger without turning her head. "But I would say she'll live."

Several of the women tittered with nervous relief at this news and started to wander back toward their own berths. Lily leaned in to Hannah. "You sleep here tonight, honey," she said. "I'll take your berth."

"I couldn't," Hannah protested, attempting to get up, but clearly a wave of dizziness prevented her from making it any farther than to a half sitting position before Pleasant eased her back down to the pile of pillows covered in satins and silks at the head of Lily's berth.

"I'll stay with you," Pleasant assured her. "Thank you, Lily."

"Hans has made arrangements for her to be seen by the town doctor as soon as we arrive tomorrow," Levi assured Gunther, although he had no idea whether or not Hans had been able to make such arrangements. "Until then . . ."

"Until then," Lily said as she corralled the three males toward the exit, "we've got things under control. Good night, gentlemen."

Levi had had every intention of taking up a position in the seat across from Lily's private berth for the night. It was separated from the rest of the sleeping car by the small toilet and galley and Pleasant would be right there. "I . . ." he protested.

"You get some sleep," Lily ordered. "If anything changes, we'll come get you, right, ladies?"

A bevy of female faces, some of them coated in cold cream like clown faces stared back at Levi and nodded. The sideshow fat

186

lady practically filled the aisle with her bulk as she took her position outside Lily's berth.

Levi tried looking past her. He just wanted to see Hannah, see her eyes meet his, and reassure himself that she was not only all right but that they were all right as well. But Pleasant was blocking his view, standing over Hannah and murmuring something to her.

"Go," the fat lady ordered and pointed one pudgy finger toward the exit. Levi saw the command mirrored in the eyes of the other women.

"Doc, you sleep here," he said pointing to the seat he'd intended to occupy. "That way," he added firmly, "no one has to go running through a moving train for help."

"I'm staying as well," Gunther said and sat down next to the window.

"Really," Lily huffed, but neither she nor any of the other women rejected the compromise. "Could we just all get a little sleep? We've got two shows to do today." She nodded toward a wall clock in the galley that showed it was past midnight.

"Take care of her," Levi murmured to Lily as he reluctantly stepped onto the platform connecting the women's sleeping car to that of the men. "And if anything . . ."

"I'll send for you," Lily promised. She

stroked his cheek with her palm. "She'll be all right, Levi."

"It's just . . ."

"I know," she replied. "I can see."

"See what?" he asked brusquely, but his heartbeat quickened like a kid caught sneaking under the circus tent without paying.

"You love her." She gave his cheek one final gentle pat and returned to the sleeping car, letting the door to the platform shut behind her.

188

CHAPTER TWELVE

Love? Impossible.

Infatuation maybe. But love? What did he know of love? Vague memories of his parents' deep affection for each other flashed across his mind. He had never really understood how a man and woman could risk such intense feelings. What if one of them died?

What if they both did?

Levi had not been able to get Lily's comment out of his head ever since returning to his car and trying to concentrate on work instead of Hannah. She would be fine. She was being well cared for and tomorrow, as soon as the train rolled into the last town on the tour, he would make sure she was seen by the local doctor. In the meantime, he had to try and make sense of the bank statement before him.

I am not in love with her.

And even if I were . . .

As dawn approached, he pushed himself away from his desk and walked out to the observation platform — the very last piece of the long train chugging its way through the night. He caught the scent of freshly plowed fields after a May rain. He saw cows heading out to pasture and farmers driving their tractors along narrow country roads.

The sun wouldn't be up for hours yet but these men had fields to be planted and cows to be milked. The train entered a tunnel and the blackness engulfed Levi, the cold dampness of the rock walls sending a shiver through him. And when the train emerged at the far end of the tunnel, he saw in the distance the signature silhouette of an Amish buggy leaving a large white farm house surrounded by large willow trees. So many years had passed, but a memory jolted him, the memory of riding just such a buggy on just such a morning as this, and his father passing him the reins. "Take over, son."

He watched that buggy until it disappeared from sight. And only when he tasted the salt of his tears did Levi realize that he was crying.

Hannah's head hurt but the very idea of spending the day in bed was so foreign to her that it made her feel anxious. "Surely I could work," she told the doctor who had arrived shortly after the train pulled into their last stop before reaching Baraboo. "All I do is sit at a desk and post numbers in a ledger and file . . ."

The doctor frowned as he put away his stethoscope. "I suppose you could go in for an hour or so. But I am warning you, young lady, this injury is not to be trifled with. At the first sign of dizziness or blurred vision I want you back in bed and someone sent to get me."

"Yes, sir." Hannah thought she would have agreed to just about anything he asked so thrilled was she to think that soon she could be out of the close quarters of the sleeping car. And most of all she wanted to see Levi.

"I'll help you get dressed," Pleasant said when the doctor had left, giving Gunther a prescription for headache powders and promising to stop by later to see that she was doing all right.

"I'm fine, really." Pleasant had been hovering over her ever since she'd cracked her head. "It wasn't your fault," Hannah added.

Pleasant burst into tears. "Please don't say anything to Father about what I said that made you sit up so suddenly and . . ."

So that was it. Pleasant was afraid that Hannah might mention her comment about possibly staying in Wisconsin. "Oh, Pleasant," she said, wrapping her arms around her sister-in-law. "Why didn't you say that you were worried about that? Of course I won't mention it."

Pleasant sniffed back tears and studied Hannah's face seeking assurance that she could be trusted. "You do understand," she said softly, and then as if a match had suddenly flamed to life, she smiled. "You understand because of Levi."

Hannah stiffened. "I don't get your meaning."

Pleasant picked up Hannah's hairbrush from the pile of belongings Lily had brought and began brushing her sister-in-law's hair. "Yes, you do. Everyone is talking about it — the way he watches you and looks at you when you're together. In the costume shop, there's even speculation that he might propose, but I told them such a thing could never happen. We are Amish. I reminded them that he is not and besides, he is engaged in a profession that . . ."

Pleasant continued to chatter on while Hannah's mind froze on the words "might propose." Of course, such a thing was unthinkable on every possible level. They barely knew one another for starters.

And yet you kissed him.

She could not deny the facts. Theirs was no stolen peck on the lips that he had trapped her into giving. Theirs was a shared kiss laden with all of the questions and curiosities that two adults who are attracted to each other can not resist exploring.

". . . And so the point is . . ." Pleasant rambled on as she wound Hannah's hair into a tight bun and anchored it firmly with hairpins she pulled one by one from her mouth even as she continued talking.

The point is, Hannah thought, *that this must stop . . . today.* And she made up her mind to go and find Levi as soon as she was free to leave the sleeping car. On the other hand, if anyone saw them talking . . .

I'll write him a letter.

Chester Tuck was at his desk when Hannah got to the payroll car. She had met him only once before when Jake had introduced them as Chester was on his way to the next stop on the tour. The man was thin and stooped and nervous, always fidgeting with his hat and always seeming to be about to run away.

"It's what makes him a good twenty-four-hour man," Jake told her. "He likes to keep things moving."

And true to his nature, the minute he saw Hannah, Chester started moving papers around on his desk, shoveling them into a top drawer as he stood and grabbed his hat from the brass hat rack on the wall. "Morning, Mrs. Goodloe," he muttered without looking at her directly.

"Good morning. I hope I won't disturb you if I take care of some filing?"

"No, ma'am. Just on my way out." He edged toward the door and then stopped. "No need to file those things there," he said with an off-handed wave toward the wire basket on his desk. "I'll take care of those when I get back later."

"I'd be more than happy to . . ."

"No." The single word carried a hint of panic, but then he smiled. "I need to clear something up with one of the suppliers before we file those," he explained. "I'll take care of it. You have a good day now."

Hannah finished the day's filing — minus the papers on Chester's desk — within the hour. In that time she had heard Levi's laughter and the low rumble of his voice giving instructions, or engaged in conversation, but he had not come to the payroll car. Jake had been in and out several times, muttering something about suppliers not living up to their end of things and asking if

194

she'd seen the invoice for the feed store delivery.

"No. It might be there," she said, pointing to the stack of papers on Chester's desk. "I offered to file them, but Chester said something about a supplier . . ."

Jake grabbed the stack of papers and scanned them, his usually easygoing nature tense and confused. "I don't get it," he muttered. "Okay," he said, putting the papers down, "if Chester comes back, tell him I need to see him right away."

He started out the door, then turned and smiled apologetically. "Sorry, Hannah. How are you feeling? You aren't overdoing, are you?"

"I'm fine," she assured him.

"Good. I'll let Levi know. The man's been jumpy as a frog all morning."

And with a wave he was gone, leaving Hannah standing at the door and thinking, *If Levi is so concerned then why not stop by to see for himself that I'm better?*

But that would indicate that he had feelings for her and she didn't want that . . . did she? She couldn't want that.

"This has to end now," she muttered aloud as she sat down at her desk — Ida's desk — and pulled out a piece of paper.

■ ■ ■ ■

Levi was not having a good day. He was worried about Hannah but had determined not to try and see her, and instead had relied on others to provide information. Lily had taken it upon herself to give him a running commentary of how Hannah had done overnight.

"Slept some but restless, you know? I expect she was in considerable pain and she has quite a bruise on her forehead. I offered to cover the worst of it with makeup but then I was forgetting myself. She and Pleasant have become so much a part of the company that sometimes . . ."

"She's fine then? The doctor saw her?"

Lily eyed him curiously. "You know he did. I saw you grilling the man not two minutes after he left from examining her."

Levi had ended the conversation by insisting the need to find Jake. It was in the course of that conversation that he learned that Hannah was at work. He had taken three strides toward the payroll car before he caught himself. "Make sure she doesn't overdo," he told Jake and turned his attention to a new employee who was mishandling the unloading of a wagon.

He kept himself occupied through the matinee and the evening performance and only headed back to his car when he saw that the payroll car was dark. That's when he found the envelope with his name on it propped against the inkwell on his desk.

Her handwriting, like the woman herself, was simple yet elegant. Block printing with each letter evenly spaced and every word perfectly aligned on the single sheet of unlined paper.

Levi,
As we near the end of our journey, I wanted to take this opportunity to say how very grateful I am for the generosity and kindness you have shown to my son, our family and to me. We could not have been more blessed. Thanks to you we are soon to be reunited with Caleb and whatever comes next for our family, we will never forget the compassion you have shown us these past weeks. May God bless you.

Hannah

It was a letter of farewell.

He read it again to be sure, then crumpled it into a ball, but could not bring himself to throw it away. Instead, he did what Levi always did when faced with a situation he could not control — he acted on instinct and headed for the women's sleeping car.

But on the way he found himself surrounded by the sounds of the traveling community he had built. A lone elephant trumpeted a late night howl, horses whinnied and stamped their feet as they jostled one another for more space. Several members of the company had gathered outside the dining tent where Fred was strumming a ukulele, and others were singing along as they sat by a campfire.

They had performed their last show of the tour and for once there was no rush to move on to the next town. The next stop would be Baraboo where they would set up for the summer, offering shows eight times a week. Some of the cast and crew would leave the show there to take other jobs. Others would supplement their incomes by offering training in acrobatics or clowning. Levi and Jake would stay for a month or so and then set out to audition new acts they might add to the show the coming season. He had always liked this last night on the road. The company of performers and crew never felt more like family than they did on this particular night.

He glanced over at the sleeping car and saw that most of the windows were open and he could hear laughter and conversation drifting out.

It would do no good to cause a scene, he decided. He and Hannah were already the subject of gossip throughout the company. He would talk to her tomorrow. He would send Hans for her and meet with her in the privacy of his sitting room. And he would tell her . . .

What?

It occurred to Hannah that neither she nor Pleasant were immune to the nostalgia that had spread through the company like a terrible cold. Emotions seemed to run the gamut from lethargy to relief and back again to outright depression. And the onset had been so sudden. Almost in concert with the sounding of the band's final notes, the performers and crew had slumped into their malaise. The women's sleeping car that was usually noisy and even boisterous as the women came back after a show was strangely subdued. And outside, instead of the usual rumble of wagons being loaded onto flatcars that had become the lullaby by which she'd learned to fall asleep, she heard the soft music of Fred's ukulele in tandem with a chorus of male voices as they gathered round a campfire.

Tomorrow.

The word had become her constant thought. Tomorrow they would leave this last town on the tour. Tomorrow they would arrive in Baraboo. Tomorrow she would see Caleb.

And the day after that she would say good-bye to Levi.

Sleep was impossible even after everyone had settled down for the night. Hannah had finally been able to persuade Pleasant that there was no need to keep watch and she had gone to sleep in her own berth. Fortunately, she had not been able to persuade Lily to return to her private room and so no one was around to see Hannah leave.

The night air was crisp and the skies were laden with stars. Under other circumstances Hannah might simply have gone for a walk, but she saw a light in the payroll car and that brought back the memory of something she had noticed the night she and Levi had kissed. It had nothing to do with the kiss. In fact, it was the kiss that had completely put the worrisome thing out of her mind.

Hoping that it was Levi working late, she headed across the compound. But when she opened the door she came face-to-face with Jake who was clearly taken aback to see her.

"Hannah? Something wrong?"

She thought about telling Jake exactly what had brought her there at such an hour, but decided to wait. After all, it might be nothing. "I couldn't sleep and the other day I didn't finish the filing. When we reach Baraboo I don't want Ida to have to do work I should already have done."

Jake frowned briefly. "Well, I suppose. But lock the door while you're in there, okay? And don't stay too long."

"I will," she said. "Lock the door," she added, "and I won't be long."

"Because Levi would have my head if anything happened to you and you just never know. Seems like a nice enough town but you just never know."

Hannah was touched by Jake's concern. "I'll be fine," she assured him.

As soon as Jake left — she waited to hear the click of the lock — Hannah hurried to the filing cabinet that held the paid bills. She pulled out the most recent folder and spread the contents on her desk. She took the invoice she recalled questioning and studied it. It was from a dry goods store and the total amount of the bill was for several hundred dollars. It was stamped "Paid in Cash" and when she retrieved the ledger from Jake's desk and checked the entry, she saw that the two documents matched. But she remembered that earlier on that day, Pleasant had gone to town with the head seamstress to find fabric that might match a ripped costume. Her sister-in-law had talked at supper about the proprietress at Danvers Dry Goods. The two of them had become fast friends, sharing stories of serving customers and handling a business. Pleasant had been fairly glowing with the experience.

The problem was that this was a bill paid to General Dry Goods — not Danvers — and the order was for the same date. And had Danvers been paid? And if so, then what was this other store?

She paced the office and as she passed Chester's desk a sliver of white paper peeped out from his desk drawer. She recalled how he'd shoved the papers inside earlier that day. What was he hiding?

She pulled open the drawer but found only blank paper. The papers he'd put away were gone. She tried closing the drawer but it stuck. Not wanting to have Chester know she'd been snooping, she bent to clear the path for the drawer and found that a rumpled invoice was the cause of the problem. She pulled it free and closed the drawer. Then she flattened the paper out and read, "Danvers Dry Goods." The date was the same. As was the list of items purchased. But the amount was half what had been paid to the other store.

Why would Chester pass up the opportunity to buy goods at half the cost? Perhaps it was because Danvers was owned by a woman. A widow like Hannah. Yes, she could see Chester not liking doing business with a woman. But to spend twice as much? There had to be some explanation.

Unaware of the passing of time, Hannah pulled out one file and then another as the trail that might lead to some logical explanation became more convoluted. She found a stream of invoices going back ten years or more paid to a "General Dry Goods" in a variety of towns up and down the East Coast and across mid-America. She found similar invoices paid to a feed company with the name "American Feed & Grain," again in a variety of towns and states.

Perhaps these were chain stores, she thought. She had heard of such businesses opening in small towns, but was the chain giving Levi the best price or was this just a convenience for Chester? He didn't seem the lazy type, but on the other hand, he did often seem harried and rushed so perhaps saving time was more important to him than saving money.

She stretched her aching back and rubbed her temples as she tried to make sense of the piles of papers she had pulled and reorganized by vendor — papers she would now need to refile. This was really none of her business after all. She had been given the task of filing but she could not help but recall comments Levi had made to Gunther when the two men sat discussing business at dinner. There had been no doubt that Levi was worried about the drop in attendance and the rising costs of goods to keep the circus on tour.

I should tell someone about this, she thought.

She could ask Chester. He probably had a perfectly logical explanation. But Jake had told her that Chester had gone on ahead to Baraboo and that she should file whatever was left on his desk.

Then she would show her findings to Jake. After all, he was the accountant and business manager for the company. Jake would know what to do.

She laid her head on her forearm, intending to give herself just enough time to rest her eyes before tackling the job of putting everything back in its place, and fell fast asleep.

CHAPTER THIRTEEN

Levi woke before sunrise, surprising Hans and the cook in the kitchen. He had just spent his last night on the train — another restless night.

"Breakfast?" the cook asked, already taking down a skillet and reaching for a bowl of eggs.

"Just coffee now," Levi replied. "I'm just going to walk the lot."

Hans nodded as the cook handed Levi a mug of black coffee. It was a long-standing tradition that on the morning after the last show of a tour, Levi would walk through the now deserted big top and sideshow tents. He would sit in the top row of seats staring down at the center ring, replaying the season's lineup of acts and already thinking about changes he would make for the coming season.

"Shall I come along and take notes?" Hans asked.

"Not today. Thanks." He saluted them with his coffee mug and swung down off the rear platform to the dusty ground below.

The truth was that Levi needed time to think — about the future of the show, but also about Hannah's future. Not that he had any say in that, of course, and yet somehow her future seemed improbably tied to his own.

Impossible.

She would never leave her faith for him and that's what he would be asking of her. The very idea that she could marry a circus owner and travel around the country with a bunch of acrobats and clowns and not be shunned by her Amish community was ludicrous. And if he loved her — and that was still an undetermined quantity in his mind — would he ask such a thing? Wouldn't the greater love be to let her go? Take her son and return home to Florida where she might find an Amish widower or bachelor waiting to marry her?

After all, she'd already made her decision. The note she'd written — the one he'd crumpled into a wad and then smoothed out and now carried with him — could not have been more clear. He'd avoided any contact or conversation with her since receiving that note. Maybe now was the time to respond.

He reversed his path and headed for the payroll car. He would take out the cash Hannah and the others would need for the train back to Florida, put that in an envelope for Gunther with a note. Then he would write a note to Pleasant thanking her for her service in the costume shop. And finally a note to Hannah — a businesslike note, similar to the one he wrote to Pleasant that would leave no doubt that they had come to the end of their relationship.

So engrossed was he in his plan that he was inside the car and opening the safe before he saw Hannah slumped over her desk surrounded by piles of papers. His first thought was that she had come in to work and been overcome by the aftereffects of her head injury. But when he knelt next to her and gently touched her shoulder, she sighed, turned her face to the other cheek and slept on. Her breathing was normal and she certainly did not look as if she were in any distress.

Levi stood up and looked around trying to decide his next move. What had the woman been thinking to drag all of this out on the day they were scheduled to leave? Everything was out of order. Neat stacks sorted by vendor rather than his preferred system of filing by date covered not only the top of her desk, but also Chester's. This would take hours to set to rights.

And yet in his heart, he knew that Hannah had to have had her reasons. He studied the arrangement of files, trying to find some sense in what she had done. And slowly he began to grasp what Hannah's digging had uncovered.

Someone he knew and trusted was stealing from him — had been stealing from him for at least a year if these documents were correct. And the first name that came to mind was his old friend and business manager's. Only Jake had full access to whatever cash reserves they kept in the safe. Only Jake could sign checks in Levi's absence.

Not Jake, he thought. *Please.*

And that was the closest Levi had come to truly praying since the day his parents had been crushed in the tornado.

He picked up the stack of invoices from Danvers Dry Goods. He had traded with Travis Danvers and his wife, Ginny, for years. He'd come to Travis's funeral and made it clear to Chester that whenever the circus came to town, all possible supplies that could be bought from Ginny should be. Yet mixed in with the Danvers invoices were others from a vendor he didn't know.

He studied an invoice for that other dry goods store dated three days earlier.

"Hannah, wake up."

The urgency in his voice jolted her upright. "What's happened? Oh, Levi, I can explain."

"No time," he said. "You need to get this stuff back in the files as quickly as possible. Don't worry about getting it right, just get it put away before Jake comes in. I have to go into town."

"I don't understand."

"I hope I don't either — I hope I'm dead wrong about this but . . ." He spotted the rumpled invoice she'd been lying on and picked it up. He compared it to the one in his hand. "I'll be back," he said tersely. "Do not mention this to anyone — not your family, not Lily and certainly not Jake, do you understand?"

She looked at him with those huge blue eyes of hers and he saw that her lip was trembling. So he retraced his steps and pulled her into his arms. "It's all right," he crooned. "You did nothing wrong, Hannah. In fact, you might have done me a huge favor. Now please get this stuff put away. I'll explain later, all right?"

She nodded and he kissed her forehead before letting her go. "If anyone asks, tell

209

them I had to go into town — nothing more."

Again, she nodded and he was relieved to see that before he was out the door, she was already starting to gather the piles of papers and put them back into the open file drawers.

Hannah's head throbbed but she suspected it was not due to the bump she'd gotten reacting to Pleasant's announcement that she might stay in Wisconsin. No, nothing was making any sense at all right now. Clearly, Levi had seen something in the papers she'd spent hours sorting through that she had missed and he had instantly known what it meant.

He did not seem upset with her. In fact, he'd shown her a kind of tenderness that had tested her will to stand firm behind the note she had sent him. Any kindness from him made her question whether or not there might be any possibility that she and he could . . .

"Hannah?"

She had not heard Jake come in. "Good morning," she said brightly, even as she scanned the room for any documents she might have missed.

"You work late and come in early. I'm going to have to talk to Levi about giving you a raise." He tossed his hat across the narrow train car and it caught the brass hat rack and stayed. "Have you seen the boss?"

"He said something about going into town." Her breath quickened. She did not like lying but she would have to watch every word if she were to avoid that particular sin now.

To her relief, Jake grinned. "Figured as much. Levi has his traditions — last town on the tour is always special to him — a place where he's connected with some of the townsfolk over the years. He always goes downtown to thank them and say goodbye."

Outside they could hear the normal cadence of tents being dismantled while animals and wagons were loaded onto railway cars. The scent of bacon and sausage and strong black coffee wafted in through the open window and Hannah's stomach growled.

"I think I'll go get some breakfast," she said, thankful for any excuse to get away from Jake and the payroll car. "Can I bring you anything?"

Jake rubbed his stomach. "Nope. Already ate. You go on. Looks like you've got everything in order here, and I imagine you've got other things on your mind right now."

Hannah tried hard not to show surprise.

211

"No. What things?"

"Your son — you'll be seeing him by supper time, Hannah," Jake said.

And suddenly, everything but the thought of reuniting with Caleb flew from Hannah's mind. She smiled at Jake. "That's right. It's always seemed as if it were so far in the future — weeks and then days away but now . . ."

"It's here. Today's the day."

Hannah could have hugged the man for setting her mind to rights, bringing her focus back to what was really important here. Caleb was all that mattered from this moment forward. "Yes," she said and she laughed. "Today is indeed the day." And when she entered the dining tent she was humming to herself.

"You're in a good mood," Pleasant observed, scowling up at her from her place at one of the long tables.

"Today we see Caleb," Hannah replied happily. She completely missed the unusually quiet reception she was receiving, not only from her sister-in-law but from Lily as well.

"I have to pack," Lily muttered, picking up her dishes and leaving just as a waiter brought Hannah a plate filled with scrambled eggs, link sausages and fried potatoes.

"Milk?" he asked, holding up a pitcher from a nearby stand and Hannah nodded as she scooted onto the bench across from Pleasant.

"I'm famished," Hannah said. "Surely that means I'm on the mend." She had assumed that Pleasant's sour mood had to do with the guilt she refused to relinquish for having caused Hannah's head injury.

Pleasant worked her lips into a disapproving pout. "I suppose staying out all night doing who knows what with who knows whom can lead a person to an appetite," she said primly, refusing to look at Hannah directly.

Hannah put down her fork. "I was working," she said, but could not help but glance around to see if anyone else might have heard Pleasant's statement.

This time Pleasant pinned her with a steely cold stare. "Do not add lying to your shame, Hannah," she ordered through clenched teeth. "I awoke after midnight and came to bring you a glass of water and see if you needed any of the headache powders. Your bed was empty and it remained so."

Hannah struggled with her sister-in-law's accusation and with the unspoken promise she had given Levi not to talk about what she'd been doing and had obviously discovered. "I was working," she repeated. "And I was alone."

"Oh, really. Then Lily must have been mistaken when she saw Levi rush out of the payroll car just after dawn and then saw you through the window."

"It's not what you think — either of you," Hannah said, and tried to concentrate on her breakfast, her appetite gone. She tried a sip of her milk. "Who else is talking about this?"

Hannah knew how quickly news spread in the traveling community. Most of the time she found it charming the way each of them seemed to care so much about everyone else, but there had been times when the gossip had been vicious — and untrue.

"I haven't spoken to Father if that's what you're worried about. As for Lily, I couldn't say. She did try and make excuses for both of you but then Lily has a soft spot when it comes to Levi — and to you."

Hannah wrestled with her options and decided that truth had always been her guiding principle. "Pleasant, you know me and I am telling you that I was working and that yes, Levi came to the office this morning. But it is business — all of it. I don't

214

fully understand it and Levi has asked that I not mention anything to anyone — a promise I have just broken in talking to you. But I would rather break a promise to him than have you believe something that simply is not true."

She watched as Pleasant's expression softened from condemnation to confusion. "But what could you possibly . . . how much filing could there be that . . ."

Hannah reached across the table and took her sister-in-law's hand. "I saw something a few days ago that raised a question in my mind. I thought perhaps I might have made a mistake and I wanted to be sure that everything was in order before turning the files over to Ida again. That's why I went there last night."

"And did you find what you were looking for?" Pleasant was leaning closer now, her eyes bright with interest and curiosity.

Oh, I found so much more, Hannah thought. "I'm not certain, but whatever has to do with that is now in Levi's hands. All I plan to concentrate on for the rest of this day is what to say to Caleb when I see him. I am going to need your strength for that, Pleasant, and Gunther's as well, if we are to be successful in reuniting our family."

Pleasant picked at the fried potatoes on

Hannah's plate. "How do you think the reunion will go? I mean, how do you expect Caleb to react to seeing you — and us — again?"

"I don't know. I have written him every day and have had only one short note back. The one I showed you."

Pleasant nodded. "The wire. 'I am fine. I miss you. And Auntie. And Gramps,' " she said in a singsong voice. "That one."

"Not exactly what I had hoped for and I suspect Ida was behind it being sent at all. Oh, Pleasant, what if he refuses to come home?"

"Father will make him."

"And then what? He'll run away again and this time things may not turn out so well." Her lighthearted mood of just moments earlier had completely disappeared. She was exhausted and confused and very, very afraid for what the day might bring.

Levi waited for Ginny Danvers to finish ringing up a sale for a customer and see her out.

"Well, Levi Harmon," she said when she spotted him. She came forward wiping her hands on her apron before offering him a businesslike handshake. "To what do I owe this honor?"

216

Levi grinned sheepishly. When Ginny's husband had been alive, Levi had made a habit of stopping by the store whenever he was in the area and spending an hour or so catching up. "It's been a while," he said.

Ginny nodded. "How about a cup of coffee? Black, right?"

"You wouldn't happen to have any of those ginger cookies back there, would you?"

Ginny laughed and minutes later the two of them were leaning across the counter, drinking coffee and nibbling ginger cookies while Ginny told him about her kids and grandkids. "You still not married?"

"Haven't found the right girl," he said, giving her the stock answer he'd always used. *Oh, but you have,* he thought.

"Clock's ticking," Ginny said with a jerk of her head toward the old grandfather clock that had stood in the corner of the store for as long as Levi could remember. "But you didn't come in here to look at pictures of my family, and you didn't come to talk about your love life." She refilled his cup. "What's going on?"

"It's nothing, really. I was wondering if you might have copies of the bills you submitted for say the past couple of years?"

Ginny lifted one eyebrow. "Sure."

"Could I see them?"

She went through a curtain where he could hear the slide of a metal file drawer opening and a moment later closing. Just then the front doorbell jangled as two customers entered the store.

"Here," Ginny said, sliding the file folder marked with his name across the counter. "Good morning, folks. How can I be of help?"

While Ginny served her customers, Levi studied the invoices. Three years earlier there had been a bill for one hundred dollars marked "paid in cash." It matched an invoice that he'd picked up from the stacks on Hannah's desk, except on his copy the amount paid was for four hundred dollars. By the time Ginny had come back to the counter to ring up her sales, he'd found three similar discrepancies.

Could Chester have pulled this off? Levi studied the changed figures closely. The four was smudged but he knew Jake's handwriting as well as he knew his own, and this wasn't his. Could they be in this thing together?

"You can take that file along if you like," she said. "I've got a duplicate."

"Thanks," Levi replied as he gathered the contents into the file and tipped his hat to the two customers. "Oh, Ginny, do you know of a dry goods business in the area called 'General Dry Goods'?"

"Never heard of 'em," Ginny replied. "Don't be such a stranger next time, okay?"

Outside the dry goods store, Levi stood for a long moment on the sidewalk trying to decide his next move. Down the block he saw a stone building that he knew held the town hall and the police department. There was enough Amish still in Levi that he hated the idea of involving outside law enforcement. He'd always prided himself on being able to manage his own security and business without having to rely on outsiders.

But someone was stealing from him — had been stealing from him for some time. And what that person had failed to understand was that stealing from Levi meant stealing from his hard-working performers and crew, as well. Fury welled up in Levi's chest until he thought he would choke. He had given every employee his trust and his loyalty, but one of them had betrayed him.

There could be only two suspects, he told the police chief. Chester was responsible for making all purchases and submitting the bills, but it was Jake who was responsible for writing the check or issuing the cash to pay those bills.

Please let there be some other explanation, Levi prayed, even as he watched the police chief fill out the warrant necessary to arrest his oldest and dearest friend.

220

CHAPTER FOURTEEN

As the train approached Milwaukee, Hannah and Pleasant decided to spend some time in the club car. It was a gathering place for the cast and more often than not, Fred could be found there strumming his ukulele while others read or talked quietly in small groups. Hannah liked the countryside she was seeing. Rolling fields, freshly plowed and planted, flashed by the wide windows like the patches of a quilt. The day was sunny and fruit trees were in peak blossom. It was late May but spring was just reaching its peak in this part of the country.

She imagined Caleb helping with chores on a farm like those they passed. Pristine, white clapboard farmhouses accented by bright red barns and tall silos and neatly fenced yards. *Please let him have found joy in this life,* she prayed, squeezing her eyes closed and clenching her fingers together.

She felt the train slow and opened her

eyes. In the distance, she could see the blue waters of Lake Michigan as they approached the city. As they reached the station, she was aware that the general buzz of conversation had grown more animated. Everyone seemed intrigued as a man in a dark suit and derby hat boarded the train. He entered their car and walked the length of it, his hands behind his back as he studied each of them.

"Where would I find Mr. Harmon?" he asked of no one and at the same time everyone.

Fred jerked his head toward the rear of the train. "Private car three cars back," he said. Then he waited for the man to leave and signaled two other male performers to follow him. The three of them gave the stranger a head start and then trailed him back through the train.

It had already been an unsettling day. Levi had returned from his walk into town accompanied by the local police chief. They had gone into the payroll office and closed the door. Minutes later Jake had emerged, slammed his hat onto his head and strode off toward town even as the last of the railway cars snapped into place and the conductor signaled that it was time to be on board.

The women who had been watching the loading of the last wagon and speculating about Jake's sudden departure, had no choice but to get on board. Now yet another law enforcement officer had arrived.

"Federal agent," Lily whispered to Hannah. "Something's up."

Hannah thought about the invoices and the discrepancies in amounts paid. *Was Levi in trouble?* "Where are Fred and the others going?"

"To protect Levi and make sure there's no trouble, I expect."

Moments later, Levi and the agent walked back through the car, followed closely by Fred and his two friends. All of the men seemed intent on the same mission as they looked neither left nor right but headed straight into the next car forward . . . the payroll car. The women all crowded onto the platform connecting the two cars jostling each other for the best position to see what was happening.

Hannah had once gone into a movie theater to search for Caleb and his friends, and had been struck by the lack of sound while actors clearly in distress poured out their stories through gesture and expression. Watching what unfolded in the next few minutes behind the closed glass door of the payroll car was a little like that.

She saw the agent approach Chester who was sitting at his desk. Chester stood and began shouting and gesturing wildly. He started toward the door but Fred and his men blocked the way. The agent took out a pair of handcuffs and put them on Chester, who crumpled back into his desk chair and began to cry. Then he raised his head and began pleading with Levi.

And all the while Hannah watched as Levi stood stone still, arms folded across his body, with no discernible expression on his face. Then he turned, saw the women crowded outside the door and abruptly turned the other way then exited at the far end of the payroll car. Hannah saw his shoulders slump just before he went through the far door and realized that what she and the others had taken for indifference was in fact an emotion so strong that he'd barely been able to hold himself together.

She pushed her way through the gaggle of women returning to their seats and entered the payroll car.

"Got it covered," she heard Fred tell the law officer. "We'll be in Baraboo by supper time. The three of us can take turns keeping watch on him until then."

Chester raised his head and spotted Hannah. "Why don't you question her?" he sneered. "Ask her what she was doing here late at night — with the boss."

Hannah felt the heat of embarrassment rise up her neck until it flamed bright pink in her cheeks.

"You are?" the agent asked not yet looking up from the small notebook where he was fanning through pages, apparently searching for some piece of information he needed.

"Hannah Goodloe," she murmured.

He glanced her way and then his eyes widened. "You're Amish?"

"Yes."

He whipped off his hat. "On a circus train?"

"Yes."

"She worked here same as me," Chester said. "Had keys same as me."

"But was not here stealing from us for the past year — same as you," Fred said sarcastically. "My understanding is that it was Mrs. Goodloe who uncovered the evidence," he added, speaking to the agent but smiling at Hannah.

"That was good detective work, ma'am," the agent said.

"And what about Jake? Anybody think to look at him?" Chester continued to rant.

"Looked at him and cleared him," the agent flung over his shoulder. "Now shut up." He gave Hannah an apologetic smile. "Was there something you needed to tell me, ma'am?"

"No. I just . . ." She peered past him to the platform outside the rear door where she could see Levi leaning heavily against the railing, his eyes closed as he raised his face to the wind. "Mr. Harmon seems to be in some distress. I thought perhaps a glass of water?"

The federal agent nodded and Hannah rushed to the water cooler. It burped and gurgled as she filled a cup and then balancing it carefully, headed for the door.

"Allow me," Fred said and pulled it open for her, giving Levi the sign that all was under control before allowing the door to close behind her.

Hannah handed Levi the water and it sloshed over his fingers a little as he drank it down. "Thanks," he mouthed, the sound of his voice carried away on the rush of wind that snatched at her skirts and prayer cap.

Hannah nodded but did not go back inside the payroll car. Instead, she stood by waiting to see what Levi might do. He had returned to the position of holding on to

226

the guardrail, his head bent, his shoulders slumped. And then she was certain that she saw a tear fly from his cheek on the wind.

"I accused Jake," he said, as if he couldn't quite believe it. "My oldest and dearest friend and I accused him of stealing from me."

She opened her mouth but words would not come.

"I ruined a friendship and for what? Some missing money?"

"How did you find out it was Chester?"

"I didn't want to think it was either man, but after the way Jake looked at me and then just walked away, I knew I'd made a terrible mistake. I just couldn't figure out how Chester had pulled it off."

"And how did he?" Instinctively, she knew that it was best to let him talk, to let him relive the whole story.

"He created a couple of front companies. It's not hard to do — pick a name and file some paperwork. And then if there was a vendor he knew dealt only in cash, those were the ones he targeted. He would rewrite the order for his dummy company charging twice what the vendor charged, then he would submit the invoice to Jake who would give him the cash to pay the vendor — himself. Chester would pay the true vendor and pocket the rest."

"But you told Jake that you wanted supplies to be ordered from Danvers regardless of the cost."

"Because Jake was the only one who could hand out the cash," Levi said. "What was I supposed to think? How could Chester pull this off — especially for so long — without his help? I thought that they were in this together."

"But Jake didn't know?"

"Chester explained the orders from his dummy company by telling Jake that Danvers couldn't supply in the amounts we needed. Earlier, he stole the cash by changing the numbers on the invoices — a one turned into a four . . . like that. But that became too risky so he set up the companies and once he did that, stealing got a whole lot easier."

He still wasn't looking at her, just flinging his story out to the wind as if in doing so he might be rid of his shame.

"Did Jake say anything before he walked away?" She was suddenly afraid that the man Levi depended on the most had left for good.

"He said that I had changed and it wasn't for the better." Levi dropped his chin to his chest and his knuckles faded to white as he gripped the railing and a shudder ran the length of his body. "He won't be back and the truth is, I don't blame him."

Hannah stepped forward and placed her palm on his back as much to steady herself as to comfort him. But when she felt his shoulders heave she left it there and moved so that she was blocking him from view of the others. "It'll all work out," she crooned, moving close enough so that her mouth was close to his ear. "Everything will work out."

And silently she prayed that it might be so.

Dusk was settling in by the time they arrived in Baraboo, but Hannah was determined to see Caleb as soon as possible. Levi was occupied with the business of Chester's arrest and she hadn't wanted to trouble him with her problems. But as always, he had made all the necessary arrangements.

"Mrs. Goodloe?"

A gray-haired woman dressed in a lavender business suit was waiting on the platform. She stepped forward and offered Hannah a firm handshake. "I am Ida Benson. Levi asked that I arrange to take you and your in-laws out to the farm as soon as you arrived. I do hope this mode of transportation suits?"

She pointed to a black hack hitched to a gray horse. Standing next to it was a man dressed in plain clothes who nodded at her but did not come forward.

"This will do just fine," Hannah assured her then turned to introduce her to Pleasant and Gunther.

"Come and meet Matthew Harnisher," Ida said. "Caleb has been staying with Matthew and his wife, Mae, and their four children."

"You are Amish?" Gunther asked, eyeing the buggy and then Ida's lavender suit.

"No," she explained. "But Matthew and Mae are Old Order Amish — like your family." She made the introductions and then while Matthew supervised the loading of their luggage, the three of them crowded into the buggy — Pleasant and Hannah in back and Gunther sharing the driver's seat with Matthew.

"Your boy is well," Ida told Hannah, grasping her hand and commanding her attention.

"But?"

Ida nodded, clearly relieved that Hannah had understood that physical wellness was not the entire story. "He is . . . anxious about seeing you again. He knows he did wrong and yet . . ." She searched for the right words. "It may take some time, Hannah."

"I understand," Hannah assured her. But as she stared at her father-in-law's straight unyielding back on the ride from the station to the Harnisher farm, she couldn't help but wonder if understanding would be enough.

It hardly mattered in the end for as they drove into the yard of the farm, Matthew's wife, Mae, came running down the steps to meet them.

"He's gone," she called. "The boys and I searched everywhere, but he's not here."

Levi had meant to go with the Goodloes when they went to collect Caleb. He had thought to ease the way for the boy. Gunther was old school and would not take kindly to the trouble the boy had put them through. He was given to lecturing — as Levi's stable help had complained more than once over the past several days. And Levi well remembered that at young Caleb's age, the very last thing a boy would heed was a lecture.

But he would have to leave that to Ida and Matthew. His first concern had to be his business. The local police had met the train and taken Chester into custody. He would spend time in jail until a trial could be arranged. In the meantime, Levi would meet with his lawyer and build the case. The more he thought about what Chester had done, the angrier he got. And when he realized that Chester's betrayal had resulted in Levi accusing Jake, fury turned to rage and he was bent on seeking his revenge.

When it had been only money he had lost, he had thought he might be able to handle the whole thing himself. But when the policeman had questioned Jake, and Levi had seen the look of utter disbelief and disappointment on his friend's face, he had known that Chester had stolen something far more precious.

At least in the midst of all this trauma he could take some comfort in knowing that Hannah was being reunited with her son. Although that reunion also had a dark side in that it meant that far too soon the Goodloe family would take the first possible train back to Florida.

A wave of loneliness washed over Levi like the surf breaking on the beach on a stormy day. The feeling was so overpowering that it took his breath away. He was a man who many would say had everything anyone could hope for — money, power, friends. But he had destroyed his best friend's trust and after his parents had died he had willingly — and foolishly — walked away from the family he had left. Over the years, he had stayed in contact with his brother, Matt, but his letters to his grandparents and his sisters had all been returned unopened. Many times Matt had urged him to come home to Wisconsin and start a family of his own, but what kind of life could he offer a wife and children? What kind of stability?

And so the circus people had become his family. Ida and Lily, like sisters to him. Hans, Jake and Chester, like brothers. But now Jake was gone. Chester had betrayed him, and truth be told, he knew none of the others thought of him as "family." He was their employer — a benevolent one to be sure — but hardly their brother. If he were gone tomorrow, what would he have left as his legacy? A circus? A mansion in Florida?

Levi had dismissed his driver outside the police station, saying he needed to walk, and for the past two hours he'd been wandering aimlessly, trying to bring some order to the chaotic thoughts that raced through his mind. It was dark now and he found himself on a country road far from the railway station and far from the compound that served as the summer quarters for the circus. He heard the wail of a train whistle moving east and recalled how, as a boy, a similar whistle had been like a siren's song for him.

He realized that he had wandered all the way out to where his grandfather's farm — Matthew's farm now — bordered the road. It had started to rain so he shoved his hands into the pockets of his trousers and hunched his shoulders against a north wind as he recognized that the person he most needed to see was at that farm. Hannah.

Turning a corner, he made out another solitary figure limping badly along the road ahead of him. "Wait up," he shouted, and the person started to run, then stumbled and fell.

"I'm not going to hurt you," Levi said as he caught up and knelt down. He saw that this was a boy, hatless and dirty. "What happened?" he asked.

"Nothing. I fell."

"Falling isn't nothing," Levi said. "Did you twist your ankle?"

The boy nodded.

"Where were you headed?"

"Train." He choked on the word and Levi realized the boy was crying. "But I just heard the whistle and now it's gone and . . ."

"My name's Levi," he said calmly as he gently probed the kid's ankle for the possibility of a broken bone. "And you are?"

"Caleb."

Levi put it together then. The plain clothes, muddy now from the two falls, the hair that hung straight and limp covering the boy's ears. The proximity to Matthew Harnisher's farm. He could take him back there but what was to keep the boy from trying to run again? From making the same mistake that he had made all those years ago? "Well, Caleb, tell you what. How about I help you get to my compound so we can have my doctor take a look at that ankle?"

"I don't think I can walk."

"Good point. Well, then let's just wait here. Somebody's bound to come along." Levi scooted his back up against the lower boughs of a sheltering evergreen tree, plopped his hat on the boy's head and then wrapped his arms around his knees. "Amish, are you?"

Caught off guard, the boy nodded.

"Me, too. Wanna hear a story while we wait?"

Again the nod.

It was quickly decided that Gunther and Pleasant would stay at the farm with Mae and the boys while Hannah went with Matthew to search for Caleb. There was little doubt which way he'd headed. Matthew's son, Lars, admitted that Caleb had told him of his plan and even tried to get Lars to join him.

"He'll have cut across that pasture and the cornfields beyond and eventually come to the road back toward town," Matthew said. "We'll find him along the road."

Hannah nodded, no longer sure of anything. She wished Levi were with them. He would know what to do, what to say to Caleb to convince him to come home with her. As the horse trotted along the narrow road, Hannah did the only thing she knew to do in such circumstances — she prayed for the wisdom to know what words would change Caleb's mind about a life better than theirs in Florida once they found him. If they found him. If he would listen.

"Are you warm enough?" Matthew asked, jarring her from her meditation and back to the reality of their journey. It had started to rain again.

"Yes. Thank you for doing this. I hope that Caleb has not been thoughtless or unkind."

Matthew laughed. "On the contrary. The boy was so good-natured and helpful with chores and all, that we found him a good addition to our family." He let the horse amble along, reins slack.

Hannah fought against the urge to ask him

236

to go faster.

"It was only as the time got closer that he changed," Matthew said.

"What time?"

"Your arrival. He got quieter then, nothing much to say, although he continued to tend to the chores and help Mae out around the house. Just went inside himself some and seemed to spend a good deal of his time following me around."

"He misses his father."

"*Ja.* That's what I told Levi." He tightened the reins and clucked softly to the horse as he peered ahead.

"How do you know Levi?" she asked more to keep the conversation alive than anything else.

Matthew glanced at her, his features shadowed by the dark and the wide brim of his hat. "He's my brother."

Hannah was certain she had heard him wrong. "You mean that you are friends — that . . ."

"Blood brothers," he said. "I see he did not tell you this."

"No." Her mind raced with myriad thoughts — Levi was Amish? But the last names were . . .

"He changed his name after he left the farm." He chuckled. "I tease him that he

237

showed little imagination. Harmon and Harnisher. For a circus man, I thought he might have done better."

"How old were you when he left?"

"Just twelve. Levi was fourteen. He would have been baptized that year."

"You must have been very sad when he left."

Again the chuckle. "I was very angry to be sure. He was supposed to be the man of the family and now that would fall to me. Your boy and I talked about that some. About that responsibility coming on so suddenly and all."

"It seems that you met the responsibility," she ventured.

"*Ja.* And so will Caleb in time. He does not wish to leave his faith, Hannah. He just wishes to try his wings a bit, find his own way rather than the way of his father or grandfather."

"But isn't that what Levi did?"

Matthew shifted on the seat. "The difference is that my brother is still out there. He is still running away. Your Caleb is not Levi. Your Caleb runs because he knows he has a place to come home to. Levi never had that until it was too late."

"His grandfather?"

"Levi blamed him for sending Pa out that

night and for not stopping Ma from follow-ing him. Our grandfather was the head of our household and in Levi's mind, the responsibility for the animals was his — not our father's. Levi couldn't forgive that."

"But you did forgive Levi for leaving?"

"He is my only brother. God showed me that I had a choice — I could hold on to my anger and disappointment or I could let it go. I chose to let it go and in time after the death of our grandparents, Levi came back to us."

Hannah thought suddenly of Jake. What if Jake never forgave Levi?

"Somebody's up there," Matthew mut-tered and urged the horse forward.

Hannah followed his gaze and saw a man standing on the side of the road waving to them. "It's Levi," she murmured, and knew in that moment that he had become such a part of her that she would know him any-where even on the blackest of nights.

"Levi!" Matthew called out and drew the wagon closer then hopped down. "Are you all right?"

"Fine." The two men greeted each other with the traditional Amish handshake — one pump of their clasped hands. Then Levi looked past Matthew to Hannah. "He's all right," he said, and stood aside to reveal

Caleb sound asleep against a tree. "Took a couple of tumbles and might have broken his ankle."

While Hannah climbed into the back of the buggy, Matthew helped Levi hoist Caleb into the buggy next to her. "Thank you," she whispered as she cradled her son in her arms. He stirred for only a minute before falling into a deeper sleep, his head resting on her shoulder. He seemed to have grown some in the short time he'd been gone, and yet he fit perfectly into the curve of her shoulder. "Thank you both."

"Let's take him into town and get that ankle looked at," Levi told Matthew as the two men climbed into the buggy. "Then you can all go back to the farm and get some rest."

"He was running away again," Hannah said as Matthew snapped the reins and they started toward town. "I heard the train whistle and I thought . . ." She could not find the words to go on.

Levi reached back and touched her cheek. "He's safe," he told her.

But for how long?

240

Chapter Fifteen

By the time they saw the doctor and got back to the farm, it was past midnight. Hannah really did not want to question Levi about his past with Matthew there, and so they did not speak of it.

"Are you all right?" he asked as Matthew carried Caleb across the yard and up the front porch steps.

"Yes. Thank you for finding him and for staying with him."

Mae was making a fuss over the boy, insisting that he get into dry clothes and have something to eat before he went to bed. Gunther waited until Matthew had gotten Caleb into the house and then turned and walked away.

"I should go," Hannah told Levi, although what she wanted most of all was to ask him why — why he had left the farm. Why he had changed his name. Why he had never told her that he was Amish. It made perfect sense now in hindsight. The way he seemed to know of their ways.

"May I stop by tomorrow?"

"Yes. Caleb would like that," she said, and ran across the lawn and into the house before he could say anything more.

But that night she lay awake trying to imagine Levi living in this house. She heard the rumble of a freight train in the distance and wondered if Levi had lain awake planning his escape — if Caleb were even now lying awake planning to run away again.

Levi did not come the next day nor the day after that. Lily stopped by with Fred, who had Caleb laughing at his antics within five minutes of meeting him. It was so good to hear her son's laughter and she realized how very frightened she had been that she might never see him again.

"Levi had said he might come to visit Caleb," Hannah ventured later when she and Lily were sitting on the porch watching Fred and Caleb toss a baseball back and forth. Caleb had begged to get outside and Matthew had brought down an old wheelchair that his grandfather had used and set it up in the yard.

"He went to Milwaukee for a few days. Someone sent word that Jake had been there. He's been like a caged tiger waiting for any news at all so when he heard this, he drove all night to get there."

"I hope he finds him," Hannah said.

"Jake is a hothead," Lily said. "Hopefully he's cooled down enough to realize that if he'd been in Levi's shoes he would have thought the same thing. Those two can be oil and water, but in a good way. Without them, I doubt the company would have made it. These are hard times," she added almost as an afterthought, as she stared off into the distance. But then she shook off her melancholy and focused her attention on Caleb. "But you have your boy back and that's wonderful."

They sipped lemonade and watched the game of catch for a few minutes. Hannah couldn't help noticing that Lily seemed wistful as she watched Caleb.

"Lily? You once mentioned that you're a mother like me, but . . ."

"My son drowned accidentally when he was four," Lily said. "He would have been sixteen now. Sometimes when I see a boy — even a younger one like Caleb — I think about my Lonnie and wonder what he would have been like. He was such a happy kid — never a tear, never a frown. It made you smile just to look at him — like looking up at the sun."

"I'm sorry for your loss, Lily."

"After that, his father left and I just stayed on with the circus. It was Brody's Circus then — a ragtag bunch of acts with a couple of exotic animals. Then Levi took over and he brought Jake in to work with him and within a year, we were playing bigger towns and bringing in enough to buy more animals and so it grew."

Hannah fought against the question she had longed to ask Lily for weeks and lost. "Were you and Levi — I mean, did the two of you . . ."

Lily laughed. "Oh, honey, he was always so out of my league. I won't deny that I was interested — more than interested. I mean, the man is gorgeous and smart and kind in the bargain. We shared a couple of dinners but a girl knows when the guy's heart just isn't in it. His wasn't and I realized that having him for a friend was going to do me a lot more good. Now Jake . . ." she said and rolled her eyes. "That is a whole different can of worms."

"You love Jake?"

"I understand Jake," she corrected. "Love?" She frowned as if she'd just uttered a foreign word. "Yeah, maybe so." She stood up and drank the last of her lemonade. "Hey, Fred, you ready to go?"

244

As Hannah walked with Lily and Fred to their car, Lily linked arms with Hannah. "We miss you," she said. "You were good for us — you and Miss Pleasant and Gunther. You were good for Levi."

"You're embarrassing her," Fred said. "It is not her way to accept compliments." He grinned as they all recalled how many times one of the Goodloe family had had to explain that something was or was not "their way."

"Let us know when you're heading for Florida," Lily said, kissing Hannah on the cheek before climbing into the flashy yellow roadster that they had arrived in. "We'll have a big send-off waiting for you at the station — brass band — the works."

"No brass band," Hannah begged and then realized her friend was teasing her.

Fred gunned the motor and it split the idyllic quiet of the countryside. "Farewell, Hannah," he called as he spun the wheels and drove away with Lily waving wildly.

Hannah turned back to the house and saw Caleb still sitting in his wheelchair, idly tossing the ball in the air and catching it. When she came close enough, he lofted the ball in her direction and smiled when she caught it.

"Not bad, Ma."

She tossed it back to him. "You should rest."

"Ah, Ma, I broke a bone. It's not like I got pneumonia or something."

If Caleb had any intention of trying to run again, he was going to be hampered by the heavy plaster cast the doctor had applied after determining that indeed the boy had broken his ankle. Hannah had never imagined she would be thanking God for breaking her child's bone, but at the moment it did seem a blessing.

He glanced toward the stables. "When do you think I might be able to help Grandpa down there?"

Since their arrival at the farm, Gunther had taken charge of the horses and spent much of the day in the barn. Hannah suspected that it was at least in part due to his indecision about what to say to Caleb. She took hold of the handles for steering Caleb's wheelchair and started rolling him down to the barn. "Let's go see. Surely there's something you can do to help."

Gunther was sitting at a carpenter's bench mending a piece of harness when they entered the barn. He did not acknowledge either of them, and Hannah could practically feel Caleb's nervousness as she wheeled him toward his grandfather.

246

Before Caleb had run away, his relationship with Gunther had been a good one. The difference in generations had made Gunther less strict with Caleb than he had been with his own son. The two of them had gone fishing together in Sarasota Bay and returned with large live conch shells for her to figure out how best to clean and cook.

How they had laughed the first time they had handed her one of the beautiful shells so large that she had to hold it in two hands. But then the animal inhabiting the shell had begun to move and extend its strange foot and Hannah had yelped and dropped the shell on the ground. Gunther had nudged Caleb and winked and the two of them had collapsed into guffaws of laughter.

But ever since they had arrived in Wisconsin, Gunther had kept his distance from the boy. He did not come to visit him as he lay in bed recuperating. He did not ask about him at the supper table, although Hannah had seen his eyes brighten with interest when she and Mae discussed Caleb's progress.

Well, it's time to put a stop to this, Hannah thought and opened her mouth to address her father-in-law.

"Caleb," he said before she could get a word out. "Hand me that awl there on that haystack."

Hannah let go of the wheelchair handles and nodded to Caleb. He rolled himself over to the haystack to retrieve the awl and then transported it to Gunther.

"Now hold this like so," Gunther said, demonstrating how Caleb should anchor the harness strap for him.

As their heads bent toward one another and Gunther's litany of instruction continued, Hannah knew that every thing was going to be all right between them. She slipped out of the barn without either of them noticing and did not see them again until Mae rang the bell calling everyone in for supper.

That night Caleb sat next to Gunther, regaling him with his ideas for how he had been thinking of offering his services for caring for horses once they got back to Florida. "If you'll help me," he added, looking shyly up at his grandfather.

"*Ja*. I can help," Gunther replied, and turned his attention back to his supper.

Caleb glanced over at Hannah and grinned, and in that moment she knew that her son was home to stay — or would be as soon as they could get a train back.

Levi was troubled. And he should have been

relieved. He had caught the thief and Chester was safely behind bars. Hannah had been reunited with her son and, after his misadventures that had led to a broken ankle, the boy seemed content to return to Florida. The company had arrived safely back in Baraboo and as always, Ida had everything under control. In short, he had nothing to worry about for a change.

And yet . . .

He sat at his desk and studied the list of potential new acts that Jake had given him. In a week or so he would head east to audition the best of the lot. It was a trip he had always enjoyed, but it was a trip he and Jake had always made together. He had spent three days searching for Jake in Milwaukee and on down to Chicago with no success.

In spite of that, his life was about to get back to its normal routine so why was he so jumpy? So out of sorts?

Outside, the rain came in a steady downpour. It had rained for days now and there was talk of flooding to the west. Perhaps the train to Florida would be delayed.

And then what?

He had no future with Hannah so the wisest course had to be to let her go. But he wasn't yet ready to do that. Oh, he was well aware that the day had to come. He just wasn't ready for that day to come so soon.

Mae had settled Caleb back into the room he'd shared with Lars, the oldest of her four boys, but now he shared it with his grandfather as well as Lars. She and Matthew made up bunks in the barn for the other children so that Pleasant and Hannah could have their room. It was a tight fit but one that Caleb seemed to revel in.

"It's a real family, Ma," he said one day as she sat with him shelling spring peas and listening to the rain that continued to fall steadily.

"We're a real family as well," she replied.

Caleb grew quiet and stared out the window to the corn field that he'd helped Matthew and his sons plow and plant. "Not like this," he said softly.

Hannah set the bowl of shelled peas aside and sat down on the edge of Caleb's bed. "You miss your father," she said, combing his silky straight hair with her fingers. "So do I."

"I don't remember him so much," he admitted, "but I guess I miss the idea of a father — and brothers. Even sisters might be okay," he said miserably.

Hannah couldn't help it. She laughed and rumpled his hair, messing up the grooming she'd been doing. "I thought you didn't like girls."

Caleb grinned sheepishly. "Some of 'em are all right, I guess."

"Really? Anyone in particular?"

"Ah, Ma," he protested, and ducked away from her.

"You've got a visitor," Mae announced as she climbed the wooden stairs.

Hannah and Caleb looked toward the door. "Levi!" Caleb shouted.

"Mr. Harmon," Hannah corrected her son firmly.

Levi handed Caleb a package wrapped in brown paper and string, which the boy tore into immediately. It was a book on horses. "Thanks, Le . . . Mr. Harmon. Thanks a lot," Caleb said, and started turning the pages of the book.

"You didn't have to bring a gift," Hannah said shyly.

Levi shrugged. "The boy and I had some time to get to know each other the other night. I discovered that he likes hanging around horses. Must have picked that up from his grandfather." He shot Caleb a look. "I thought maybe you might like to share that with your grandfather," Levi added. "Word has it the two of you might be going into the horse business."

Caleb grinned and Hannah could have hugged the man for validating her son's idea. "Thank you," she said.

"Well, those peas are not going to cook themselves," Mae announced from her position in the doorway. "If you'll excuse me I need to start supper." She reached for the peas.

"I'll help," Hannah said.

"No, you've been cooped up in this house all day. It looks like we've finally a break in the showers so Levi, take the woman for a walk so she can get a little fresh air. It's a lovely spring day for all its dampness and we aren't always so blessed here in Wisconsin with such balmy breezes."

"Sounds like a fine idea," Levi said.

Hannah was torn, reluctant to let Caleb out of her sight. In spite of his plans to care for the horses of neighbors back in Sarasota, Hannah could not help but wonder if that would be enough excitement for the boy.

"He's not going anywhere," Mae said. "Are you, Caleb?"

Caleb blushed. "No, ma'am."

"I won't be long," Hannah promised, leaning in to kiss his forehead.

"Ah, Ma," he fussed and turned his attention back to his book.

Outside, she and Levi strolled toward the

orchard, taking care to avoid the soggier parts of the lawn. All around them, cherry blossoms past their peak showered down like snow, their sweetness perfuming the warm spring air. Levi walked with his hands clenched behind his back while Hannah kept hers folded piously in front of her.

"It was kind of you to think of Caleb," she said, unable to bear the silence that stretched between them like a tightwire.

"He's a good boy. A bright boy," he added.

"Things between Caleb and his grandfather have not been easy, but with time I think perhaps . . ."

"I gathered as much. I ran into Gunther in town. He was making arrangements for your trip back to Florida and told me about the boy's idea. He seemed hopeful — but cautious, like you."

Hannah had known the day would come when they had to leave, but so soon? Caleb was still in the cast and . . .

"I can't let you go quite yet," Levi said, not looking at her but focusing instead on the horizon.

"I don't understand." But, oh, how she hoped. Was he going to ask her to stay? And what if he did?

Levi stopped walking and turned to face her. "I need you to testify in court in the case against Chester."

For an instant, it felt as if she had been doused with a bucket of cold water. Her mind had been so full of what if's and maybes but not in her wildest imaginings would she have expected such a statement.

"I couldn't possibly," she said, the words no more than a whisper around her shock that he would even ask such a thing. "We are Amish," she added as if he hadn't known that. "We do not take part in the English legal system. It is our way. You, of all people, know that we cannot swear an oath and we cannot . . ."

"Stop telling me what you can and cannot do," he snapped impatiently. "Without your testimony we may not have enough evidence to . . ."

"I cannot do this and you must not ask it of me," she interrupted and turned to head back to the house.

"You would let a thief go free — someone who stole not only from me but from people who have befriended you these past few weeks?"

She stopped and turned to face him. "It is . . ."

". . . not your way. I get that." He removed his hat and ran his fingers through his thick hair in frustration.

"It is not *your* way." She covered the distance between them, wanting to shout the words at him. Instead, she pressed her fists to her skirt to stem the tide of her anger. "You are Amish."

"Was," he corrected. "I made my choice long ago. I am as much an outsider now as anyone in my company."

His bitterness surprised her.

"And at the moment," he continued, "it is my company I must think of. Chester has taken more than money. He has stolen the trust I worked so hard to build with these people. They look at each other now with suspicion and doubt. They look at me differently."

His pain was so obvious in his haggard features that Hannah had to resist touching his face. As if touching him would do anything to smooth away the exhaustion and distress she saw there.

"Levi, think of it. Chester has been your good friend and a valued employee. He was not always a thief. Why did he steal? Have you asked him that?"

"I don't know — greed, selfishness, because it was easy. What do the reasons matter? He did it and kept doing it. And I didn't see it. Nor did Jake. That's the point."

"And so he must go to jail? That is the

only possible recourse? That will make things right with you?"

"What would you have me do, Hannah? Forgive and forget? This is not just about my selfish interests. These people work for me — if they see that nothing is done about a man who steals, then what?"

"It is not for me to say what you should do — only God can tell you that. But you must be willing to listen." She took half a step closer and stood her ground. "And I must ask that you respect that I cannot and will not break with my traditions to do what you think must be done."

He stared down at her for a long moment and then carefully picked an errant blossom petal from her hair. "I would walk through fire for you, Hannah," he said and had Mae not chosen that moment to sound the dinner bell, she realized that he would have kissed her.

Levi had thought that he could keep her close by insisting that she testify. He didn't really need her to do that. Chester had confessed to opening accounts for dummy companies that he'd established, as well as confessed to forging by changing the amounts on certain invoices.

When Levi realized the extent of Chester's

deceit, he was furious. But just then in the orchard he had seen in Hannah's eyes and heard in her question, the truth of the situation. This was not about justice. It was about revenge. Chester had betrayed him, and Levi had the need to make an example of the man lest anyone else think they could hoodwink him in the future. His anger and hurt carried over to Jake who he felt should have questioned the bills, the higher prices.

But he'd seen the bills as well, noticed the higher costs. Had Levi questioned anything? No, he had trusted a man who had worked for him for over ten years. And yet throwing the man in jail did not feel right. Chester behind bars did not make Levi feel any sense of peace.

Only God can tell you what to do, Hannah had said.

Later that night Levi wandered into the kitchen of his modest Wisconsin home — a home far less elegant than the mansion in Sarasota. Hans sat at the kitchen table reading.

"Sir?" He was immediately on his feet ready to serve.

"Just came for some water," Levi said. "What are you reading there?"

"Scripture from the book of Matthew," Hans answered.

257

"I didn't realize you were a religious man, Hans."

"It was a habit I developed on the trip here. Gunther — Mr. Goodloe — read some every night. I found that it was a good way to set aside the worries of the day. We also started each morning with a reading," he added.

"So read me a passage," Levi said, as he leaned against the sink and drank his water.

Hans cleared his throat. "Blessed are the poor in spirit, for theirs is the kingdom of heaven. Blessed are they who mourn, for they shall be comforted. Blessed are the meek, for they shall inherit the earth. Blessed are they who hunger and thirst for righteousness, for they shall be satisfied. Blessed are the merciful, for they shall obtain mercy. Blessed are the pure of heart, for they shall see God. Blessed are the peacemakers, for they shall be called children of God. Blessed are they who are persecuted for the sake of righteousness, for theirs is the kingdom of heaven."

Levi stood for a long time staring out the kitchen window at the rain sluicing down the glass. "Thank you, Hans. Sleep well," he said softly.

"And you," Hans replied, and left Levi alone.

CHAPTER SIXTEEN

On Sunday, families came from all around the area to crowd into the Harnisher home for services. It was their turn to host the services and Mae had been cleaning for days. As the others arrived, Lars and his brothers took charge of unhitching the horses and getting them out of the rain into the barn. Men unloaded the backless benches from the bench wagon that moved with the services from house to house. Mae had insisted on leaving some of the more comfortable chairs in place for older members of the congregation.

The benches replaced the large table where the family normally gathered for meals. Men sat together at the front and women at the back. This was a small group and so everyone was able to crowd into the one room.

Three chairs had been placed at the very front of the room for the ministers and the bishop to occupy. While the first hymn was sung, the two ministers, bishop and deacon retired to another room to decide who would preach that day and in what order. During the hymn, people continued to arrive and find their place in the crowded room.

Caleb leaned on his crutches and took his place next to his grandfather. As the first hymn began, Hannah watched Caleb carefully, worried that it might be too soon for him to be up and around, when she heard Pleasant gasp.

"It's him," her sister-in-law whispered, her eyes darting quickly toward the door and then back again to her hands folded tightly in her lap. The hint of a smile tugged at the corners of her normally tight-lipped mouth.

Hannah watched a jovial young man greet several of his peers and elders gathered in the outer hallway. He was at least two inches shorter than Pleasant was. He had a ruddy round face and an easy smile, and Hannah could understand how a woman as reserved as Pleasant might be taken by such an easygoing and gregarious young man.

She nudged her sister-in-law with her shoulder and smiled her approval. Pleasant covered a girlish giggle of delight by pretending to cough. But then her eyes darkened, her face reddened and she went as still as a stone.

"What?" Hannah whispered, thinking Pleasant might have choked. She glanced toward the door ready to cry out for help when she saw the reason for Pleasant's distress. Or rather the reasons.

For following the young man into the room was a woman, small and heavy with child and three additional children who could not have looked any more like their father.

Pleasant threw off Hannah's hand of comfort and as the pregnant woman and her two youngest children slid on to the bench next to her, Pleasant sat up even straighter. Her jaw was firm, her eyes pinning the man with accusation. He glanced their way then, and clearly recognized Pleasant. To Hannah's shock, he smiled and nodded as he might in greeting someone he hadn't seen in some time but was pleased to see now.

All through the services Hannah tried to concentrate but she went through the rituals by rote. All the while next to her, Pleasant simmered with indignation and fury.

As the main sermon was being delivered in a singsong style and in the High German preferred by this group, Hannah could think

261

only of what Pleasant had told her of the man. He had come to Florida to visit a sick uncle and offer help with the crops that winter. He had talked of looking at some land to buy, of possibly coming to Florida to live. She knew that he had come to the bakery every morning that he was in the area and that he and Pleasant had talked of the weather and the crops and his uncle's improving health. She knew that he had complimented Pleasant on her cake donuts, claiming they were lighter than air.

But there had been no more to it than that. He had not walked with Pleasant or taken her for a ride in his uncle's buggy. Pleasant had admitted as much, hoping that perhaps if they could see each other again in Wisconsin, things might move to that next level of official courting. In the days that they had spent traveling north, Hannah could see now that Pleasant had built an entire picture in her mind of how things might develop between her and the boyish-looking farmer.

The hope that romance awaited her had been behind her announcement that night that she might just stay in Wisconsin. She stole a look at her sister-in-law as the second minister droned on. Pleasant's face was composed, her eyes seemingly riveted on the preacher while her hands writhed as she twisted a lace handkerchief into a coiled rope of her misery.

Hannah's heart went out to this woman who, over the duration of their journey, had become her friend. And then she had a thought that made all other thoughts fly away like the sound of the minister's words through the open windows in the close little room.

What if she had also misjudged Levi's feelings for her? What if she, like Pleasant, had taken his attentions for something more than was intended? What a fool she must appear to someone so worldly. She thought back to those moments when she had been most susceptible to his kindness, his gentle touch, his kiss . . .

In every case it could be said that he had wanted something from her, needed something. Like in the orchard the day before when he had told her he needed her to testify in court. Mortified, she closed her eyes tightly as she recalled how her heart had soared at the touch of his lips on hers that night in the payroll car that now seemed a thousand years ago. Why would a man like Levi have the slightest interest in a plain woman like her? He had his pick of the women in his company and of the women in the towns they traveled through. And there were the wealthy society women Hannah had seen on the streets of Sarasota riding through town in their fancy cars, the tops down and their laughter trailing behind them like expensive perfume.

As he had said, he had made his choice. It had been years since he had run away to the outside world and he had never come back.

Fool.

She felt Pleasant's eyes on her and realized that she, like her sister-in-law, had suddenly sat up a bit straighter and clenched her fingers into fists. Pleasant reached over and covered one of Hannah's fists with her open palm. Clearly, she thought that Hannah's anger was an expression of solidarity and perhaps in a way it was, for they had both been foolish and naive.

When the services finally ended, the room was transformed once again in preparation for the noon meal to be shared before everyone started for home. Because converting some benches to tables took more room and left less seating, the congregation would be served in shifts. While some stood talking on the covered side porch that ran the length of the house, others had their meal and then the order reversed until all were fed. Again, everyone squeezed onto the long benches set next to tables laden with a variety of dishes that would serve as a light lunch. Mae's best jam, apple butter and pickled beets filled dishes up and down the length of the table. There was homemade bread and cheese. Knowing that in just two days she and her family would be on a train back to Florida, Hannah stood a little to one side of the gathering taking it all in. Their gatherings in Florida were not so different from this one and she could not help wishing that Levi could somehow realize that this was where he belonged.

While everyone else was at church or sleeping in for the morning, Levi entered the small cell where his front man was being held. Chester's face was lined with exhaustion and remorse. "I'm so sorry, boss," he muttered without looking directly at Levi.

"Then you are done with trying to throw the blame onto others?" Levi asked.

Chester nodded. "I'm so ashamed of what I did. I just . . ." He lifted his shoulders and let them drop as if words could not be found to explain what he had done.

Levi bowed his head for a moment and then certain that he was doing the right thing, he reached for Chester's hand. "Then

I forgive you. I am dropping the charges against you."

This time Chester looked at him, his eyes wide with disbelief. "Why would you do that?"

"Because someone recently reminded me that the Bible teaches mercy and forgiveness. For a long time I had forgotten that and when I realized how you had betrayed my trust, all I wanted was justice. But that kind of justice is no more than revenge and makes me no better a man than you were when you decided to steal from me."

"But . . . thank you, Levi. Oh, thank you. I promise you that . . ."

Levi held up his hand. "I don't want your promises," he said, "but you can do something for me."

"Anything."

As Hannah helped serve the light lunch, she saw Pleasant's lost love approach her in-laws and make the introductions to his wife and children. It was obvious that he was none the wiser for the heartache he had left in his wake as he ushered his little family back inside to the table they shared with another family. But Hannah saw Pleasant make some excuse to her father and hurry off into the kitchen.

She thought of going after her, to comfort her, but she saw Caleb leaning on his crutches surrounded by a circle of girls and younger children at the far end of the porch. He appeared to be telling them a story and Hannah could not help but be curious. She moved closer.

". . . And then the tornado came," he said as every child leaned closer. "It smashed across his father's farm sounding like the roar of a hundred freight trains. It destroyed livestock and the house and then it hit the barn . . ."

". . . Where his parents had gone," one girl murmured.

Caleb nodded. "And when the storm had done its worst the boy crawled out from the cellar with his brother and sisters and saw that nothing was left."

Hannah inched closer. Where on earth had the boy come up with such a tale?

"What did he do then?" a child asked.

"For a while he lived with his grand-parents but he was very very sad and lonely for his father and mother and so he ran away."

"What happened then?"

Caleb's face went blank, but he recovered quickly. "Oh, he had many adventures and became a very rich man. He had his own car," Caleb said in an awed tone and several of the young boys in his audience gasped with appreciation. "And a big house — two big houses," he added.

"But he was not happy," a girl prompted and Hannah saw Caleb glance at her and smile.

"No. He was not happy for he had gone into the outside world — and no matter what he did, he did not belong. He had no family there."

"And what happened then?"

Caleb faltered again and Hannah realized that he had no grand ending to his tale. "Nothing. He was trapped in that world. He wanted to go back but he couldn't."

The children started to grumble. "That's a terrible story," one boy groused as he got up and brushed the dust off his good Sunday trousers. "I'm going to see if there's pie." One by one the other boys followed him and the girls wandered away. Hannah stepped forward.

"Where did you hear that story, Caleb?"

"From Levi — Mr. Harmon. He told it to me the other night while we were waiting on the side of the road but I fell asleep and never heard the true end of it."

He eased himself to a sitting position and Hannah sat next to him. "What if that was the end of it? What if Mr. Harmon was telling you that story to teach a lesson?"

"Like in church?"

"Something like that. Maybe he wanted you to think about the true cost of running away — at least for that boy."

"That boy was him," Caleb said. "He turned out okay."

"How do you know the story was about Mr. Harmon?"

"Because he told me so. He told me that he used to be Amish, too, and when he ran away he didn't think about how he would never be able to go back. He was older than me and said he should have known better because once a plain man chooses the English world, that's it."

Hannah felt as if her breath could not find its way through her lungs. "And what do you think of that?"

Caleb shrugged. "I don't know, Ma. I like being who I am. It's just that sometimes I wish there was some adventure. But then it was sometimes pretty scary being out there by myself. When I came here, it was like coming home again, like a real family and I liked that better."

"Did you not miss your grandfather . . . or me?"

"Oh, Ma, I missed you a lot and I just

269

kept thinking how perfect it would be if you could come live here with the Harnishers, too. Then maybe you wouldn't be so sad and we could be a family with them and . . ."

"We have our family," she reminded him.

"I know but I think about how Pa used to teach me stuff like Lars's dad does. Grandpa is always so busy. And there are only a few boys my age back home. Most guys my age live somewhere else and just come to Florida for visits."

It was true. Caleb's cousins lived in Ohio and the community in Florida was so new that it was either older couples who had raised their families and come south to farm in a warmer climate, or single men or young marrieds who saw Celery Fields as their future as Caleb's father had.

"It is the life God has chosen for us, son," Hannah said.

"I suppose," he said glumly.

Hannah looked around, trying to think of some distraction that would bring back Caleb's smile and saw the girl who'd been listening to his story coming from the kitchen.

"I brought you snitz and ice cream," the girl said, offering him the plate. "I made the snitz myself."

Caleb took a bite of the dried apple

270

concoction and grinned. "Not as good as my Ma's," he said with a wink at Hannah.

"Oh, Mrs. Goodloe, I should have thought . . . I didn't bring you . . ."

"It's all right. If you'll sit with Caleb and make sure he doesn't overdo, I'll get some for myself. It looks delicious."

When she looked back, Caleb was teasing the girl by offering her a bite of the ice cream and then pulling the spoon away at the last minute. It was something his father would have done and Hannah smiled at the memory. And then she turned back to the house and saw Levi talking to her father-in-law and the bishop. But the most astonishing sight was that standing with them was Chester Tuck.

Levi seemed uncommonly nervous and kept wiping the palms of his hands against the sides of his suit trousers as Hannah approached. She was aware that her expression was one of confusion but she could not hide her curiosity at the strange assembly of men standing on the Harnisher's porch.

"Ah, Hannah," Gunther said when she reached the foot of the steps leading up to the porch. "Levi has been waiting for you."

In another time, the words might have been music to her ears. "Levi has been waiting for you . . ." would have been enough to launch her heart into flight. But that morning during services she had seen plainly the reasons for his interest in her. She wondered what it was that he wanted from her now.

"Chester," she acknowledged as she climbed the steps without looking at Levi.

"Ma'am," he murmured and started to say more but Levi placed a restraining hand on his sleeve.

"Shall we go inside?" the bishop suggested.

Hannah was perplexed by the seriousness of the mood and the unexpected presence of Chester, but when the four men turned and entered the house, she had little choice but to follow them.

Inside, Gunther led the way to a bedroom where benches had been added for the bishop, deacon and ministers to congregate before the services. Gunther indicated that Hannah should sit on one low bench while Chester and the bishop sat on the side of the bed facing her. Levi and Gunther remained standing.

"Mr. Tuck has something he wishes to say to you, Hannah," the bishop told her as he placed his hand on Chester's shoulder.

"Ma'am," Chester began, then cleared his throat and started again. "I've come to ask

272

you to forgive me for accusing you the other day. I was the thief and I tried to throw suspicion onto others."

Hannah's heart went out to the man who looked so small and miserable sitting there. "Chester, I . . ."

"I thought I had good reason for the stealing," he said, "but the very idea that I could try to accuse someone like you — someone so pure and honest. I was just lashing out because you were the one who found me out."

Hannah looked to the bishop and Gunther and finally Levi, trying to understand this strange confession.

"Chester has asked to face those he accused and try and make amends," Gunther explained.

"It was his idea to come here," Levi added. "All I asked him to do was write letters to you and the others. He already met with the rest of the company earlier this morning."

"Was Jake there?"

Levi's eyes darkened with sadness and he shook his head. "No one has heard from him."

The bishop cleared his throat. "Do you forgive this man, Hannah?"

"Of course. He did me no real harm, but

Levi, I still cannot testify in court."

"There will be no trial," Levi said. "I have dropped all charges. Chester was desperate. His mother needed an operation and medicine. His father was out of work. The doctor insisted on payment up front. He meant to pay it all back but then it just got ahead of him."

Levi turned his attention to Chester. "You have been my friend for many long years," he said so softly that Hannah found herself leaning forward to catch the words. "We have seen many things together and had many adventures."

Chester nodded, his head bent low, his folded hands dangling between his knees.

"You stole from me and in taking from me you also stole from others who had been your friends. You could have come to me. I would have helped."

Chester sniffed back a choked sob and cleared his throat but he did not look up. "I was too proud."

"Pride goeth before a fall," the bishop said in German.

"And I meant to pay it back. I thought I could." He buried his face in his hands and burst into racking sobs.

Levi knelt next to Chester. "I forgive you," he murmured rubbing his friend's back.

"It's over, Chester. I forgive you. It will do no one any good for you to go to jail. I won't recover my money. Your parents will be even more destitute. And I will have lost the best twenty-four-hour man working the circuit today."

"You mean it. It's over?"

"You can keep your job," Levi said as he reached into his pocket and handed Chester a check. "This should cover the medicine and expenses your parents might have for the next six months. During that time, I expect you to work on setting up some kind of budget and payment plan that you can live with."

Levi stood and offered Chester his handshake. Chester stood and accepted it. Levi delivered the traditional Amish handshake but then Chester embraced Levi, thanking him profusely. Then Chester turned to Gunther and Hannah and blubbered out his promise to mend his ways and make it all up to Levi and anyone he might have harmed through his actions. Unable to go on, he collapsed back onto the chair and broke down completely.

While Gunther and the bishop calmed Chester, Hannah found herself alone with Levi for the moment.

"Why?" she asked as the two of them

moved out onto the porch.

He smiled and spoke to her in the language of her ancestors. "Because it is your way," he replied, "and as you now know it used to be my way, as well."

Hannah thought of the story he had told Caleb, recalling Caleb's words. "He was older . . ."

"It's hard to explain my reasoning, Hannah," he said in English. "This . . ." He waved a hand over the land. "This was my father's and grandfather's land but after my parents died . . ."

"I know the story, Levi. Matthew told me." She stared at the barn for a long moment.

"It was rebuilt," he said softly. "There was a barn-raising not long after . . ."

"Oh, Levi, how very painful this must all be for you — coming back to such memories."

"Not so much anymore. I made my peace with it years ago. It's partly the reason I decided to settle the circus here in Baraboo. I wanted to be close to what family I had left. Matthew and I worked it all out after our grandfather died. At least here I could see them from time to time."

It had started to rain again as a deputy escorted Chester down the porch steps to a

276

car that had been parked around the side of the barn out of respect for the Amish. All around them people were clearing the tables, loading the benches and preparing to leave.

Levi touched Hannah's arm. "I have to take care of some things — since I pressed charges in the English court, that all has to be legalized before Chester will be truly free," he said, "and I need to find Jake."

"You haven't seen or heard from him?"

"I doubted him, Hannah. My best friend — the one person who has been with me through all of this and I questioned that loyalty and friendship."

"He just needs time," she said, but wasn't sure that she was right. Jake was a proud man, especially when it came to all that he and Levi — "two dumb stowaways" as he liked to refer to them — had accomplished together. "He'll come around. The two of you are like brothers. In time . . ."

Levi clearly doubted that. "Perhaps. The first step is to find him."

"No one has seen him?"

"Lily says he left as we all boarded the train and she hasn't seen him since."

"You said he once worked in Chicago. Perhaps he went back there."

"That was a long time ago. No, he could

be anywhere by now."

She rested her hand on his arm. "Give him some time," she advised.

He covered her hand with his, the warmth of his touch seeping through her like the balm of the first true spring day. "Hannah, could I come back later?"

"Oh, Levi, perhaps it would be best if . . ."

"I want to say a proper goodbye to the boy," he said, interrupting her and once again she realized that what she had taken for his feelings for her were really just a good man's concern.

Hannah thought her heart would surely break at the reminder that soon she would leave him — for good. She looked around at the others climbing back into their buggies and heading down the lane in a single line of identical black-topped, horse-drawn carriages toward home. She looked beyond the parade of vehicles to the surrounding countryside, green and verdant after the rain. And she looked up at the sky where a break in the clouds had freed the afternoon sun. *Maybe if we stayed . . . in time . . .*

She turned to face him, the words on her lips. But then over his shoulder she saw Pleasant, her shawl covering her head and shoulders as she stood beneath a weeping willow and watched as the young man and

his family drove away. Two naive women —
she and Pleasant — taken in by men who
had meant no harm — only kindness.

"Yes," she told Levi. "Come and say goodbye." And she gathered her skirts and ran
back inside the house before he could witness her tears.

CHAPTER SEVENTEEN

When Levi returned later that evening it was evident that he would have no time alone with Hannah. She had made sure of that. Almost as soon as he arrived, Matthew called for him to come help with the evening milking. Once that was done and they returned to the house, Mae had supper prepared, a supper that Hannah and Pleasant helped to serve. After supper Hannah insisted that Caleb needed his rest and she had packing to do.

She thanked him profusely for all of his kindness and his help in finding Caleb and seeing that he was so well cared for. She prompted Caleb to do the same and that, in turn, prompted Gunther to add to the chorus of appreciation. They left him with little choice but to wish them all safe travels and ask that they write and let him know of their return.

And then she was gone. She followed Caleb down the dark narrow hallway to his room and closed the door. It was as if she could not get away from Levi fast enough. Her actions confused him. He had thought that once she knew that he was Amish, that once he publicly forgave Chester, then she would see that he could change, that they could have a future together.

He had come to his brother's farm, not to say goodbye, but to ask her to stay and marry him. He loved her and he had been certain that she returned those feelings. *Had been . . .*

He glanced up to see pity in the eyes of his brother and his sister-in-law. "Tell me what to do," he pleaded, but Mae simply shrugged and Matthew wrapped his arm around Levi's shoulder and walked him out to the porch.

"Let her go," Matthew murmured. "In time you will both understand that it's for the best. We cannot go back, my brother." He gave Levi two sharp claps on the back and went inside the house.

Levi stood there for a long moment. The words his brother had just uttered went against everything Levi believed. Wrongs could be made right. Had he not just seen that with Chester? And how was it for the best for two people who loved each other to be torn apart? He glanced toward the barn — the ground where his parents had died. They had been together because they could not be apart and they had paid a terrible price, but sometimes love demanded such a price. No. Perhaps in taking them both, God had actually given the two of them the blessing of not having to go on alone.

He stepped off the porch and instead of heading down the lane toward town, he walked across the yard to the small cemetery where his parents, grandparents and five other generations of Harnishers were buried. He had lost almost everyone he'd ever cared about — his parents, his best friend and now Hannah. He found his parents' graves and knelt between them. And for the first time in all the years since he'd run away, Levi prayed for God's guidance.

And when he left the little graveyard and headed back to his compound, he knew beyond a shadow of a doubt what he must do to make everything right again. It would take some time, but all he had was time. The first step was to find Jake.

Hannah finished packing Caleb's things and tucked him in for the night. Back in the room she shared with Pleasant, she packed her own clothing and then stood at the window looking out at the dark. She watched as Levi crossed the lawn and stopped near two headstones in the little cemetery she had noticed on her first walk with Caleb to try out his crutches.

She saw him kneel and bow his head and every fiber of her being tugged her to go to him. The roar of her need was so loud in her head that she failed to hear Pleasant enter the room until her sister-in-law was standing behind her with her hands resting lightly on Hannah's shoulders.

"You love him," Pleasant said.

"Yes."

"And he loves you?"

"No." She had never been more certain of anything. "He was only being kind like the young man who came to the bakery."

"But he's free to love you and in time . . ."

"But I am not free to love him," Hannah said and turned away from the window. "I can't live in the world he has chosen, Pleasant, without abandoning everything I believe in." She saw her misery reflected in Pleasant's eyes. "If God wills it, you will find love, Pleasant." *And perhaps, so shall I.*

"I've been such a fool," Pleasant said. Her eyes welling with tears.

"You were naive," Hannah corrected.

"I thought that Noah's attentions were . . .

something more. All he meant was friendliness — a man who enjoys making people smile. He never intended . . . it was all in my head."

Hannah embraced her sister-in-law. "I know. We've both learned hard lessons on this journey. And yet, had you not persuaded Levi to convince Gunther that we should all come, I would still be waiting to see Caleb. You did that, Pleasant, and I am so very grateful."

Pleasant snorted derisively. "I didn't do it for you. I thought . . ."

"Whatever your reasons, it got me here. Oh, think of it, Pleasant. Think of the friends we have both made and the adventures we have shared. Think of what might have happened had Caleb not ended up here with Levi's brother or had Levi not told Caleb his story. I might have lost my son forever."

"I guess," Pleasant said, sniffing back her tears. "Do you think they will write to us? Lily and the others?"

"Of course. And next season when they are in Florida, we will have a reunion," she assured her.

"And will you invite Levi to that reunion?"

"Levi will always hold a special place in my heart," Hannah admitted. "I think that for some reason, God led me to his house that day. I think there is some purpose we can't begin to know in this journey we have made with Levi's circus, Pleasant."

"But will you see him when he comes back to Florida?"

"Oh, that's the future, Pleasant," Hannah replied, knowing that she was avoiding a question that she couldn't begin to answer. "Tomorrow we head home to Florida where we will both start again all the wiser for the experiences we've shared." She hugged her sister-in-law. "This I am certain of — we are sisters as we have never been before and that in tandem with bringing Caleb home, makes everything worth whatever price we may have paid."

Levi had not made it in time. Torn between word that Jake had been seen in town and that Hannah's train was leaving, he had thought he could settle things with Jake and still make it to the station in time.

In time for what?

To beg her to stay.

Jake had been at the barbershop for a shave and haircut. Rather than try and approach him in front of others, Levi had waited outside, sitting on a park bench in the square and keeping an eye on the barbershop door. Finally, he saw Jake emerge.

"Jake?"

His friend hesitated, squinted into the sun and then turned and kept walking away.

"Give me a chance to explain," Levi said as he caught up to him and fell into step.

"This oughta be good, because from where I'm standing you have no explanation. How could you think I would ever . . ." Jake bit down on his lip and kept walking, his hands thrust into the pockets of his suit trousers.

"You're right," Levi admitted. "I couldn't figure out how Chester could pull it off since he had no direct access to the money."

"And I did," Jake said bitterly, then he wheeled around, stopping Levi in his tracks. "Do you know how it felt being questioned by the police? How it felt that other people — people I know and care about — knew?"

His face was almost purple with his suppressed fury.

"Would it help if you punched me?" Levi asked quietly.

Jake looked startled at the suggestion, then shrugged. "Naw. That'd be no fun because you'd never punch me back. You've got that much Amish in you."

They walked along for several blocks in silence.

"I can see only one way to make this right," Levi said after a while.

"Yeah? What's that?"

Levi pulled a document from his pocket and handed it to Jake. "I'm giving you my shares in the business. It's yours — all of it. I work for you now."

Jake thrust the paper back at him. "I don't want your business, Levi. I want your friendship and your trust."

This time it was Levi who put his hands in his pockets. "You have both right there in your hand. It's the only evidence I can offer — that and my apology. Think about it," he said. "I have to go to the train station, but when I get back . . ."

"I'll be there," Jake replied. "You never could run this thing by yourself."

Levi started off down the street at a trot.

"Hey," Jake shouted and Levi looked back but did not stop running toward the station. "Good luck."

But as Levi ran through the streets and into the station and then out the door to the platform, he saw that he had come too late.

"She's gone," Lily said, touching his arm as she and the others headed back to their cars. "Maybe it's for the best."

Levi walked to the edge of the platform and stared after the train. He saw a lone figure — a woman in a plain gray-blue dress and white prayer covering — standing at the very back of the train. She did not wave, but she was watching and he knew that she knew that he had come.

The summer had flown by and at the same time it had seemed a lifetime since she had last seen Levi. On the day they had left Baraboo, Lily and Fred had organized a little impromptu parade to see them off. Fred had shown up at the station in full clown makeup and costume while Lily had presented them with a basket loaded with cheeses and sausages and breads.

Hans had been there and Chester, as well. But there had been no sign of Levi. He had offered Gunther the use of his private car to transport the family, but Gunther had turned him down. Still, she had hoped that he might . . .

"All aboard!" the conductor had shouted, and Gunther had hustled them onto the crowded car, anxious to get the seats that faced each other in the center of the car.

The train had chugged to life and slowly started to pull away from the platform when

288

Hannah saw Levi.

He emerged from the train station, glancing up and down the track until he realized that he had arrived too late. As the others turned to go, he remained — a lone figure staring after the departing train.

"I'll be back," Hannah had told her father-in-law as she climbed over Pleasant and practically ran to the rear of the train. There she stepped out onto the little metal platform and craned to see him. She did not wave or try and catch his attention. It was enough to know that he had come.

"Goodbye," she had whispered as he grew smaller and smaller and finally disappeared from view altogether as the train rounded a curve.

Since then she had had letters from Lily filled with gossip and news — except about Levi. These two performers had eloped. This one had left the circus to become a nurse. Someone else had developed a new act. She chattered on excitedly about returning to Florida and seeing them again, but she said not one word about Levi.

And Hannah was reluctant to ask. After all, she knew what the gossip had been and now that it had calmed, why stir things up again by showing interest or curiosity? On the other hand, wasn't it odd that she didn't inquire about him?

In the end, she had decided against raising any question. After all this time, to do so surely would be cause for gossip. But oh, how she longed to know if he was well, if he and Jake had reunited, if he ever thought of her.

She forced her thoughts aside and went through her day's routine — washing, cooking, cleaning, ironing, tending the kitchen garden she had planted and taking care of the bookkeeping for the bakery.

Hannah could not recall a hotter, more humid September. Every morning she washed out the clothes the family had worn the day before, hung them on the line and then went inside the small house they all shared to start breakfast. Pleasant and Gunther left for the bakery at four and Hannah packed them a breakfast that Pleasant's half sister, Lydia, delivered on her way to her new job as the community's schoolteacher. At the same time, Hannah packed a lunch for Caleb who spent his days going to school and then working the celery fields and carefully putting away what little money he could to buy a horse of his own.

Horses had healed the breach between Caleb and his grandfather. Their common love for the animals had brought them closer and Gunther had encouraged Caleb's dream of one day owning his own breeding stable by giving him sole responsibility for the care and feeding of the family's mare, as well as the team of Belgians that Gunther used for business.

That afternoon, Hannah was making the month's ledger entries when she heard the bell over the bakery door clang. She waited for Pleasant's usual, "We're closed," then remembered that her sister-in-law had left early that afternoon to deliver a cake for the birth of a neighbor's first child. Caleb and Gunther had gone to a horse auction.

"I'm sorry," Hannah said as she stepped from behind the curtained area that served as the bakery's office. "We're . . ." The words froze on her tongue.

For standing in front of the counter was Levi. Or was it only that her eyes and mind were playing tricks on her? Too much sun, she thought. The oppressive heat, she assured herself.

For this man who had Levi's face and Levi's smile was dressed plain. His dark, loose-fitting trousers were held up by black suspenders. His collarless shirt a deep shade of navy. His face clean-shaven as always but his copper highlighted hair hung straight and smooth covering his ears under a wide-

291

brimmed Amish straw hat.

"*Guten Tag,* Hannah Goodloe," he said softly.

She grasped the countertop, her only defense against giving in to the overwhelming urge to race around the counter and into his arms. "What is this?" she asked, unable to find the words as she nodded toward his unusual attire.

He removed his hat and spoke to her in the familiar Swiss-German dialect of the Amish. "*Ich bin* Levi Harnisher," he said and his eyes pleaded with her to understand something she could not begin to fathom.

Her uncertainty made her irritable. "You should not make light of . . ."

"I am not making light of anything, Hannah," he said, reverting to English. "I have come to ask you a very important question. I have come back."

"To what?"

"To my faith, my family and with God's blessing — to you."

"I don't understand."

"It's simple, really. I . . ." The doorbell jangled and together he and Hannah snapped, "We're closed."

"Well, I know that," Pleasant said and then she saw Levi and her mouth fell open.

" 'Tis I," he said with a nervous laugh and

292

a slight bow.

Pleasant considered him for a long moment. "I know that you are not a cruel man, Levi, and therefore I must assume that you have not come costumed like this to make fun of our ways."

"It is no costume," Levi said. "These are my clothes, made for me by my sister-in-law, Mae."

"And your fine suits?"

"Gone."

"And your private rail car?"

"Under new ownership."

"And the circus?"

"It all belongs to Jake now."

Pleasant studied him carefully while Hannah forced herself to breathe.

"And what about your mansion here on the bay?"

"I have donated that to the state as well as my other land holdings here, with the exception of one small parcel that I have kept for myself and another that I gave to Hans."

And after quizzing him, Pleasant came away with the same conclusion Hannah had voiced earlier. "I don't understand."

"Would it be presumptuous of me to ask myself to supper where I can explain everything?"

"Yes, it would be presumptuous," Pleasant said, "but you'll do as you please. You always have."

"That is the past," Levi said. "Hannah?"

"I will set another place," she said.

Levi smiled at them as if they had just handed him the moon and stars. He replaced his hat and moved to the door. *"Danke,"* he said and there could be no doubt that relief colored the breath he released as he opened the door and stepped outside.

CHAPTER EIGHTEEN

For the rest of the afternoon, Hannah pondered this strange turn of events. While she scrubbed the bakery floor, Pleasant prattled on about Levi's changed appearance and short answers to her questions.

"Why would he abandon everything he's worked his entire life to build?" she asked repeatedly.

"Perhaps it was because he wanted to reunite with his family," Hannah guessed.

"He already has a relationship with Matthew and Mae," Pleasant argued.

"But not his sisters."

"But they all live in Iowa or Wisconsin. What's he doing here in Florida?"

Hannah saw the light then. He had come to take care of his business holdings — the mansion and other properties he owned. He had come to put all of that to rest. But he had mentioned keeping one plot of land for himself and another for Hans. Amish men were not given to establishing second homes the way some in the outside world did.

"I should go," she said, putting away the ledger and files she had been working on. "Someone needs to tell Gunther that we will have a guest."

Gunther Goodloe was sitting at the kitchen table playing a game of dominoes with Caleb when Hannah entered the small house.

"Levi has come back," she said without preamble. On the walk from the bakery to the house she had practiced half a dozen ways of delivering this news, but in the end she had stated it plain and Gunther simply nodded.

"*Ja*. He was here." He placed his final tile, winning the game. "Time for chores, Caleb," he said.

"Levi looked plain," Caleb said as he put away the dominoes and picked up his hat. "Do you think that means that . . ."

"I don't know what it means," Hannah replied. "Now go."

She put on her apron and began assembling the evening meal.

"He's come back for you," Gunther said softly.

"He said that?"

"Didn't need to. Why else would a man like that change his entire life?"

"Then he has made a mistake," she said as she set the table, counting the places as if the addition of one were monumental.

"You do not care for him?"

"I . . ." She had almost said that she loved Levi but then she had realized she was talking to Gunther — her late husband's father.

"My son has been dead many years, Hannah. His memory lives on in Caleb. You are still young — young enough to start a new family. If Levi is the one . . ."

"He cannot think that it is enough to simply change his clothes and grow his hair to cover his ears," she said, rubbing her palms over her apron. "Anyone can dress up on the outside. It is what is here that counts." She patted her heart.

"He . . ."

"Besides," she continued more to herself than to Gunther, "he ran away from his family and his faith." Everyone knew that in the Amish faith, choosing the outside world over the faith and community of one's birth could not be forgiven.

Gunther pushed himself to his feet. "Do not be too hard on him, Hannah. There may be more to his change than you know." He said no more as he walked slowly down the hall to his bedroom.

Supper was a quiet affair. Caleb and Gunther generated what limited conversation there was, while the women — Hannah, Pleasant and Pleasant's half sisters, Lydia and Greta, remained silent.

"How is Lars?" Caleb asked.

"He has grown another two inches," Levi reported. "He's taller than his mother now."

"I'm almost as tall as Ma," Caleb said, grinning at Hannah. "And taller than Lydia or Greta."

Gunther asked after the men he had worked with in the horse tent and after Levi assured him that they missed his help and expertise with the horses, silence fell over the table. Even Caleb seemed at a loss for words. Hannah felt as if every bite she took clogged her throat, leaving her unable to speak at all. She had made sure that Levi was not sitting next to her for the very idea of his taking her hand during grace was more than she thought she could bear.

Instead, she had taken her place at the far end of the table next to Pleasant and across from Caleb. But that position had its problems as well for she could watch him — watch him watching her.

Finally, Gunther signaled the end of the meal with a loud belch — a compliment to

Hannah for another good meal.

"Ma," Caleb said, his voice cracking. "I was wondering. Some boys from town are playing baseball this evening with our guys — just until dark and . . ."

"Have you done all your chores?" Hannah asked, relieved to be able to concentrate on something other than the overwhelming presence of Levi.

Caleb nodded, then ducked his head a moment. "Could I take the buggy?"

Hannah's emotions warred between knowing her son was growing up and needed some independence and the fact that once the game ended it would be dark and Gunther's buggy had only two dim side lanterns.

"I wouldn't mind watching the game," Levi said. "Perhaps your mother and I could come with you."

Caleb's eyes pleaded with Hannah to agree to this plan.

"All right," she said. "As soon as the dishes are finished."

"I can do the dishes," Pleasant's half sister Lydia volunteered. It had been clear from the moment she'd heard that Levi had returned that every romantic ideal she'd ever entertained had fully blossomed.

"Can I come to the game, too?" Greta

asked. Greta found the games and activities — even the chores — usually assigned to boys far more interesting than those activities reserved for girls. "I can catch," she announced.

Levi chuckled while Caleb made a face.

"Yes," Hannah decided. "You can come as well, Greta." She couldn't help but take some small pleasure in the look that Caleb and Levi exchanged. Taking Greta along had clearly not been in either one's mind.

The baseball field was a makeshift affair on the edge of the celery fields. Several boys from Sarasota had already gathered and were tossing a ball around from player to player. Another smaller cluster of Amish boys stood on the sidelines talking and knocking sand off their shoes with handmade bats.

Caleb was out of the buggy and off to join his friends almost before the horse had come to a full stop. Levi helped Greta and then Hannah out and together they walked over to the edge of the playing field. Hannah saw several of the boys talking to Caleb and looking their way. After a while, Caleb broke away from the group and started toward them.

"We're a player short," he said to Levi without really looking at him. "The others were thinking maybe you might . . ."

"Sure," Levi said. "What position?"

"First base?"

"Okay," Levi agreed. "You ladies will be all right?" he asked.

Hannah nodded as Caleb and Levi trotted off toward the other players.

"He's cute," Greta said.

"Handsome," Hannah corrected her without thinking. "A man of Mr. Harmon's age . . ."

Greta looked up at her and laughed. "I didn't mean Mr. Harmon. I meant Caleb." The girl considered Levi for a moment. "I suppose for someone that old, Mr. Harmon is nice-looking. Better than some, anyway," she said. Then she studied Hannah for a long moment. "You two would make a good match."

"Really? I didn't know that you had decided to serve as the community matchmaker," Hannah teased. Anything to turn Greta's interest to some other topic. "I thought you planned on raising horses."

"Well, just until I marry Joshua Troyer," she announced with such certainty that Hannah thought it just might come true.

Hannah sat on the grass and Greta did the same, each of them pulling their skirts down to cover the tops of their shoes and

301

wrapping their arms around their knees as they watched the game in progress.

"And once Joshua and I marry, then our children will help out as well," Greta continued as if the match with the bishop's grandson were already decided. "The boys can work in the stables and cut the hay in fall and the girls can help me in the house and with the little ones."

"You seem to have this all planned out," Hannah said, trying hard not to let her amusement show. "Does Joshua agree with these plans?"

"Oh, he hardly knows I'm alive," she said, resting her chin on her knees. "But he will. Someday."

Hannah watched the girl watching the game and thought back to when she and Caleb's father had shared dreams of a large family and a lifetime together. But they had not been blessed with many children — only Caleb. And she understood how that had put undue pressure on her son. There ought to have been siblings for him, but she had miscarried many times and then Caleb's father had died.

Greta nudged her as Levi came up to bat and before facing the pitcher, he glanced back at her and pointed to the far right side of the field.

"Oh, that's so romantic," Greta squealed. "He's going to hit a home run just for you, Hannah."

The pitch came low and fast and Levi swung. There was a crack as ball met bat and then the ball was sailing in a high arc between first and second base. The fielder backed up but the ball stayed aloft until it landed several yards behind the fielder.

"Home run," several players on both teams crowed as Levi trotted around the bases, grinning like a schoolboy. They did not care about scores. They only cared about the sport of playing and when Levi crossed home plate both teams gathered to congratulate him.

Moments later he and Caleb walked back toward Hannah and Greta. They were rosy-cheeked and Levi was still breathing hard but he had his arm around Caleb's shoulders and Hannah could not help but think that he would make a good father.

And it hit her suddenly that Levi *should* be a father and if he insisted on pursuing her, he never would be. She had proven that she was barren save for Caleb. Any idea that she might entertain his attempts at courtship was sheer selfishness and she would have none of it.

They let Caleb drive the buggy home and

once there, he and Greta set about unhitching and stabling the horse for the night.

"I have something to tell you," Levi said as he walked Hannah back to the house. "I have been taking instruction to be baptized."

Hannah stared at him, thinking this must be some sort of joke. He had run away and abandoned his family and his faith. Surely he understood that he could not simply go back . . .

"When I ran away I had not yet been baptized," he explained. "In fact, it was my grandfather's insistence that I prepare to join the church that was part of my reason for leaving. Once Bishop Troyer realized that, he reminded me that never having been baptized or never having accepted the responsibilities of living in the Amish faith, I was never shunned. It was he who suggested that it is never too late to join the church and accept the obligations that come with such an act."

"But how could you ever . . ."

"I have divested myself of anything connected with the outside world — the English world, Hannah. Jake owns the circus and the state has the mansion here and most of the land holdings I once owned. I have been preparing myself for this moment ever since that day when I watched your train leaving

Baraboo. I . . ."

She placed her fingers over his lips unable to hear more. "You cannot come into the faith for false reasons, Levi. Being baptized and joining the church is not a means to an end — it is a commitment to live your life a certain way no matter what. Do not do this because of me."

"There was a time when I would have done anything if it meant that we could be together," he said. "When I first realized that I was in love with you . . ."

"No," she cried. "This is wrong and I will not allow it." She gathered her skirts and ran back to the house, closing the door behind her.

"Hannah?" Gunther glanced up from reading his bible. "Are you unwell?"

"I am . . ." She had meant to assure him that everything was all right, that she was simply tired, that she would see him in the morning. But instead she started to weep and could not seem to stop.

Between her sobs she told him what Levi had told her, adding that she was certain he was doing this only because he thought he was in love with her. "And even if he were to return to the faith for the proper reasons, any idea that he and I might . . ."

"Why not?"

"He is a man catching up to the life he left behind. He wants marriage and a family." She broke down completely.

Gunther remained silent and slowly she regained control. "It's impossible," she finished on the hiccup of a sob.

"And yet, it seems to me that there is another way to look at this," Gunther suggested, stroking his gray beard. "Think of it, Hannah. Think of how Levi came into our lives. Think of how many times along the way he should have simply disappeared from our lives but did not. What if God has led the two of you to one another? What if God has used you, and Levi's love for you to bring him back to his faith? Where is the harm in that?"

Her head was spinning. "But surely if his only reason for . . ."

"And do you know for certain that you are his only reason, Hannah? That speaks of arrogance that you could have such influence."

Hannah bowed her head. Of course, Gunther was right. How immodest of her to set herself on such a high pedestal. She should have rejoiced in Levi's decision, not degraded it with her own conceit. "I can see your point. I should apologize," she said. "Thank you, Gunther."

Outside, she could hear Levi's laughter as he talked with Caleb and Greta in the barn. She followed the golden light of the lantern the children had taken with them when they went to stable the horse. They were talking about the baseball game and when she stepped into the open door of the barn, she saw Levi showing Greta how to grip a bat properly.

"Children, it's late," she said when they looked up at her and the two of them nodded and headed for the house.

"I should go," Levi said as he put on his straw hat and rolled down his sleeves. He did not look at her as he passed her on his way out.

"I'm sorry to have doubted you," she said, and he stopped but did not turn around. "It is good that you have heard God's call for you to return to the faith of your ancestors. I am happy for you."

He picked up the lantern and used it to light her face. "You've been crying."

"Yes, but my tears were tears of pride and arrogance."

He stroked her cheek with the backs of his fingers. "Hannah, there are two things you must believe about me. I am serious about returning to my faith. For some time now I have been unsettled. In spite of everything I bought or acquired — success, power, material things — I was never able to find the one thing that makes life worth living. Contentment with who I am and how I pass my days."

She closed her eyes and leaned into his touch. "And the second thing?"

"I love you, Hannah. I think I fell in love with you the day I saw you coming up the drive of my mansion. I think I knew that somehow you were going to change my life in ways I could not begin to fathom — and you have."

He kissed her then, his lips warm on hers as he cradled her cheek and angled her face to receive his kiss and return it.

"Marry me, Hannah," he murmured.

Reality hit her like a slap and she drew back from him. "I cannot," she whispered. But this time she did not run from him. After everything they had shared, everything he had done to bring Caleb back to her, she owed him an explanation. "I love you," she began and realized that was not the best choice of a beginning to her explanation.

"But?" He ground the word out through gritted teeth.

Levi Harnisher might be plain on the outside but there was still some of the proud and powerful Levi Harmon that lived

308

within. Hannah heard impatience and resistance in that single word.

"Hear me out," she pleaded.

He left one hand resting on her shoulder but gazed beyond her for a moment. Then he looked down at her. "All right. I'm listening."

"The Ordnung teaches us that marriage is meant for a clear purpose — the purpose of bringing children into the world."

"Seems to me for some it's also for the purpose of companionship," he argued.

"That's true — for someone like Gunther, for example. But you are not old, Levi."

"Neither are you." He ran one hand through his hair, a habit she'd found endearing when she'd first met him.

"I cannot have more children." There, she had said it but she should have taken into consideration that Levi never accepted easy answers.

"Because? What did the doctor tell you, Hannah?"

His question exasperated her because, of course, no doctor had told her anything. She had simply gathered the facts of her many miscarriages and drawn her own conclusion.

Levi hooked his forefinger under her chin and lifted her face so that the light from the lantern shone on her.

"My late husband and I tried to have more children," she said softly. "Except for Caleb, we lost them all."

Levi frowned and she thought perhaps she had convinced him and wondered why instead of relief, she felt only sadness.

"I am not your late husband," he said. "We will follow God's plan for us and if that brings children, so be it."

"And if not?"

"So be it," he said, biting each word off precisely so that there could be no doubt of his commitment. "Now, do you have any other reasons not to let me court you properly over the coming weeks?"

"Oh, Levi, you can't want . . ."

To her surprise he set down the lantern and cupped her face with both hands. "This is me you are speaking to, Hannah. Pleasant was partly correct when I asked to come for supper and she said I would do as I please anyway."

Hannah leaned into him. "Only partly correct?" she teased.

"In this particular circumstance, I cannot do as I please unless you are also doing as you please. So I will ask once more, Hannah. Will you marry me?"

And because her heart took flight on

wings of pure joy and because she was more certain than she had been of anything she had ever done in her life, she wrapped her arms around him and whispered, "Yes, Levi Harnisher, I will marry you."

CHAPTER NINETEEN

During the years he had owned the circus, Levi had prided himself on doing whatever manual labor might be necessary to keep things running smoothly. Often when they were short a man to unload the wagons, Levi had stepped in to help. He had worked with the animals, especially the elephants and horses that the company depended on to do the heavy work of setting up and tearing down the huge tents. But all of that had been child's play compared to the unending work of farming. From well before sunup until well after dusk it seemed there was work to be done — work that could not be postponed.

He had forgotten how great a factor a change in weather could be. A deluge of rain could ruin a day's work if the soil and seeds got washed away. In the aftermath of such a storm the plow could get mired in deep pockets of sandy mud left behind. It was a

312

little like stepping into wet concrete. And no rain at all was even worse. He had set out to plant his fields with celery because that was a proven crop in these parts. But celery thrived in this part of the country because of the boggy, mucky, semiwet fields. Days of no rain dried those fields and left the tender young plants struggling to survive.

Levi was plowing the last rows of the field closest to the modest house he'd completed and thinking about his grandfather as he often did these days. As a boy, Levi had thought his grandfather was far too serious, too stern, too joyless. But now he was beginning to understand that along with the responsibility of a family came an enormous weight. The weight of "what if." What if there were a hurricane that wiped out everything? What if there were a fire in these dry days? What if the crop prices dropped? What if he failed?

Of course that was only half the worry. The other half came with fitting into a culture he had abandoned long ago. It was more than simply putting on different clothes or reverting to the language of his youth. There were times when he had found himself thinking about assigning some task to Hans or about a new marketing ploy that

313

might help fill seats at the next performance. There were times when he missed the life he had so willingly handed over to others. Life among the Amish was so . . . plain.

As he pushed the plow through the muck, the muscles in his arms and legs screaming with overuse and exhaustion, he wondered if he and Hannah could be truly happy or if he — like his grandfather — would one day turn into a beaten down and bitter old man.

No, he thought as he pulled back on the reins looped around his shoulders and the team of horses paused. He took off his hat and wiped sweat from his brow with the back of his hand and gazed up at the sky — a cloudy gray sky that held the promise of rain before evening. *Show me the way,* he prayed. *The rest of the way on this journey You have set me on. Show me how to be a good husband to Hannah and father to Caleb.*

The heat and humidity of the midday sun distorted his view of the horizon as he stared at the house. It wavered as if it were no more than a mirage. But then he saw Hannah coming across the fields toward him. She was carrying a bucket and stepping carefully over the furrows he'd plowed. The hot west wind carried snatches of the hymn she was humming, soothing away his worries as if they — not the house or the fields or the life he had chosen — were the mirage.

"I brought you some water," she said, filling the dipper and handing it to him. "You're not used to being out in the hot sun, Levi. Perhaps you should —"

"I'm almost finished," he assured her. He drank down the water and handed her the dipper, which she refilled and handed back to him. "And if I can finish the plowing today, then tomorrow I can start the planting and then —"

"Caleb could help you," she said. "He's only waiting for you to ask."

He knew that she was asking another question entirely. The question of why he hadn't asked the boy to help. She shaded her eyes with one hand and stared up at him, waiting.

"I don't want Caleb to feel that I'm trying to take the place of his father."

"His father died, Levi, as did yours. I had thought — hoped — that you might understand what that means for him. He misses —"

"It's because I understand, Hannah, that I'm taking it slow."

She wrinkled her brow into a quizzical frown.

Levi touched her cheek. "After my father

315

died, my grandfather treated me as if nothing had changed. He was my father now and that's all I needed to understand as far as he was concerned. I had his assurance that he would protect and provide. That was supposed to be enough."

"But it wasn't."

"No. I missed my father's patience, his humor, his assumption that I would grow up to be a good man. And from what Caleb told me about his father that night we sat in the rain along the side of the road, he misses those same things."

"Then give him those things," Hannah said. "His father is gone, Levi, but you are here and if we are to truly be a family, then Caleb needs your love and guidance."

"I've never been a husband or a father," Levi said. "It's a lot of responsibility and I'm —"

Her eyes widened with fear. "Do you regret leaving that other life, Levi? Because if you're not sure . . ."

He cupped her jaw and forced her eyes to meet his. "I have never been more certain of anything as I am that I love you and that my life without you would be unendurable."

"Then, what is it?"

"I'm afraid I might fail you — and Caleb. What if . . . ?"

She laid her fingers on his lips and shushed him. "Our love for one another and God's love for us will see us through whatever lies ahead, Levi. We are starting from a good place. We have a home and this land and an entire community to help us through whatever may come. We're going to be all right."

The horses snorted and stamped, and Hannah laughed. "See? Even the horses agree. Now come in out of this heat and rest for a bit. You and Caleb can finish plowing this evening after the rain."

Together they unhitched the horses and led them back to the yard. "Caleb?" Levi called when he spotted the boy sitting alone near the barn, working on a piece of harness. He looked up, an eager smile on his face, and Levi wondered why he hadn't recognized that look. It was the same look he had given his grandfather in the days following his parents' death. It was a smile filled with hope. *Let me in,* that smile said. *Let me be part of your life.*

Hannah breathed a sigh of relief as she went to washing the windows of the home they would share and watched Levi and Caleb tend the horses. They would be all right. And even if God decided not to bless them with more children, it would be enough. They would be a family. And with Gunther and his daughters and her cousins and aunts and uncles back in Ohio and Levi's family in Wisconsin . . .

She polished a pane of glass and thought about Levi's family — his sisters who had joined their grandparents in shunning a boy who had never been baptized into the faith in the first place. As she and Levi had set about planning their wedding, she had noticed how he carefully avoided any mention of his sisters.

"Matthew and Mae and the kids could make the trip," he'd told her, "and then maybe we could travel back with them and visit your people in Ohio as we work our way back here." Tradition called for them to leave the day after their wedding and spend several weeks traveling around visiting family and friends. Jake had insisted that they allow him to provide transportation on what was now his private railway car for the journey. "I'll even make it plain for you," he assured Hannah.

But there had been no mention of Levi's sisters and their families. "Well, this won't do," Hannah muttered as she polished the glass panes. "If we are to truly be a family, then we need to mend these fences."

That night, after Levi had taken her and Caleb back to Gunther's house and everyone was asleep, Hannah wrote a letter to Mae Harnisher and enclosed separate letters for each of Levi's sisters that she asked Mae to deliver. She introduced herself to them and invited them to come for the wedding, making sure to note that she realized it was a long trip and certainly she and Levi would understand if they could not get away. Then she asked if she and Levi might call upon them when they came to Wisconsin after the wedding. She was about to end the letters there when she decided that she had perhaps been too circumspect. And before she could change her mind she added the following note to each letter.

The one thing that our families share is the pain of great loss. And had it not been for Levi's kindness, I might have lost my only child as well to a life that would have taken him away from me as Levi's choice took him from you. I cannot know what your thoughts may be, but I do know that Levi thinks of you often and misses you. I am asking you to open your hearts to us as we begin this new chapter in our lives and join us in celebrating the great joy that God has given us.

She sealed the envelopes before she could rethink a word of the letters. As soon as Yoder's Dry Goods opened, she would post the letter to Mae and then pray that Mae would take it from there.

In his career with the circus, Levi had stood before crowds of hundreds — even thousands — of spectators, making speeches or acting as ringmaster for the show. But never had he been more nervous than he was on this Sunday morning sitting in the front row of the small Amish congregation that had gathered for services in Gunther's house. And yet, he had never in his life felt more certain about the path he had chosen.

When he had run away from his grandfather's farm, he hadn't been certain of anything except the strong need to get away from the memories and the pain of loss. From that day to this he had lived his life on the move, making decisions based more on expediency than what the long-term consequences might be. For years it had all seemed to work in his favor.

He had met Jake, and the two of them had eventually become a formidable business team. He had acquired assets beyond anything he might have dreamed. He had become a respected figure in the communities where he had established bases for his business. But through it all he realized now that he had never stopped running, never stopped searching for whatever it was that he had left the farm to find.

And then Hannah had walked up that driveway and into his life. It occurred to him now that on that day he had felt something shift. He had not understood it, but there had been no denying it. Now he felt more certain than ever before in his life that God had sent Hannah to him that day, not to find her lost son — but to find him and bring him home to his roots.

After the last sermon and hymn, Bishop Troyer rose and cleared his throat. "We have a special request to consider," he said. "Levi Harnisher has asked to be accepted into this congregation. If you agree, he will join those applicants already accepted in being baptized at our next service."

Behind him, Levi was aware of a rustle of whispers as the men murmured comment in their Swiss-German dialect to their neighbors.

"Circus . . ."

"Wisconsin . . ."

"The widow Goodloe . . ."

He held his breath and closed his eyes, praying silently that they would accept that this was what he wanted for himself — whether or not he had won Hannah's love in the bargain.

"We will vote by show of hands," the bishop said, silencing the murmured discussion. "Those in favor?"

Levi did not dare turn around.

"Opposed?"

He squeezed his eyes more tightly shut and realized he was clenching his fists as well.

"Then it is done," the bishop intoned.

Levi's eyes flew open and he glanced around, confused. What was done? Had he passed or not?

The bishop smiled and offered him the traditional one-pump Amish handshake. "Welcome, my brother."

Levi released the breath he'd been holding and pumped the bishop's hand up and down. *"Danke,"* he murmured. He looked around for Hannah and found her among a cluster of women, all dressed in dark, plain dresses with identical prayer coverings and yet, she alone was the woman he saw.

Their eyes met, hers sparkling blue with a tenderness and caring that he realized had been missing for far too long in his life. He saw the future then — the two of them and Caleb, of course, building a life together.

Two Sundays later at the next biweekly services, Levi joined a small group of teen-aged boys and girls to receive baptism. As soon as the hymns and sermons were completed, the bishop asked the applicants to kneel, and reminded them that they were about to make their promise to God before this congregation. He moved down the row asking the four questions that signaled their commitment to the church. With the help of the deacon, Bishop Troyer poured water from a wooden bucket onto the head of each applicant. He did this three times in the name of the Father, the Son and the Holy Ghost.

Then Bishop Troyer helped each applicant to stand, uttering the traditional words in German. "In the name of the Lord and the Church, we extend to you the hand of fellowship. Rise up and be a faithful member of the church."

When the bishop leaned in to bestow the Holy Kiss on his cheek, Levi felt a rush of such utter contentment and peace pass through him that he could not hide the tears that filled his eyes. He had come home at last.

On her wedding day, Hannah went about her chores in the usual way. She was up before sunrise, gathering eggs from the hen house and scattering feed for the chickens before starting breakfast for the family. Only her memories accompanied her through this daily routine.

Hannah's marriage to Caleb's father had taken place in Ohio in early December. There had been a heavy frost that morning in contrast to the heavy dew of humidity that clung to everything on this wedding day. Two years later, after Hannah had already suffered two miscarriages, the bakery had burned to the ground and Gunther's second wife was not fitting into the community. So the entire family had migrated to Florida for what Gunther had assured them would be a fresh start.

A year after that, Caleb had been born and eight years and no other children later, her husband had died when a reckless driver ran his buggy off the road one dark night. She had thought of taking Caleb and moving back to Ohio — back to where her sisters and brothers still lived. But Caleb had balked at moving from the only home he'd ever known and on top of that, Gunther's second wife had died a year earlier and in spite of her ability as a baker, Pleasant was not much of a housekeeper or cook. Gunther had needed Hannah to mother

Lydia and Greta, his children with his second wife, even though Lydia had then been fifteen and Greta was Caleb's age. And so she had stayed.

She could not help but think how wondrous were the ways that God led his children in directions they could not imagine and often fought against. Take Levi . . .

"Good morning," he said, coming alongside her and relieving her of the basket she'd used to gather the eggs.

"Levi Harnisher, you startled me," she chastised him, but she was smiling and she reached up and caressed his cheek with her fingers.

Levi set the basket down and wrapped his arms around her, "Hello, wife," he murmured.

"Not yet," she said, "but before this day's over."

Their kiss spoke of all the promise and hope they both held for their years together. Hannah even dared to hope that there might be children and she knew that Levi wanted that as well. He would not speak of it because he knew that it upset her to think she might not be able to give him the family every Amish man hopes for.

The rumble of metal wheels and clop of horse hooves on the shell-packed path that led to Gunther's house announced the arrival of their first guests — the wedding party come to help set up and welcome the others. Because this was her second marriage, theirs would be a quieter ceremony with far less of the usual fuss that came with a first wedding.

Hannah had made herself a new dress, apron and covering — items she would wear on Sundays for the coming years. Levi had bought a new suit barren of the lapels and buttons that had decorated the suits he'd worn as a businessman.

"Wife," he whispered against her temple as he released her and gave her back the egg basket. He greeted the men and helped unload the benches that would need to be set up for the ceremony, and later would convert to tables for the two meals to be served in the daylong celebration.

Behind the church bench wagon, women were spilling out of a small parade of buggies. They talked softly but excitedly as they started toward the house bearing covered dishes of food, and carrying the good Sunday clothing they would change into once the work of setting up was done.

An hour later, the members of the wedding party had all had their breakfast and changed into their finer clothes. They took up their posts, waiting to greet the guests as they arrived. And arrive they did — on foot, by buggy and by three-wheeled bicycle — all anxious to witness the marriage of the widow to the reformed circus baron. To Levi's surprise, his sisters and their families had arrived along with Matthew and Mae a few days earlier. They had quietly embraced the brother they had not seen in decades, and Levi had welcomed them back into his life with open arms.

Now Hannah and Levi waited with the bishop in Gunther's small bedroom. While Bishop Troyer spoke to them of the duties and obligations of marriage and family, Hannah could hear the guests singing hymns. She found herself thinking of the times she had sat in the business car of Levi's circus train, the strains of the circus band's brass fanfares surrounding her. But the sound of voices raised in song without benefit of instrumental accompaniment seemed twice as sweet.

"Shall we?" Bishop Troyer rose and indicated that they should follow him into the larger room where their guests waited. Hannah's smile widened as she saw Hans, Fred and Jake seated together in the back row of the men's section. Then spotted Lily and three of the other women she had befriended seated in the very center of the women's section, their floral hats standing out like parrots among the more somber coverings of the Amish women. She squeezed Levi's hand and nodded and he grinned down at her.

"Surprise," he mouthed. "I got special permission."

To either side of the room sat the attendants or *newehockers* for each of them. Pleasant, Lydia and Hannah's soon-to-be sister-in-law, Mae, sat opposite Caleb, Gunther and Matthew. Hannah smoothed the skirt of her new deep blue dress and straightened her cape and apron before taking her place on the bench reserved for Levi and her.

The ceremony began with prayer followed by one of the ministers reading a passage of scripture. Levi had requested the Beatitudes for he reminded them all that it was this passage that had turned his life around and brought him home to his faith and to Hannah.

The sermon seemed to go on forever and Hannah could not help but smile as she recalled how Levi had admitted that the lengthy sermons was one part of being Amish that was going to take some getting used to. She couldn't help but wonder how their friends from the circus were surviving the closeness of the room and the droning of the minister's words when she heard a distinct snore coming from somewhere behind her, and then Jake's startled yelp when Fred obviously nudged him.

The minister paused for a second to allow the titters of laughter to die and then droned on. Finally, he called Hannah and Levi forward, administered the required questioning that was akin to an English couple stating their vows and then blessed them. As soon as the bishop stepped forward to offer the final prayer, Hannah felt an aura of excitement permeate the room. And the moment the prayer ended, the room exploded into action.

Women hurried off to the kitchen while men transformed the benches into tables set in a u-shape in the yard. As soon as the tables were in place, the women filled them with a feast of roasted chicken, mashed potatoes, gravy, creamed celery, coleslaw, fruit salad, tapioca rice pudding, applesauce, and bread, butter and jam. For dessert there was Pleasant's cherry pie and hand-cranked ice cream.

"Who gets married at the crack of dawn on a Tuesday?" Jake asked as he made a show of stretching and yawning and then grabbed Levi in a bearhug.

"Eight o'clock is hardly the crack of dawn," Levi told him. "And Tuesday's a day as good as any other day."

"Hello, Hannah," Jake said. "I've missed you — Ida's okay but not nearly so pretty."

Hannah blushed and Levi leaned in to explain Jake's mistake to him. "It is not our way . . ."

". . . to pass out compliments," Jake finished. "Just stating the facts, my friend. Nothing more."

"We're so pleased you came," Hannah said, noticing the other guests hanging back and whispering among themselves, reluctant to approach the newlyweds with the outsiders around. "We . . ."

". . . need to attend to your other guests," Lily said, taking Jake firmly by the arm. "Go talk horses with Gunther," she instructed, and winked at Hannah as she and the other women from the circus headed off to see if they could help in the kitchen.

Once the tables were set up and the food had been brought out, Hannah and Levi took their places at one corner of the "u" with the women sitting down the side of the table next to Hannah and the men next to Levi. Hannah sat on Levi's left as she would now whenever they went anywhere in the

330

buggy. As tradition dictated, Hannah's family from Ohio and Matthew and Levi's sisters and their families ate in the kitchen.

At first, Hannah had worried that Lily and the other circus women might be uncomfortable. Jake, Fred and Hans could easily take part in the male conversation about baseball, livestock and such, but the women were a different matter.

"They'll be all right," Levi whispered, reading her mind as usual.

And then she heard Lily say, "The one thing I have never been able to understand is how you get all that stuffing inside the chicken." That led to a sharing of recipes for stuffing a chicken, which led to a discussion of the variety of recipes for stuffing which led to Lily's memories of her mother's Thanksgiving turkey and so on, until Hannah knew she had nothing to worry about. She could not remember a time when she had been happier in her life. And she could not imagine that the future might hold any more joy than she was experiencing at that very moment.

As soon as everyone had eaten, the crowd broke off into small groups. The younger guests played games or flocked to the shade of a tree to talk, while single men and women paired off or gathered in small clusters. Hannah and Levi made the rounds visiting with each guest until it was time for yet another meal, then more visiting, and finally around ten o'clock, the guests took their leave.

As Hannah stood with Levi saying their goodbyes, she could not help but marvel at the fact that on this day she had become Mrs. Levi Harnisher. Her life had changed so much in just a few short months and yet she had never felt more certain of her path than she did on this night standing side by side with Levi.

"You must be exhausted," Levi said, wrapping his arm around her waist as she waved to the last of the buggies making its way down the lane.

"Oh, no," she protested. "I want this day to go on and on." But she could not stifle the yawn that forced its way through her lips, and Levi laughed.

"Walk with me," he invited, holding out his hand to her.

From this day forward, I will always walk with you, she thought as she took his hand and walked with him down the now-deserted lane.

"Looks like we'll have good weather to begin our journey north tomorrow," he mused, glancing up at the clear, starlit sky and crescent moon.

"Not a cloud in the sky," she replied. But although the heavens were filled with stars, there was only one cloud hanging over the perfect day. Regardless of what Levi might say, she wanted so much to give him children. At Levi's insistence, she had been examined by a doctor and told that there was no physical reason she could not conceive. But the problem had never been conceiving. The problem had been bringing the child to term, and the doctor had admitted to her in private that he could not predict such a thing.

Levi felt the tension that had gripped her as they walked. He let go of her hand and wrapped his arm around her shoulders. "Let's sit awhile," he said, leading her to the tangled roots of a large banyan tree where they sat side by side on one of the giant tendrils running out from the tree's base, their arms around each other.

They were both nervous, he realized — a product of the fact that they did not yet know each other's habits. "Are you happy?" he asked.

She shifted until she could look up at him. "Yes. And you?" She traced the shape of his mouth with her finger, and he smiled.

"I cannot recall a time when I felt more at peace, more content with what the future might bring as I do at this moment, Hannah. Whatever challenges life may present to us, I know that with you at my side we can meet them."

"And God's blessing," she reminded him gently.

"For me, you are that blessing," he said. "My wife — my love," he murmured as he kissed her.

Her prayer covering scratched his chin as she laid her cheek against his chest and sighed happily.

"Hannah?"

"Mmm?"

"Now that I'm a married man, I'll have to grow out my beard," he reminded her.

She laughed, the sound muffled against his shirt until she raised her face to his and stroked his smooth cheek. "Perhaps you can give your razor and shaving brush to Caleb. I saw him running his hand over his jaw the other day the way you sometimes do."

"Peach fuzz," Levi said and laughed. "But then, he is growing up."

"It will be another bond between you," she reminded him.

"*Ja.* I'll give them to him before we leave tomorrow." He pulled her close again, but after a moment she sat up and faced him.

"I have a gift for you, my husband," she said softly. Then she reached up to remove her prayer covering and his breath caught as he realized that for the first time he would see her hair undone.

"Let me," he said.

She dropped her hands to her sides and waited while he removed the long hairpins that held the weight of her hair in place. He took his time, laying each pin in a cup of her hands so none would be lost.

He pulled the last pin free and watched as her hair tumbled to her waist, thick and heavy against her back in waves made permanent by years of the same twists and turns. He looked forward to the morning when he would watch her tame it all into the precise bun that he had come to love. And for all the days and nights of their lives this would be their special moment — that moment of release when he and he alone would know the full blossom of her beauty. And then in the morning she would tuck it all away again. They were man and wife and for as long as God gave them, neither of them would ever be alone — or lonely — again.

They sat together in silence, him stroking his fingers through her hair as she rested her head against his shoulder. He kissed her temple.

"We should go in," she murmured. "It's been a long and wonderful day."

"With more to come tomorrow and the day after that and the day . . ."

She sat up and pulled the weight of her hair over one shoulder. Then she took his hand in hers. "Pray with me," she said softly. She fit her fingers between each of his and turned so that her forehead and his were touching as they bowed their heads and silently thanked God for the blessings He had given them.

CHAPTER TWENTY

They returned from their wedding trip two days before Christmas and as far as Hannah was concerned the best gift she could possibly receive was seeing Caleb again.

"Look at you," she kept saying as Caleb rolled his eyes and Levi gave him a sympathetic smile. "Why, you've grown and filled out so much."

"Ma, it's only been six weeks," he reminded her.

"Still, look at you," she repeated and hugged him.

"How's the horse business?" Levi asked.

"I've got eleven customers," Caleb reported.

"Twelve," Levi corrected and nodded toward their newly built barn. "I bought a pair of Belgians from Jake to help with the planting, and there's a mare in there you could ride from farm to farm. Might save you some time and make it possible to add new customers."

Caleb's eyes grew huge with delight. "Really?"

Levi shrugged. "Go see for yourself." He wrapped his arm around Hannah's shoulder as they watched the boy take off for the barn at a run. A moment after he entered the barn, they heard a loud cheer and a moment after that, he came out leading the gray dappled mare by a lead rope.

"You'll spoil him," Hannah said.

"We'll consider it an early Christmas present. Besides, all I'm doing is encouraging his work ethic," Levi protested. Then with a wink, he added, "The only person I'm interested in spoiling is you." He pulled her close and kissed her forehead.

His soft beard brushed her skin and she looked up at him. In the six weeks since their wedding he had grown the beard that all married Amish men had. But Levi's beard was a rich shade of copper and she would not have believed it possible, but he was even more handsome with it than he had been clean-shaven.

"How are you feeling?" he asked, the wide brim of his straw hat shading his worried expression.

"Better," she assured him. She was well aware of what her problem was but Levi

338

had not yet caught on and she was not yet ready to tell him.

She was pregnant. By her count, she was entering her second month and as had always been her pattern, she was suffering from morning sickness. She knew she should explain it to Levi but then what if she lost this baby as she had all the others? He would be devastated. Watching him with his nieces and nephews and then hers as they traveled around during their wedding trip, she had seen how very much he enjoyed being around children. He would be such a wonderful father — already was one to Caleb. How could she disappoint him? She almost wished she weren't pregnant.

The thought shocked her and she silently begged God's forgiveness. *Thy will be done . . .* she reminded herself firmly. Whether or not she carried this child to term was not in her hands or Levi's — it was God's will and there was a reason for whatever way things went. But she could not help praying nightly for their child's health and well-being.

"Are you sure you're up to having everyone come here?" Levi was asking her as they watched Caleb mount the horse bareback and ride around the farmyard.

They had insisted on hosting the celebration known as "second Christmas" held on the twenty-sixth. "Of course. Everyone is bringing something to share so there's not much work to do."

"And you're sure having Lily and the others is all right?"

"They are our friends," she said firmly. "And they have no place to go for the day. If that is upsetting to anyone, well, then . . ." Actually, she wasn't sure. She knew there were some in the small Amish community who did not care for their ongoing association with these outsiders.

"Too worldly," she had heard one matron hiss to her neighbor as she passed the two women after last Sunday's services.

And Pleasant had told her outright that there were those in the community who were less than convinced that Levi's baptism had been legitimate. "Merle says that several of the men think he came back to the church because of you. Merle also says that if Levi were sincere, he would have no further association with his former employees."

Hannah had learned that "Merle says" had become a staple in Pleasant's conversation over the weeks that she and Levi had been gone. Merle Obermeier was a widower who had made no secret of his decision to pursue Pleasant as his second wife and the mother of his four children. He was a decade older than Pleasant, a dour and suspicious man who always seemed to look for the dark side of things.

"Do you love him?" Hannah had asked Pleasant after becoming aware of the relationship.

Pleasant had shrugged and Hannah's heart had gone out to her. Did Pleasant not deserve the same happiness that Hannah had found with Levi? Surely there was a man out there somewhere who could give her sister-in-law that kind of happiness.

"Don't just settle because you think . . ."

"I don't just think," Pleasant had replied bitterly. "I know. Merle Obermeier may be my last chance. He's a good man, Hannah."

And Hannah had understood that the discussion of Pleasant's future was closed. Well, Merle Obermeier might think otherwise but she knew that Levi had genuinely found his faith. He seemed almost relieved to be back living the plain life of his youth. As for Lily and the others, Merle could disapprove but Hannah and Levi would not turn their backs on their English friends. People would just have to understand. And if they didn't? Well, she had no doubt that Levi would deal with that if the time ever came.

Levi was aware that Hannah might be pregnant. The signs were all there, and yet she said nothing. In the mornings when she fought against waves of nausea, she mumbled something about a virus and sipped ginger tea to settle her stomach. He knew why she was keeping the news to herself. She was afraid of miscarrying and nothing he could do or say could quell that fear.

He had talked to the doctor privately, seeking the man's assurance that there was no medical reason why Hannah could not give birth. The doctor had advised patience. "The one thing you don't want to be doing is adding to her fears."

But Levi felt such a compulsion to care for his wife and unborn child that it was all he could do not to tell Hannah what he suspected and demand that she allow him to worry with her. *Demand,* he thought as he watched her hanging laundry on the clothesline he had stretched like a tightrope between two large palm trees outside their back door. Demanding was the way of Levi Harmon, a man used to having his way. A man used to others giving him his way as if that were somehow his right.

But Levi Harnisher understood that such thoughts were a part of the outside world. In the Amish world it was not his will, but God's will that mattered. "Well, then," he prayed quietly, "if it be Your will, give us this baby, this child that we share, and let us raise him or her in the way of our ancestors."

He pushed himself out of the rocker on the porch and went to help Hannah. The wind had caught a sheet she was trying to hang and it whipped away from her like a sail broken free of its mast.

"Got it," he called as he rescued the damp sheet from its landing place in her herb garden and carried it back to her.

"It will have to be washed again," she fussed as she wadded it into a ball.

He picked it up and spread it over the clothesline, pulling clothespins from where she had clipped them to her apron and anchoring it there. "It's fine," he told her and then he placed his hands on her shoulders until she looked up at him. "Everything will be fine."

The tears welled in her blue eyes and he pulled her into his embrace and rocked her side to side.

"How long have you known?" Her voice was muffled against his chest.

"A while now."

"And yet you said nothing."

"Nor did you," he reminded her. "But now we know — the three of us and . . ."

She pulled back. "You told Caleb?"

He chuckled. "No."

"Then who are the three of us?"

"You. Me." He placed one palm gently over her midsection. "And this child of ours."

She covered his hand with hers. "Tell me again," she said softly.

"Everything will be fine," he repeated then added, "whatever happens. We have already been blessed beyond all measure just by finding each other, Hannah. If God sees fit to give us a child, then I would have to say that our cup would runneth over."

The sheer relief Hannah felt at being able to share the worries and joys of her pregnancy with Levi had the surprising effect of making her feel much better. On Christmas morning she hardly had any nausea at all, but she was glad that the routine called for prayer, fasting and quiet reflection on the true meaning of the day.

With Gunther and his three daughters, Hannah, Levi and Caleb attended services at Merle Obermeier's farm. He had the largest house so that everyone could be in the same room. The yard was already filled with buggies, unhitched and parked in a circle when they arrived, and more buggies had followed them up the lane. Caleb joined his friends to help lead the horses away either to the barn or to pasture. Hannah was relieved that Caleb had made new friends. New families had come to Florida in the last year — young families with children. The settlement growing up around the celery fields was becoming its own little community.

Inside the house the air was warm because of so many people crowded into one room and also because Merle refused to open any windows, assuring everyone that the house would stay far cooler if they would simply come in quickly and close the door behind them. He stood sentry at the front door to see that his instructions were followed.

"All that fanning of the door — opening and then closing it only to immediately open it again. That's the cause of all this hot air — that and Obermeier's lecturing," Gunther grumbled.

"Papa, please." Pleasant squeezed her father's forearm. "It's his house."

Hannah could not help looking around and trying to imagine Pleasant living here.

Merle had been a widower for less than a year. There had been a time when rumor had it that he had cast his eye on Hannah as a possible second wife. But then she had boarded the circus train to go and find Caleb and Merle had made it plain to Pleasant that he could not tolerate such open trafficking with outsiders.

Of course, Hannah pointed out the fact that Pleasant had made that same journey, but she explained that Merle saw her participation as unavoidable. After all, Gunther could hardly expect Hannah to travel alone. In his view, Gunther had gone along to keep an eye on Levi, and Pleasant's role was to watch over Hannah.

Hannah noticed that Merle's two youngest children were running in and out of the house and up and down the stairs without one word from their father. Would Pleasant be able to teach them some manners and discipline them? Would Merle allow such a thing? For although he regularly reprimanded his eldest son and only daughter and cast sour looks in the direction of any mother whose baby was crying or whose toddler was making faces at another child, he turned a blind eye to the shenanigans of his own toddlers. Lydia had reported that the older two often missed school. The older boy was often ill, and Lydia worried that Merle's daughter was being expected to take on far too much responsibility at home.

Surely, Pleasant could do better than this, Hannah thought, and then she immediately sought God's forgiveness. It was not for her to say whether or not Pleasant and Merle should wed. No more than it was for her to say if she and Levi would be blessed with the birth of their own child.

Levi and Caleb sat shoulder to shoulder on the bench in front of her. Levi glanced back, his deep chocolate eyes inquiring as to her health.

"I'm fine," she mouthed and motioned for him — and Caleb — to turn their faces forward. But the truth was that the oppressive heat that was building in the room with each new arrival was getting to her. She felt flushed and lightheaded. The women were seated so close together on the bench that there was barely any room for what little air there was to circulate.

She heard others singing the opening hymn and tried to follow along. Then Bishop Troyer said, "Shall we pray?" And suddenly the room began to undulate as if she had been pushed underwater and was trying to fight her way back to the surface. A thud and then nothing until she felt blessed fresh air and smelled the scent of newly mown grass.

"Hannah?"

Levi was on his knees cradling her in his arms. Pleasant arrived on the run, spilling half of the glass of water she carried. Caleb was fanning her with his broad-brimmed Sunday black hat.

"Ma?"

"I'm all right," she told him. "Just overcome by the heat is all."

Caleb heaved a sigh of relief and grinned. "You weren't the only one." He pointed across the yard where others were attending to three other people — a woman, a girl and an older man.

Levi chuckled. "When the fourth person went down, the bishop told Merle to open the windows or he was moving the services outside."

Hannah glanced toward the house and saw that every window had been opened wide. From inside she could hear the drone of the sermon the first minister was delivering. He was quoting the story of Jesus's birth as recorded in the book of Matthew.

"Hannah?" Levi leaned near. "The baby?"

"We're fine," she assured him. "Now shush. I want to hear the story." She clasped hands with Levi and leaned against him as the familiar words rolled out through the open windows and across the yard. She couldn't help thinking that even though most people thought of snow and cold weather when they thought of Christmas, Jesus had been born in the tropics — a place not so very different from this place. Somehow that gave her a measure of comfort.

When the services ended, Hannah insisted that she help the other women lay out a light lunch for everyone to enjoy before they headed for home. The meal was plain and sparse and the talk was of the feasts they would all enjoy the following day after the children presented their Christmas pageant at the school.

"Let's go home. You need to rest," Levi told her when he came looking for her after the meal and found her scrubbing pans in Merle's kitchen — pans that she suspected had nothing to do with the meal just served.

"Yes, go," Pleasant urged. "I can finish this."

"Where's Caleb?" Hannah asked as Levi helped her into their buggy.

"He's walking home with a couple of his friends."

On the ride home, Hannah was overcome with exhaustion and within minutes of leaving Merle's farm, her head rested on Levi's shoulder and she was fast asleep. When they reached their farm, she roused enough to realize that Levi was carrying her into the house and up to their bedroom.

"I have to . . ." she protested sleepily.

"You have to rest," he said. "We have a full day tomorrow." He laid her gently on their bed, removed her shoes and then her prayer covering and pulled the pins from her hair, fanning it over the pillow. "Merry Christmas, my Hannah," he whispered as he kissed her lightly on the lips and then tiptoed from the room.

Hannah woke the following morning and realized that she had slept through most of the afternoon and all of the night. The first thing she noticed was that Levi was not in the room, although it was obvious that he had slept next to her as always. Then she heard muffled laughter and whispers in the hallway outside the closed bedroom door.

Something clunked against the wall and then she heard Levi announce, "Special delivery!" followed by Caleb's giggle.

Hannah got up and put on her robe as she padded barefoot to the door and opened it. Caleb and Levi were standing there, both grinning broadly and each holding one end of the most beautiful cradle Hannah had ever seen.

Her first instinct was to protest that it was too soon, that they could not be sure, that there might be no baby to fill such a wonderful cradle. But then she looked at Caleb and saw his pride in what he had obviously helped Levi build. "Do you like it, Ma?"

"It's wonderful," she said.

"It's also heavy," Levi added.

Hannah swung the bedroom door open and stood aside while they carried the cradle into the room.

"Where do you want it?" Caleb asked, glancing around the sparsely furnished room.

"I think there," Hannah said, pointing to her side of the bed. "That way I can rock the baby and go back to sleep."

"Ah, then I suppose the other piece will be on my side of the bed," Levi said as he and Caleb set the cradle in place.

"What other piece?" Hannah asked.

Caleb was already back out in the hall and came through the door carrying a bentwood rocker. "This one." He set it down in the corner. "Go ahead, Ma, give it a trial run — or rock, I guess."

Hannah sat in the beautifully crafted chair, running her palms over the smooth wood of the arms and pushing the chair into motion with one foot. "I love it," she said huskily. Then she looked over at the cradle. "I love them both. But how . . ."

"We worked on them down at the circus shop," Caleb said. "Levi said we weren't ready to let folks know about the baby yet and Jake — Mr. Jenkins — and the others promised to keep it secret so it all worked out just fine."

He was beaming. Hannah had not seen her son so happy since they had returned to Florida. "Thank you," she said and held out her arms to him.

"Ah, Ma," he protested but he came to her and accepted the kiss she gave him on each cheek.

Levi had stepped out into the hall again and returned with packages wrapped in brown paper and string. "I found these in the closet where you keep your sewing," he said. He turned one package over, eyeing it curiously. "I thought just maybe . . ."

"Yes, there's one for each of you," Hannah said, laughing. "That one's Caleb's."

Levi tossed the boy his package and Caleb sat on the side of the bed tearing off the string and paper. Inside were three new shirts and two pair of trousers.

"You're growing so fast," Hannah said.

"Thanks, Ma. Can I wear one outfit today

for the pageant?"

Hannah nodded.

"There's one more thing," Levi said, handing Caleb a small package.

Caleb unwrapped it to reveal a pocket-knife. "It was my father's," Levi told him, and Hannah thought her heart would burst with joy at this sign that Levi had come to think of Caleb as his son.

Caleb studied the knife for a long moment, turning it over in his hand. Then he looked from Hannah to Levi. "You know I was thinking," he began, his voice cracking, "I mean with a new baby coming and all . . ."

"What is it, Caleb?" Hannah felt her throat close with fear that maybe Caleb would not welcome a new child — another child.

"It might be confusing for the kid if I'm calling you 'Levi' and he's calling you 'Pa,' so I was thinking maybe — I mean if you wouldn't care, I was thinking I could call you Pa?"

Levi wrapped the boy in a bear hug and Hannah heard her husband's voice crack as her son's had when he said, "I think that would be a fine idea, son."

Hannah sniffed back tears of joy and rose from the rocker to complete the circle, wrapping her arms around the two of them and laying her cheek against Levi's back.

"Hey," Caleb said as he wriggled his way free, his cheeks flushed with embarrassment at having caused such a scene, "you didn't open your present from Ma yet."

"So I didn't," Levi said as he picked up the last package and turned it slowly over in his hands. "What could this be?" He squeezed the thick soft package.

"Open it," Caleb urged.

Levi grinned and tore off the paper, revealing a large cotton quilt. He spread it over the bed and examined it. The background was a patchwork of solid dark blues, greens, browns and purples — the fabrics commonly used to make Amish clothing. But the center was a feast of brilliant reds, yellows and oranges.

"It looks just like one of the wheels on the circus wagons," Caleb said.

And when Levi realized that the boy was right, he looked at Hannah, his eyes full of questions.

"I wanted you to have something to remind you of how we came together — of how we became a family," she said shyly. "I can change it and make it all plain," she added, suddenly afraid that he didn't want to be reminded of those days.

"Don't change it," he said huskily. "I was just thinking that maybe you could make a smaller one for the baby."

"And one for my bed," Caleb added.

"We're going to raise some eyebrows when that quilt is washed and hanging on the line," Hannah warned them.

Both Caleb and Levi shrugged.

"I'm not one to live by what others may think of me, Hannah."

"Neither am I," Caleb chorused.

Hannah smiled. "Neither am I."

EPILOGUE

June, 1929

Hannah awoke with a start, her gown soaked through in the oppressive heat that even at daybreak was overwhelming. Her hair clung to her cheeks and sometime during the night, she and Levi had both kicked off the covers.

She rolled onto her side and saw that Levi was already up. There had been no rain for weeks now and Levi and the other Amish farmers worried constantly about their crops. It was odd to think of the parched fields when it felt as if she were swimming in dampness.

She sat up and was gripped by a pain so sharp that she bit down on her lip to keep from crying out. She could hear Caleb passing her bedroom door on his way downstairs and she did not want to alarm him.

But oh, the pain came in waves that threatened to pull her under like the heavy undertow in the Gulf. She clutched the edge of the bed and rode out the pain. Then when it seemed to have passed, she pushed herself to her feet. But she was only able to make it as far as the foot of the bed where she was reaching to retrieve the circus quilt when the next wave hit.

Her knees buckled and this time she cried out.

"Ma!" She heard the pound of Caleb's footsteps coming back up the stairs. He flung open the door and froze.

"Get your father," she managed.

Caleb stood there, his eyes focused not on her but on the bed. Hannah followed his gaze and saw the dark stain of blood. "Go," she said. "Now!"

She eased herself onto the floor and clutched the quilt against her as she heard Caleb's cries for help echoing across the farmyard.

"Please," she prayed, "please not when we've come so far. Please."

But they had not come far enough. The baby was not due for another six weeks, at least. It was too soon and there was blood and . . .

Hannah wept.

Levi's boots hit each stair in rhythm with Caleb's horse galloping off.

"I sent Caleb for the doctor," Levi said, kneeling next to her.

"It's too soon," she said.

"Maybe not," he replied and held her close.

They stayed that way, him tightening his hold on her as together they rode out every labor pain, her collapsing against him once the pain had passed, until they heard voices in the yard, then in the house.

"Up here," Levi bellowed, and Hannah heard for the first time in his voice the fear and panic that he had spent the past several minutes swallowing down as he tried to convince her that everything would be all right.

"Let's get her on the bed," the doctor said, taking charge as Pleasant followed him into the room.

They both looked at the soiled sheets.

"Caleb's room," Pleasant said and led the way as Levi carried Hannah, and the doctor followed. In the hall Caleb hung back, his eyes wide with fear.

"Go get your grandfather now," the doctor ordered, and Caleb raced down the stairs. "It'll occupy the boy," the doctor explained when Levi seemed about to question why Gunther should be called. "He can keep the boy calm."

Levi lay Hannah on Caleb's bed and sat next to her, gripping her hand as yet another pain hit.

"You should wait outside," the doctor said as he prepared to examine her, and Pleasant rushed about gathering towels and a basin.

"Not leaving," Levi said and refused to look at the doctor.

"Stubborn," Hannah managed when the doctor met her eyes, his bushy white eyebrows questioning what she would prefer. "Let him stay. He'll just worry."

"Very well. Pleasant, I'll need your help. Are you up to this?"

"I've participated in deliveries before, but . . ." Pleasant huffed. "Not human babies perhaps but . . ."

"Fine. Do exactly as I ask and don't hesitate, all right?"

Hannah saw Pleasant's lips narrow into the familiar line of determination that was her trademark and felt comforted by that until the pain came again and threatened to rip her in half.

"I'm here," Levi said, his eyes filled with tears as he witnessed her pain. "Doc, do something," he growled.

"All right, Hannah, now the next time you feel the pain I need for you to push hard.

Ready?"

Hannah nodded and waited as she might wait for the next wave to crash onto the beach in a tropical storm.

"Now!" the doctor coached.

Hannah fought with everything she had to push past the pain and when it passed, she felt exhausted. And then she heard a sound she had thought would never be hers to hear again. She heard the cry of her baby.

"Not done yet," the doctor said when she raised herself half onto her side to see her child. A fresh wave of pain hit her, knocking her flat.

"Push!" the doctor bellowed.

Hannah had little choice but to follow his command. But this time the effort was more than she could take and she felt the pain pulling her under and then everything went dark.

Slowly, Hannah became aware of movement in the room and yet everything seemed quieter, less chaotic. She opened her eyes and saw Levi talking quietly with the doctor. She glanced around Caleb's room.

There was no sign of the baby.

Tears leaked from the corners of her eyes as she understood that they had almost made it this time. The baby had lived at

360

least for a moment for she had heard the cry, but then . . .

"She's awake," Pleasant said as she dipped a cloth in water and used it to wipe Hannah's brow.

Levi was next to her in an instant and the doctor stood at the foot of the bed. "Well, young lady, you gave us a bit of a fright there," he said. "We thought we'd lost you."

Hannah ignored him and turned to Levi. "The baby?"

Levi smiled. "Looks like Caleb and I are going to have to build another cradle."

"I . . ." Hannah was confused. Levi was smiling. So was the doctor. So — miracle of miracles — was Pleasant.

"It's twins," Pleasant told her. "A boy and a girl."

"Twins?" Hannah fought past all the fears and anxieties of the past several months as she tried to accept what they were telling her. "And they are all right?"

As if on cue, she heard the wail of two different babies coming from across the hall. And then Greta and Lydia were standing in the doorway, each of them holding a bundle that looked for all the world like a sack of flour.

"They are hungry," Levi said as he stood and took the bundle that Greta held and placed the child in Hannah's arms. "And they would like to know their names," he added.

Hannah had put off Levi's attempts to choose names for their child in advance. Now there were two of them.

"What was your father's name?" Hannah asked as she examined her son, counting his fingers and toes to be sure he was as perfect as he appeared.

"Reuben," Levi whispered.

Hannah held out her free arm for the baby that Lydia held. "And your mother?"

"Emma."

"Then hello, Reuben and Emma Harnisher," she said softly, kissing each. She looked up at Levi then. "All right?"

Unable to speak, Levi nodded and then sat on the edge of the bed and took his daughter in his arms and rocked her slowly from side to side.

Out in the yard they heard a commotion, as several buggies seemed to arrive at the same moment. Pleasant went to see what was happening and the doctor chose that moment to take his leave as well, leaving Levi and Hannah alone with their babies.

Levi cupped Hannah's cheek with his free hand. "Are you truly all right?"

"A little sore and tired," she said, "but I

have never been happier, and I have never loved you more."

As Levi leaned in to kiss Hannah, Emma started to squirm and fuss and Levi looked so utterly lost that Hannah couldn't help but laugh. "Here," she said, exchanging son for daughter. "She favors you," she said, stroking Emma's tuft of copper-colored hair as her daughter settled into the curve of her arm.

Downstairs they heard voices.

"Truly, I don't think . . ." Pleasant was protesting as they heard footsteps in the lower hallway.

"Let them come," Levi called out.

There was quiet for one long moment. Then one by one they shyly entered the small room.

First Caleb and then Gunther followed by the bishop and a parade of their neighbors.

"Come meet your brother and sister," Hannah said, coaxing Caleb forward after Levi had introduced the twins to everyone.

"Do you want to hold him?" Levi offered, holding Reuben out to Caleb.

Caleb looked panicked and then swallowed hard. "Maybe later," he muttered as he leaned in for a closer look. "They're really tiny."

"They'll grow," one of the women said

and the other women all giggled.

From outside, came the unmistakable sound of a motorcar approaching the house.

"It's Jake and Lily and Fred and Ida," Caleb announced from his position by the window.

Hannah did not even bother to remind her son that he was being too familiar using their first names like that. She saw one or two of the neighbor women raise their eyebrows and scoot a little closer to each other.

"They are family," she said quietly. "Levi's family — and mine."

Their circus family crowded into the room explaining that they had come as soon as Jake had returned from seeing the doctor and reported that his appointment had been cut short when Caleb had burst into the doc's office and announced that his Ma was having the baby. The way they told it — interrupting one another to supply every detail — it was impossible not to be charmed. And when Lily produced two rattles — one pink and one blue — for the babies, the neighbors crowded in closer.

"Not much of a present but it'll do until we have time to shop," Lily said as Fred gently shook the rattle in front of Reuben and the baby seemed to actually smile.

"Ah," chorused the neighbors and they smiled at Lily.

After that, conversation seemed to flow naturally among the gathering as Pleasant announced that Hannah needed her rest and herded everyone from the room. For several moments after they left, Levi and Hannah could hear voices outside their window. Gunther asking Fred about someone he had worked with in the horse tent. Lily telling Pleasant about one of the women from the costume department who had left the circus to marry a Chicago banker. And the buzz of the neighbors — talking among themselves, but no doubt taking in the easy exchange between the Goodloes and the circus people.

Hannah held out her hand to Levi, who stood at the window cradling Reuben as he watched the departure of their guests. "Come sit with me," she said.

Levi nodded but then leaned out the window. "Caleb? Come up here, okay?"

A moment later Caleb stood at the door.

"Bring that rocking chair over here," Levi said, and the boy did as he was asked.

"Now have a seat," Levi said with a wink at Hannah.

Caleb eyed him suspiciously but sat.

Levi placed Reuben in his brother's arms.

Then he crossed the hall and carried the cradle into the small room. He placed Emma in the cradle, then sat on the bed with Hannah. Gathering Hannah into his arms, he rocked the cradle with the toe of his boot.

Hannah cuddled into his shoulder. "Our little family," she murmured happily.

"It's a good start," Levi answered, and then he grinned and to Caleb's obvious embarrassment, Levi kissed his wife.

ABOUT THE AUTHOR

Anna Schmidt is an award-winning author of more than twenty-five works of historical and contemporary fiction. She is a two-time finalist for a coveted RITA® Award from Romance Writers of America, as well as a four-time finalist for an *RT Book Reviews* Reviewer's Choice Award. Her most recent *RT Book Reviews* Reviewer's Choice nomination was for her 2008 Love Inspired Historical novel *Seaside Cinderella,* which is the first of a series of four historical novels set on the romantic island of Nantucket. Critics have called Anna "a natural writer, spinning tales reminiscent of old favorites like *Miracle on 34th Street.*" Her characters have been called "realistic" and "endearing" and one reviewer raved, "I love Anna Schmidt's style of writing!"

The employees of Thorndike Press hope you have enjoyed this Large Print book. All our Thorndike, Wheeler, and Kennebec Large Print titles are designed for easy reading, and all our books are made to last. Other Thorndike Press Large Print books are available at your library, through selected bookstores, or directly from us.

For information about titles, please call:
  (800) 223-1244

or visit our Web site at:
  http://gale.cengage.com/thorndike

To share your comments, please write:
  Publisher
  Thorndike Press
  10 Water St., Suite 310
  Waterville, ME 04901